VIRAGO
MODERN CLASSICS
385

Emilie Rose Macaulay (1881–1958) was born in Rugby, Warwickshire. She was educated at Oxford High School for Girls and Somerville College, Oxford, where she read Modern History. She wrote her first novel, *Abbots Verney*, in 1906 whilst living in Great Shelford, near Cambridge. Rose became an ardent Anglo-Catholic and here her childhood friendship with Rupert Brooke matured and through him she was introduced to London literary society. She moved to London and in 1914 published her first book of poetry, *The Two Blind Countries*. In 1918 she met the novelist and former Catholic priest Gerald O'Donovan, the married man with whom she was to have an affair lasting until his death. Her last and most famous novel, *The Towers of Trebizond* (1956), was awarded the James Tait Black Memorial Prize and became a bestseller in America. She was created a Dame Commander of the Order of the British Empire in the 1958 New Year's Honours, but seven months later suffered a heart attack and died at her home.

Books by Rose Macaulay published by Virago

The World My Wilderness

CREWE TRAIN

Rose Macaulay

Introduced by Jane Emery

virago

VIRAGO

This paperback edition published in 2018 by Virago Press
First published by Virago Press in 1998
First published in Great Britain by William Collins in 1926

3 5 7 9 10 8 6 4 2

A CIP catalogue record for this book
is available from the British Library.

ISBN 978-0-349-01002-1

Typeset in Goudy by M Rules
Printed and bound in Great Britain by
Clays Ltd, St Ives plc

Papers used by Virago are from well-managed forests
and other responsible sources.

MIX
Paper from
responsible sources
FSC® C104740

Virago
An imprint of
Little, Brown Book Group
Carmelite House
50 Victoria Embankment
London EC4 0DZ

An Hachette UK Company
www.hachette.co.uk

www.virago.co.uk

INTRODUCTION

Rose Macaulay was fond of her fictional character, Rome Garden. This empathy is not surprising, for although the insouciant and ever-inquiring Miss Garden of *Told by an Idiot* (1923) and *Crewe Train* (1926) is not a fully rounded self-portrait, in picturing her Rose Macaulay drew a sharply outlined sketch of herself as a figure in the London literary life of the Twenties. Describing the manner and mind of Rome Garden at thirty-one, she openly refers to their affinities:

> She was a woman of the world, a known diner out, a good talker, something of a wit, so that her presence was sought by hostesses as that of an amusing bachelor is sought. She had elegance, distinction, brain, a light and cool touch on the topics of her world, a calm, mocking, sceptical detachment, a fastidious taste in letters and persons. She knew her way about as the phrase goes, and could be relied upon to be socially adequate, in spite of a dangerous distaste for fools, and in spite of the 'dancing and destructive eye' (to use a phrase long afterwards applied to one whose mentality perhaps a little resembled hers) which she turned on all aspects of life around her.

Like Rose Macaulay, Rome Garden rarely loses her aplomb. Although in the last chapter of *Told by an Idiot* she is knowingly headed, at sixty-three, towards death within the year, she maintains her smiling distance from life's 'queer, absurd show' and the cool sense of her own relative unimportance as a player on its stage. The tone of her thoughts at the end of her life is not that of tragedy but of comic irony, the consistent tone of Rose Macaulay's most popular light novels.

Despite her prophesied demise, Rome Garden proved to be too valuable a witness of folly to disappear from Rose Macaulay's fiction. Three years after her gallant farewell soliloquy the nonchalant and stoic Miss Garden is resurrected in *Crewe Train* as an attractive middle-aged country house guest, and she once more casts on the scene her 'enigmatic regard (was it amused, ironic, or merely expectant?)' Although she plays only a cameo role in this satire of literary society, her candour and sanity remain in our consciousness throughout *Crewe Train*, for the narrative voice of the novel is that of just such a quizzical observer as Rome. The first paragraph reminds us of Jane Austen, the last line recalls Evelyn Waugh. Both passages are vintage Rose Macaulay.

And the reader is grateful for that authorial voice, for the keenest pleasure of reading Rose Macaulay's writing comes from her wry commentary on 'all aspects of life around her'. Why, then, we may well ask, did she choose to use as the leading character of *Crewe Train*, a novel about the talky, sophisticated milieu she knew so well, not Rome Garden but a young woman who seems to be an anti-self? Denham Dobie is gauche, silent, non-social, 'an untutored savage' who goes unwillingly to literary parties, made miserable by the strain of inventing small talk for the entertainment of her egocentric, bookish dinner partners. She prefers swimming and pottering about the seacoast alone in a small boat.

Harold Nicolson suggests an answer. He begins his Rose Macaulay obituary essay, 'One of the many things that we shall all remember about Rose was her combination of opposites.' Denham Dobie, the very centre of *Crewe Train*, seems to be the social and intellectual obverse of gregarious and scholarly Rose Macaulay; she visits the Zoo to escape talkers and those who would civilise her. She muses, 'There would always be a part of you, a secret, hidden part which would never put on anything, but would stay as it was born, naked, savage, sceptical, and untutored.' Rose Macaulay was mostly Rome Garden, but (although far from untutored) partly her opposite, Denham Dobie. 'Nobody ever zigzagged more,' said Alan Pryce-Jones of her.

Her idyllic childhood on northern Italy's Mediterranean coast, in the midst of a large, well-educated English family had created at least two selves – both the serious young book-lover who perched in the orange trees in the Villa Macolai garden to read, and the daring amphibious tomboy Rose never wholly outgrew. In addition to praising Rose as a cultivated guest, Harold Nicolson offers a hilarious example of her passion for spontaneous lone bathing under any conditions of weather or risk, in oceans, pools and ponds, wherever she travelled. She was known throughout her long life for her impulsive and intrepid deeds as well as for her wise and witty words. Her daring as a driver was notorious; in her sixties she drove an ambulance in the worst havoc of the London Blitz.

In part, Rose Macaulay created Denham Dobie to fit the

plot of *Crewe Train* – the adventures of the barbarian who goes to the city, a classic form of satire. In addition, she was at ease describing both Denham's adventurous outdoor pleasures and her plight as an outsider entering a small, self-absorbed and self-satisfied community. Young Denham, orphan and expatriate, arriving in bustling London from isolated Andorra, is puzzled by the lives of book-mad, gossipy writers, publishers and reviewers, and asks disconcerting, literal questions, seeking the reasons for their frenetic schedules and their time-wasting social customs, domestic arrangements and dress codes.

When, at forty-five, as an increasingly successful London writer, Rose Macaulay published *Crewe Train*, she herself could look back on having adjusted to a number of identities and milieux, beginning as a Somerville student doing Modern History Honours at Oxford, and later a published neophyte poet and novelist from the provinces who occasionally came down to London as what she called 'an innocent from the Cam'. Then during the First World War, she took on new roles, serving first as an ineffectual V.A.D. nurse in a military hospital, then as a Landgirl (more to her taste) working on a Cambridgeshire farm. From 1916 on she had lived less happily with her widowed mother in Hedgerley as a commuting suburbanite and, until the war's end, as a civil servant in the new Ministry of Information. (She was sometimes unable to keep a brisk individual comment out of her official memos.) In 1922 she became a Londoner and an active, successful member of the literary establishment.

These worlds appear in her novels, and in each Rose Macaulay surveys the scene and records her perceptive views. In all she published thirty-six books; twenty-three were works of fiction, and fourteen of these, like *Crewe Train*, were social comedies and high-spirited novels of ideas which became increasingly popular with her upper-middle-class liberal audience. Three of her first five novels were conventional, rather moral in the Victorian mode, yet, not surprisingly, the heroine of her first book, published in 1906, is a young woman who looks around her with 'quizzical, comprehending eyes'.

Many found Rose Macaulay's enigmatic gaze formidable, but Harold Nicolson said, 'She amused everybody and offended no one. There was an acid element in her intelligence, but it was citrous merely and never poisoned.' As book after book appeared, her lively intelligence and *joie de vivre* gradually lightened and brightened – but did not entirely obscure – her underlying ethical seriousness. In 1920 *Potterism*, her murder mystery-cum-satire on the sensationalised postwar British press and its corruption of thought and language, was a bestseller in England and America.

In 1926 when her fifteenth novel, *Crewe Train*, was published, Rose Macaulay was at the height of her popularity as a writer and a celebrity dinner guest. She was to become known as a woman of letters: a novelist, a biographer, a literary critic, a literary and social historian, a political commentator, a reviewer of books, films and radio programs, an essayist, columnist, anthologist, travel writer, and a star of the BBC wireless quiz programme, The Brains Trust. But in the midst of this intellectually sophisticated, hard-working, and fast-moving life, the memory and influence of the outdoor freedom and joyful reading of her childhood remained alive. Her characteristic libertarian individualism, comically represented in the behaviour of Denham Dobie, was foreshadowed by her ancestry and had been nurtured by her childhood.

In 1881 Emilie Rose Macaulay was born at Rugby where her father, a former Fellow of Trinity College, Cambridge, was a schoolmaster. She was the second child and the second girl in what was to become a family of nine. (Rose's mother Grace longed for sons and her first three children, all daughters, knew from early childhood that they should have been boys.) When Rose was six, her mother's ill health prompted the dramatic move of the whole ménage, servants and all, from damp, grey England to warm, golden Italy where they were the only English residents in the fishing village of Varazze, southwest of Genoa. The children's lives at once moved out of doors, and, fortunately, Grace Macaulay's admiration for male bravery and sportsmanship encouraged Rose's natural delight in dauntless physical freedom. For seven years she played, in and out of the sea, like a young apprentice pirate or fisherman.

But she was a more complicated tomboy than Denham Dobie. Rose Macaulay's paternal grandfather was the first cousin of Thomas Babington Macaulay, a descendant of what Noel Annan calls England's 'intellectual aristocracy', generations of upper-middle-class clerics and dons who educated their daughters as well as their sons. And Rose's mother, from the same admirable stock of Macaulays, Coneybeares, Darwins, Trevelyans, Huxleys and Vaughans, was an educated woman for her day. Tutored by both parents, Rose began her schooling early, and as an adult she could be described as learned – but never as pedantic.

Grace Macaulay gave her children their elementary lessons and instruction in poetry, Italian, and the Book of Common Prayer as well. The donnish George Macaulay daily read classics aloud to them and told them the stories of old myths and legends. But although they loved hearing of the voyage of Jason and his Argonauts in search of the Golden Fleece, the tales most prized by what Rose called 'our savage tribe' were from boys' adventure books like *Treasure Island*, *The Swiss Family Robinson*, *The Prisoner of Zenda*, and *Masterman Ready*. 'The Five', as the Macaulay children nearest in age called themselves, spent their mornings in study and their afternoons on the shore with their canoe, the Argo, acting out the quests and encounters in those pages. In later life Rose kept all these cherished childhood volumes on her top bookshelf, until years later when, along with her irreplaceable antiquarian library, they were destroyed in the London Blitz. Denham's excited discovery of 'the useful hideaway', the secret passage in *Crewe Train*, recalls an episode in one of the clan's favourite tales, *The Coral Island* by R.M. Ballantyne.

But this prelapsarian bliss ended when the family moved back to England in 1895 to settle in Oxford. Rose was fourteen and loath to become a proper young lady. She wrote of that mandatory transformation with comic melancholy, reminiscent of Denham's dismay in contemplating convention-bound town life:

Later they took us to England and school, and we lived in a University town, where we wore shoes and stockings all day, and where, did we lapse (and we did), in the streets from respectable behaviour, a schoolfellow from the girls' High School or the boys' Preparatory was sure to pass and put us to shame. We could, and we did, be Sherlock Holmes and track criminals unobtrusively (or so we hoped), but it was a poor kind of life.

Only the double shock of the Oxford High School's rules of decorum and her father's lecture on the necessity of acknowledging the undeniable fact of her gender at last awakened Rose from the dream that she would some day become a naval lieutenant. In *Told by an Idiot* she describes the adolescence of Imogen Garden, a character much like her young self, who 'had always meant to be a sailor, and who even now blindly hoped that somehow, before she reached the age for Osborne, a way would be made for her (either she would become a boy or dress up as a boy, or the rule excluding girls from the senior service would be relaxed)'. Shamed by her relatives for playing Indians in the woods, Imogen thought, 'A tomboy. Imbecile word. As if girls didn't like doing nice things as well as boys ... Oh, it was rotten being grown-up. Grown-ups had such a hideous time. They became so queer, wanting to go to parties, and even meetings, and all kinds of rotten shows.'

Almost all of the heroines in Rose Macaulay's books have androgynous Christian names, and more than one resists maturity. The waif Barbary, in Rose Macaulay's post-Second World War novel, *The World My Wilderness* (1950), is a dark version of this *puer aeternus*; she is an uncivilised child who plays life-and-death games aiding the French Resistance, half adolescent girl and half wild creature.

At school, a bastion of propriety, Rose remained almost as shy and silent as Denham, and only began losing what a friend called an 'almost intelligible torrent of words' when, in 1900, she entered Somerville College, Oxford, to become a passionately engaged student, thanks to her wealthy Uncle Regi Macaulay's generous recognition of her quick mind and her literary talent. He knew the family lore; the first sentence Rose had ever printed was, 'I CAN WRITE.'

The dedication *of Crewe Train* – 'To the Philistines, the Barbarians, the Unsociable' – although an accurate description of the pleasure-loving, indolent, and awkward Denham, obviously does not apply to the well-educated Rose who 'knew her way about' the social scene. But these phrases are followed by another category in smaller type –'and to those who do not care to take any trouble', a category which includes both author and character. Both believed that most duties conventionally assigned to women were boring and tiresome.

And so in *Crewe Train* Rose Macaulay created a near caricature of a young-woman-as-a-twelve-year-old-boy in order to put in Denham Dobie's mouth and mind words and thoughts echoing her own criticisms of fussily conformist adult society. We find the same complaints in the sprightly, even flippantly exaggerated essays in *A Casual Commentary*, published a year before *Crewe Train* appeared. In the essays and in the novel, she mocks herself as well as other Londoners.

She was a great traveller but she often laughs at British tourists; she derides popular novelists and in *Crewe Train* praises the admirable Rome Garden for being too fastidious to write novels.

Although *Crewe Train*'s jokey dedication to the happy slacker and the anti-intellectual is clear enough, the book's title is certainly puzzling to those who do not know the popular ballad of the same name which describes the troubled state of a misdirected traveller:

Oh, Mr Porter, whatever shall I do?
I want to go to Birmingham, but they've sent me on to
Crewe!

Crewe Train plots the adventures of a life traveller who sets off meandering contentedly alone up a mountain path with only mindless pleasure as a destination, and ends dismally in a suburban drawing room into which unwelcome visitors, pointing out tedious social and housekeeping duties, may at any time intrude. It is the story of the trapping of a child of nature by sex, love, marriage, social convention, domesticity, pregnancy, and gossip. But however pathetic are Denham Dobie's attempts to escape her imprisonment and go her own happy, irresponsible way, until the last chapters the novel never departs very far from comedy, because few readers can wholeheartedly identify with Denham's childlike behaviour. Her lover and husband, Arnold Gresham, is no domestic tyrant but an intelligent, well-educated, conventional, affectionate, quite reasonable young publisher whose myopic failure to understand what a gypsy life his feckless wife dreams of is understandable. And besides, Rose Macaulay's comments about the obstacles to women's freedom are diverting black humour. She is a playful and rueful observer, not a reformer.

As a young woman Rose Macaulay had not joined the suffragettes, for although she thought it absurd that women should be denied the vote, she did not believe that, under the British system, the vote would do them much good. More importantly, she disapproved of the 'noisy fuss' the suffragettes made. But she always held a brief for women, knowing them to have been unfairly disadvantaged throughout history; her writings record the injustices. Her central belief about gender was that most men and most women of the same class were more alike than different; she hoped that the reader would not be able to guess whether the sympathetic first-person narrator in her last novel, *The Towers of Trebizond*, was a man or a woman.

Until the closing chapters of *Crewe Train* we are really not meant to take Denham very seriously as a representative societal victim; there is, after all, an attractive and successful young career woman in the story, Audrey Gresham, who is not hobbled by the customs, etiquette, and dictates of taste which so irk and puzzle Denham. Denham Dobie's careless, vagabond ways are not offered as a model for independent young women but as a comic scenario of an attempted escape from female duties unpalatable to Rose Macaulay. Only towards the end of the story do we realise Denham's pain in being trammelled and thwarted by a loving but incompatible marriage. In the end she discovers the wife's life is forced to conform to that of the husband.

In *Crewe Train* Rose took bold risks with the sympathy of her readers. Always seriously interested in religion, she nevertheless showed the non-spiritual and commonsensical Denham's scepticism about some rules of life prescribed by the Roman Catholic Catechism. Not surprisingly, some Catholics found this tasteless; others were indignantly offended. And in 1926 even more readers were shocked at Denham's not wanting to have a baby – she thought her dog Jacob was a better companion. (One humourless male reviewer called Denham 'a mental case' and expressed his deep disgust at the author's allusions to morning sickness.) But down-to-earth, literal Denham is completely consistent and, despite occasional jokes at her heroine's expense, Rose Macaulay clearly believes that Denham's principle of living without taking too much trouble is a sensible and appealing one.

Today's women cheer at Rose's epigram from 'Problems of a Woman's Life': 'At the worst a house unkept cannot be so distressing as a life unlived'. (She was meticulous about the use of the English language, the state of the cupboards was another matter.) Rose Macaulay was ahead of her time. The rigour of fashion's dress code for ladies in the Twenties seems as laughable to us as it was to Denham. Rose Macaulay entertained in restaurants, did without live-in servants, was untroubled by the litter of books and papers in her flat, and advised those who lived alone to avoid cooking by foraging for tinned soup and biscuits at home and enjoying party food abroad. Indeed, she made the radical statement, 'If someone has got to housekeep, there is no reason why it should be a woman rather than a man'.

But the mind-deadening and joy-killing effect of household routine is not *Crewe Train*'s only satirical target. Denham's exposure of the narrowness of publishers' and writers' lives is wonderfully subversive as she attempts to persuade her young husband that travelling about English coastal villages on a motorcycle and selling books in order to survive would be preferable to a London life spent bringing out such slim volumes as *Mildew* (someone's poems) and *Maunderings* (someone's essays). And her indifference to the wounds suffered by her husband on reading a tepid review of his first novel provides one of the funniest scenes in the book. The vanity of all writers was one of Rose Macaulay's favorite subjects.

She also exercised her authorial role as a satirical critic of the publishing world by using Denham to mock the Dorothy Richardson-type stream of consciousness passages in Arnold's trendy novel. After reading a paragraph of associational gibberish, Denham says doubtfully, 'I suppose Jane did think like that. I suppose she was a little queer in the head'. And Aunt Evelyn's lush unconscious parody of the overripe prose of a best-selling romance novel in the late chapters of *Crewe Train* is one more joke for critics: 'The youth was handsome, bronzed and brawny; he was a lusty young seagod. The girl was a jocund Chloe. They teased and romped: then bending her face backwards, he crushed her in his arms and kissed her lips.'

However, although witty, the narrator's world-weary observations on sex, love, and marriage are rather less comical. Denham observes that love is the cheese that baits the marital trap and discovers that 'the mutual intoxication' of the honeymoon inevitably wears off. At the last Denham cries out, rebelling against the inescapability of love's fetters: 'One was trapped by love, by that blind storming of the senses, by that infinite tenderness, that unreasoning, unreasoned friendship ... If you had never loved, you could be happy, idle, loafing and alone, exploring new places, sufficient to yourself.' The closing chapter, which dramatises the coercion of conforming suburban life, is shot through with Denham's claustrophobic wretchedness, yet its final line is hilarious. *Crewe Train* comes close to being the 'tragic farce' which was Rose Macaulay's definition of life.

To understand the source of her disbelief in the possibility of a happy marriage for everyone and of her unsentimental compassion for lovers and husbands and wives, we can consider her twenty-three years of love for a married man. And *Crewe Train*'s portrayal of the irrevocable damage gossip can do to love and friendship is also a part of Rose Macaulay's private history of what she called 'love and no ties'.

Neither Rose Macaulay nor any of her siblings married. She described her view of the ideal relationship between men and women in 'People Who Should Not Marry':

> Some men and women might well prefer to live alone, meeting their beloved only when it suits them, thus retaining both that measure of freedom (small though any human freedom is) enjoyed by the solitary and the delicate bloom on the fruit of love which is said to be brushed off by continual contact.

She sacrificed neither her liberty nor her privacy in her long secret relationship with her 'beloved friend', Gerald O'Donovan, with whom she fell in love in 1918.

He was then her superior officer in the Italian Section of the Department for Propaganda in Enemy Countries in the Ministry of Information. As a young man he had been a magnetic, eloquent, visionary Catholic priest in western Ireland, and an active leader in movements for clerical, economic, educational, and social reforms. Opposed by his bishop, he left his parish in 1904 and, somewhat later, he left the Church. He became sub-warden of Toynbee Hall, the workers' education settlement house in East London. In 1910 he married Beryl Verschoyle, a daughter of the Irish Protestant gentry and fifteen years younger than himself. When Rose met him the O'Donovans had three young children.

By 1918 Gerald O'Donovan had already published two of the five novels he was to write. In addition to sharing literary interests, he and Rose had the same angle of vision; H.G. Wells said that the sardonic Gerald had 'an eye like a rifle barrel through a bush'. As a reader for Rose's publisher, Collins, he became responsible for her novels and was an important influence on her work, encouraging her to write the irreverent light fiction which established her reputation. (She herself was more interested in her scholarly non-fiction writing.)

There is no dependable evidence that Rose Macaulay and Gerald O'Donovan ever planned to marry, and through the years Rose became a warm family friend. Her last and best book, *The Towers of Trebizond* (1956), which she identified in a letter to Rosamond Lehmann as 'my story', celebrates the joy, and foreshadows the inevitable painful aftermath of her close relationship with Gerald: 'We were so glad to be together, and we each understood what the other said, and we laughed at one another's jokes, and love was our fortress and our peace, and being together shut out everything else and closed down conscience and the moral sense'. But for all Gerald O'Donovan's support and for all her rejoicing in his company and in her travels abroad with him, in the end Rose Macaulay controlled her own life, made many friends, and did not depend completely on him for a sense of herself.

A friend's gossip about them had been a damaging force in the early stages of their relationship, and Rose Macaulay makes rather bitter use of that memory in portraying the meddling of Evelyn Gresham in the lives of Denham, Arnold and Audrey. In 1921, when Rose was living in Hedgerley, she let a room in the London flat of Naomi Royde-Smith as a *pied-à-terre*. Naomi was the powerful and brilliant editor of the *Westminster Gazette* and had been Rose's generous and helpful patron ever since she had published her poems when Rose was still a cub living at home in Cambridge. When the two women lived together they held a successful weekly literary salon in Kensington at which they entertained such lions as W. B. Yeats, Arnold Bennett and Walter de la Mare (Naomi's devoted admirer), and helped introduce such aspiring writers as Elizabeth Bowen to literary society. Rose played the much applauded jester.

In 1922 when Rose moved into her own flat, Naomi exercised what friends called her social talent as 'a great romancer' to spread speculative rumours about what was at that point becoming an increasingly intense friendship between Rose and Gerald. This widespread 'talk' made it embarrassing for the two to continue to appear together at literary lunches and meetings and forced Gerald out of Rose's public world. Rose, who, friends say, 'hated a row', quarrelled with Naomi and they were never good friends again. Evelyn Gresham of *Crewe Train*, Denhams talkative and presumptuous aunt who 'saw and intuitively understood' whatever suited the sentimental and sensational clichés of her busy imagination, is hardly a perfect replica of Naomi Royde-Smith, but she has the chic facade and the 'large, wondering eyes' for which Naomi was admired and like her, was a Francophile, educated abroad. She is the rumour-mongering manipulator of the plot; she dooms Denhams hopes for solitude and freedom. (One of the four novels Rose later wrote is entitled *I Would Be Private*.)

But neither *Crewe Train* nor any other Rose Macaulay novel succeeded merely because it had elements of the *roman à clef* (ironically, another form of gossip). The intelligence of her dancing eye, her sense of the absurdity of what she observed, her mockery of cant, her forgiving magnanimity, her lightly carried erudition, and her elegant, witty style continue to delight. What finally secures her place in the admiration and affection of her committed readers is the lasting excellence of her last two novels, and the human drama of the sorrows, gallantry, and climactic triumphs of her final years.

In the early Forties Rose lost her favourite sister after tending her through months of suffering, lost her flat and her treasured library to bombs and fire, and lost her lover to another prolonged death. Although worn by grief and illness after these disasters, she nevertheless wrote three travel books and two novels. One was her poignant novel of the dark night, *The World My Wilderness* (1950). The following year she was awarded a Litt. D. from her revered father's university, Cambridge. And at last, seeking absolution for her life with Gerald, she rejoined the Anglican Church, which she had always loved but from which she had excommunicated herself, and wrote the internationally acclaimed comic-tragic novel of travel and spiritual quest and love and adultery and remorse, *The Towers of Trezibond* (1956). Her deep religious sense combined improbably and brilliantly with her talent for generating laughter. In 1958, the seventy-eighth and last year of her life, she was made a Dame Commander of the British Empire.

However given the literary world is to jealousy, as the author of *Crewe Train* often wryly observed, no one is known to have begrudged Rose Macaulay these final honours.

Jane Emery, Stanford University, California, 1994

To
THE PHILISTINES,
THE BARBARIANS,
THE UNSOCIABLE,
AND THOSE WHO DO NOT CARE
TO TAKE ANY TROUBLE

CONTENTS

PART ONE

BARBARIAN

CHAPTER I

Preliminary

A Mr Dobie, a clergyman, wearying of his job, relinquished it, ostensibly on the grounds that he did not care to bury dissenters or to baptise illegitimate infants, but in reality because he was tired of being so busy, so sociable, and so conversational, of attending parish meetings, sitting on committees, calling on parishioners and asking them how they did – an inquiry the answer to which he was wholly indifferent.

Having relinquished these activities, and having just enough money left him by his lately dead wife to exist penuriously without industry, Mr Dobie looked round for an agreeable and peaceful spot in which to reside. Abroad was best, he decided, for abroad you are less surrounded by inquisitive and sociable persons who wonder why you do nothing, and insist on conversing with you. So abroad Mr Dobie went, with his seven-years-old daughter Denham (named after her mother's favourite Buckinghamshire village), a very self-sufficing and independent child, who made remarkably few demands on her father's time and attention. He recalled the island of Mallorca, where he and his wife had once spent a very pleasant spring holiday, and which had certainly been both agreeable and cheap. Thither, therefore, he made his way, and took up his abode in a small pink house on a hill above the little town of Soller. There for three or four years he lived, very cheaply, in a wonderful climate, on the side of a fragrant hill, embowered in orange and lemon gardens, with the picturesque little town at his feet and the mountains at his back, and a small old fishing-port huddled round a blue bay a couple of miles to the west.

At first he was very happy and peaceful; peaceful as only a widower can be peaceful, and as few widowers who are also fathers are peaceful. But, as time went by, and his knowledge of the Mallorquin idiom improved, and he was accepted by Soller as one of its inhabitants, he discovered that Mallorquins are almost the kindest and most sociable people in the world, and would not let him alone. They were not content with being kind to Denham, and loading her with invitations to the company of other children, which annoyed her a good deal, but they were kind to him too. He could not so much as walk through the town without being accosted on every side with greetings, and, when he walked on the hills, he was at the mercy of the friendly peasantry who traversed the fragrant paths between the vineyards. It began to tell on Mr Dobie's nerves. So did the chatter of the loquacious old woman who did his cooking and ran his house.

But there was a worse thing. The English came.

Here is one of the points about this planet which should be remembered; into every penetrable corner of it, and into most of the impenetrable corners, the English will penetrate. They are like that; born invaders. They cannot stay at home.

4

So that even in the desert heat of hottest Africa you shall see little wigwams bearing the legend 'Grand Hotel of London. Five o'clock tea,' and if you visit the Arctic regions, you shall find Esquimaux infants babbling broken Anglo-Saxon, and huts inscribed W.C. Every train running over the globe is full of them, and the world's roads, plains and mountains are dense with knapsacked British walkers, burnt brick-red by sun and air.

Yes; the English will go everywhere. So it was not to be expected that they should not go to Soller. They went first, of course, to Palma, Mallorca's capital and port of arrival. Some of them remained there, and went on excursions from it, believing it to be the only place on the island with inhabitable hotels; but many explored the whole island, and stayed continually in Soller, since Soller was obviously a charming place to stay in. Artists came, spreading themselves over the town and the port, painting their foolish pictures of the landscape and the natives. Busy people came for holidays, idle people for whole winters, and for an agreeable and cheap life. Of course they discovered Mr Dobie, the retired clergyman in mufti, and of course they insisted on making friends with him and his grave, square-faced, brown-legged little girl. Other clergymen discovered him, and talked about church matters with him, and asked questions about his past. The local priests were bad enough, but these stray visiting English clergy and their families were intolerable to Mr Dobie. He took counsel with himself, wondering whether there was any place to which the English did not go, or, at any rate, went less. He paid visits of investigation to the other Balearics, but Iviza and Minorca he found full of British archaeologists, and the smaller islands

5

were so extremely small as to herd disagreeably together those who lived on them.

At last, studying a map of Europe, he discovered the republic of Andorra, in the eastern Pyrenees; inquiring about it, he ascertained that it was very difficult of access, being snowbound from November to May and mountainous all the year round, and that the approach to it was by mule.

So, reluctant, but seeing nothing else for it, Mr Dobie and his daughter left their beautiful island home and made for this ancient mountain republic, and took up their abode in an old farmhouse which they found on the bleak hill above Andorra town.

Certainly it was cold there, but also certainly it was, on the whole, peaceful and lonely. The Andorrans, though sociable (for all nations are this), were not nearly so sociable as the Mallorquins; and the English, though they came there sometimes (as they always will), did not come often and did not stay long. Mr Dobie dug himself in with a sigh of relief, and led an apathetic and contented life.

But – for life, is after all, very unreliable, and will, with a sudden giggle, bring to nought all one's careful arrangements – within two years he had slipped somehow, entirely unexpectedly to himself, snared by passion and a desire for household comfort, into a second marriage, with the handsome daughter of a prosperous local smuggler, who gave him, a good deal to his distress, four hybrid children, and, which was more distasteful to him still, involved him in local society, for her friends and relations came continually about his house. He despised himself for that madness of the blood which had thus trapped him into folly, and evaded, so far as might be, its results. More and more he drew back into himself, offering silence to his wife when she spoke, which was continually, and ignoring her friends. To his young daughter he felt apologetic, knowing that he had done her grave injury. Her stepmother was not particularly unkind to her, but she was always there, and that, to Denham, was worse. Also she was a busy, fussing woman (the fact being that you cannot, in Andorra or anywhere else, run a house, let alone children, without being busy and fussing, which is an excellent reason for running neither), and she made Denham, when she was not at the school she attended in Andorra, help with the work. Denham, who disliked work as much as she disliked company, evaded it so far as she could, and sulked when she could not. Her stepmother punished her for disobedience and laziness, but, finding this quite useless, gave it up as being too much trouble, and confined herself to nagging, which was to her no trouble at all. Denham saw no kind of reason why she should help with activities which she had no desire to have performed; for her part, she would as soon have the house dirty as clean, and as soon eat bread and cheese as cooked foods, so why bother? As to her half-brothers and sisters, she regarded them as useless and worthless objects to have about, and certainly had no intention of exercising on them any of those beneficent activities which infants demand and require. She let them alone; which was her inherited policy in dealing with the whole world, and all she asked of anyone else.

So the years slipped by, chilly and same, until Denham was twenty-one. Then they were same no more, though still chilly, for years are that even outside Andorra.

7

CHAPTER II

The Dobies

I

The relations of Mr Dobie's first wife were coming up to lunch from Andorra town, where they were staying. So the daughter of Mr Dobie's first wife took some bread and cheese and went out at twelve. She had no particular dislike of her mother's relations, who made her shy, but were no more tiresome to her than most other people; but she was bored when people came to lunch, or, indeed, to anything else. They talked, and had to be talked to. They didn't let one alone, and one wasn't allowed to let them alone. Denham's Aunt Evelyn looked at her out of big, long-lashed, childish green eyes and said things that were hard to answer. Perhaps they were clever things, perhaps stupid things; anyhow, Denham had no answer to them. Aunt Evelyn chattered. So did her elder daughter Audrey and her son Guy. Only Noel sat silent, looking like a small carved flower. But she, too, was there, and this is precisely where relations and, indeed, other acquaintances, should not be. Only Humphrey, the second son, a dark and quiet youth of twenty-three, was not there, for he was always somewhere else. This family was, in brief, troublesome; and Denham, holding the view that people should not visit the homes of other people, went out. This is often the only effective course, and one cannot blame those who take it.

So, on this June afternoon, Denham was strolling up the rocky path of Monte Anclar behind Andorra town, full of bread and cheese and the kind of animal content which one experiences when out alone in the country. She was a long-legged, lounging, loosely-built young woman, brown-skinned, blunt-featured, with small dark eyes sunk deep under sulky black brows and a big mouth screwed up into a whistle. She looked and was a loafer. She was untidy; she was probably stupid; she might well be sullen. From the immense quantity of bread and cheese she had just devoured you might infer her greedy. She was obviously no lover of her kind; when she saw anyone whom she knew approaching, she plunged aside off the path and lurked hidden until they were passed by. If you had asked her why, she would have replied, 'Dunno. It's a bother speaking to people when you're out.' And so, of course, it is. Denham Dobie had no intention of giving herself unnecessary trouble. She evaded even the British and American tourists whom she did not know, and who passed from time to time, as they will even in the Pyrenees, for fear they should ask her the way to somewhere. They would begin, cumbrously, 'Perdoneme, Señorita, por donde se va para . . .' and then break off into, 'Oh, you're English, aren't you? What a comfort. Can you direct us to . . . ?'

That was a great nuisance. Denham, looking bored and impassive, would direct them curtly, and turn aside herself in another direction. Why the devil, she speculated, couldn't people look out their own ways on maps? The fact that they enquired she put down partly to congenital idiocy, but more to that strange love of human intercourse, of making talk, which so oddly moves much of mankind and womankind. Talk, talk, talk – how they do go on!

Denham had something of the sly, secret air of a poacher, as she slouched softly in her old sandshoes up the rocky path in the hot sunshine. The afternoon was all right. In the grey house above the town, the relations of her mother would be sitting about after the meal, talking of nothing to her father and stepmother. Of nothing or of something – it made no odds. Few things were worth talking about, anyhow. Denham wondered whether her father had managed to escape yet and go out. Probably he had, and was now walking away from his relations-in-law, having left them to be entertained by his second wife and her children. He felt awkward and shy with them. His sister-in-law, Evelyn Gresham, thought he had behaved stupidly in bringing up Denham in a remote republic only (till lately, when the routes had been improved) to be reached by mule. Her staccato, inconsequent cultured chatter reminded him of his wife's, but it was more resonant and bizarre. She was a graceful, pretty chic creature, in the middle forties, and looking thirty-five; she was black-haired, white-faced, red-lipped, and of a reedy slenderness. She found her brother-in-law and his wife and family surprising, and stared at them round-eyed. He thought her irritating, and was not sure that she was quite right in the head. She lacked shadow and repose; she clacked. Her son Guy, a dark, conceited and mocking young man in the Foreign Office, he found antipathetic, and her daughter Audrey altogether too facile and glib and competently all there. He preferred the younger son and daughter, who did not utter. He failed to see why they should all come bothering him like this, climbing continually up the hill to his house and sitting there just because Denham was their relation. He preferred that Denham should visit them at their inn. Sometimes he made her do this, but usually she refused. Denham was selfish; she was not like those people in stories who consent to be thrown to the enemy on condition that the rest of the garrison are spared. On the contrary, she would even, as we have seen, evade her share of the trouble by stealing off by herself when it was threatened. A selfish girl.

2

Denham stole cautiously in by a back door, lest the visitors should still be there. It is better to pay visits than to suffer them, for if you pay them you have the closure in your hands, whereas if you suffer them, a lunch party may last till after tea. It is not playing the game to make it do so, but not everyone plays the game.

In the patio Denham stopped to listen. The family were drinking coffee within. Through the door drifted a fragment of a familiar discussion, carried on mechanically in the resonant voices of Andorrans speaking their own tongue. The visitors, then, were gone.

'*What* wouldn't father bury?' That was Pepe, probably

endeavouring to change the subject from one inconvenient to himself.

'Heretics, of course, you bad boy.'

'But father's a heretic. Tia Lucia says so.'

Denham went in.

She was overwhelmed with a flood of abuse in Catalan, which ran, approximately, 'Well, by God, Denham! A beautiful way to act, indeed! Sneaking out without a word to anyone, just when your aunt and cousins were coming, and leaving them on my hands. Are they, then, *my* relations, dear God? Jesus Mary, no, they are not. And your father is no better, for he, too, makes off the moment we have eaten lunch, and here was I left with the family of his deceased wife on my hands for the afternoon, waiting on in case you should come in. Was it, then, me that they came to see? No, my God, they look down their noses at me all the time and are thinking of the deceased wife. Because they are English skeletons, they think me too fat.' She ended in English, 'Vulgaire – common – Andorran – how de doo, Meessees Dobee, vairy find day, ees eet not? Good-baee!'

The children laughed, finding their mother witty. Denham, who was not listening, drank coffee.

'No one would think,' continued Mrs Dobie, resuming her native tongue again, 'that you were right as to the head. Pepe, put that cake down till I give it you, greedy boy.'

'Still,' said Pepe, a thoughtful child, 'people ought to be buried when they die. Even heretics ought. If they're not, they smell.'

'Hombre, what chatter! As if your father couldn't decide who should be buried and who should not. Teresa, let Gina's hair alone or I'll smack you. Here comes your father, so now.'

Mr Dobie came in. He was tall and stooping and fifty-five. His face was weak and pale, his eyes looked perpetually away. He sat down and drank coffee, with an air of mild distaste for his company.

'Well,' said his wife, 'you are a nice pair, you two.'

Mr Dobie drank his coffee. Like his daughter, he went his way, and took no notice of complaints.

'Father,' said Pepe, 'will you please tell us about how you wouldn't bury heretics?'

'No,' said Mr Dobie, absently.

Denham's brooding eyes met his, and he looked away. He knew that she knew, though they had never discussed it, that neither reluctance to give dissenters a Christian end nor bastards a Christian beginning had been the reason for his abandonment of the clerical profession. She had long since divined the real reason, for it was the same as her own would have been. He had been bored with having to take trouble, and with doing all the dreadful things that clergymen have to do, and that she dimly remembered her father doing long ago. Clergymen are at it all the time; never an hour to themselves; a desperate life. Of course, he had given it up. The only question was why in the world he had ever taken to it. Bury dissenters? Baptise bastards? He hadn't wanted to bury or baptise anyone at all. But it was a silly-sounding reason he had thought of for ceasing to do so; why not, as Evelyn Gresham enquired, Roman Catholicism, or Doubt? These, however, would have distressed him and disturbed his mind, for he was quite Anglican, though lazy and shy.

Denham finished her coffee and loafed out.

As to poor Mr Dobie, he had a stroke that night, and died. The worry of all these visitors and all this nagging about them had been too much for him. Certainly, people should stay in their own homes.

CHAPTER III

The Greshams

The Greshams sat on the veranda of the Hotel Sièco de Sans after lunch, talking. 'Don't you see, darlings,' Evelyn Gresham was saying, in her clear loud, staccato voice, 'I've got to take Sylvia's girl. Mind you, I don't want to. But I've got to. You see, don't you?'

'What about her paternal relatives?' said Guy. Guy was twenty-five and in the Foreign Office, where he was more capable and industrious than he liked people to think. He was a clever fellow, though a dandy, with trifling and elegant whiskers.

'Impossible,' his mother replied. 'His father was a vet or something. They were quite nothing, and of course are still. Denham can't go to *them*. Even if they'd take her. She's quite uncouth enough as it is. You wouldn't believe she was Sylvia's girl. No, she must come to Mulberry Square.'

'She won't *like* Mulberry Square,' said Audrey. 'Can you see her in London at all? I can't.'

'She probably won't come,' Noel suggested, hopefully. 'She'll be very stupid if she does.'

'I expect,' Audrey said, 'that she *is* very stupid. Those fine-animal types often are. I admire her enormously, in a way. But I think she'll be difficult in London, and not really happy.'

'We'd better board her out in a country home,' said Guy. 'She ought to be chopping wood and pasturing flocks. To keep her in Mulberry Square would be cruelty to animals.'

'Oh, don't keep calling her animals, children. It's silly, do you see? And unkind. She's your cousin, and your aunt Sylvia's girl. Yes, Sylvia's girl. She must come to us. It's a home she wants. A home, away from that awful woman and dirty house.'

'Certainly,' said Audrey, reflectively, 'it is rather dirty. But perhaps Denham likes dirt. She's not very well washed herself. All the same, I like her. Do you, Noel?'

Noel thought for a moment. Then, 'Not specially,' she answered, in her neat, small voice. 'I shall wait and see.'

Noel's personal relationships were a fastidious and restrained business. She committed herself slowly, if at all. Audrey liked more people, and sooner.

'Well,' said Evelyn, 'I shall go up there this afternoon. You'd better come with me, Audrey. A girl of her own age.'

'I'll come if you like,' said Guy.

'No, Guy. That's silly. Audrey must come.'

'All right, mother, if I must. I'm not very keen on it, though. Our step-aunt may not want us.'

'Oh, she won't. She won't want us. I'm sure she hates me. For being Sylvia's sister, you know. Hates me. Spanish women get terribly fat. That reminds me – where's Humphrey?'

'Why ask?' Guy murmured. 'You have said it.'

His mother sighed. 'I wish Humphrey wouldn't. There'll be another scandal. You might try to stop him, Guy.'

'I stop Humphrey from pursuing a lovely creature? My dear mother!'

'She certainly is a lovely creature,' Audrey said.

'He told me he hated her,' said Evelyn. 'I don't understand Humphrey. Simply, you know, I don't understand him.'

'Humphrey,' said his brother, 'has his own meanings for words. By "hate", as applied to lovely females, he means the desire to pursue and capture.'

'Though it makes him quite miserable and angry,' Audrey added. 'And he despises them and himself all the time. He finds women disillusioning. He thinks it's women in general, but really it's because he goes for the wrong sort. He won't ever fall in love with civilised, intelligent, nice women. So of course he comes down with a bump every time. It's quite his own fault. He's silly.'

'Everyone's silly about love,' said Evelyn, brightly. 'In one way or another. Yes. Everyone's terribly silly about love.'

'A terribly silly subject,' said Guy. 'But the difference between Humphrey and, say, me, is that I enjoy my silliness and his makes him unhappy. I mean, hang it all, if you can't enjoy your love-affairs, why have them?'

Noel got up and walked away. She had had no love-affairs yet, nor desired them; but she read poetry, and she found that Guy made the subject common. She saw love as a wild and high adventure, not as something agreeable to eat.

'I shall start at once,' said Evelyn. 'If I don't go at once, I shall never go. I don't want to, a bit, but I feel I must.'

She threw away her last cigarette stub and got up from her low chair. She was very graceful, from her small dark head to her small scarlet-shod feet. Her ankles and wrists were slim like a child's. She wore a white silk knitted jumper and a scarlet frieze skirt. Her skin was smooth and white and shining, and the lashes over her big green eyes long and black. Her dark hair was brushed sleekly back from her round forehead and closely cut. She had high cheekbones and a small thin mouth and a charming smile. Audrey always said that she looked decadent, and like a Beardsley woman shingled. Audrey was proud of her mother for not looking ordinary and undistinguished and middle-aged. She herself was just a pretty and pleasant-looking girl; but Evelyn had a cachet. Noel's head and face had the delicate, clear beauty of a cameo, and Guy had his elegance and his whiskers and Humphrey a kind of sad, tormented, clever look. Besides looking well, they were artistic, literary, political, musical and cultured. So, as families go, they were all right, in Chelsea, though, except Humphrey, they were not quite fit for Bloomsbury. Evelyn and Audrey set forth up the hill path.

CHAPTER IV

The Snare

I

Denham was stupid and sullen and dazed. She felt that it was forward of these people to have come over so soon, with Mr Dobie lying dead in his bedroom and Mrs Dobie wailing in hers. However, Mrs Dobie, perhaps desiring distraction from her grief, put on a thick layer of mauve powder, came downstairs to see the visitors, and was very rude to them in two languages.

'My God,' she remarked to Mrs Gresham in Catalan, 'is it I who have lost my husband, or your deceased sister? I think that it is I. This, by God, is my affair, and not by any means yours. If you have come to see your niece, there she is. *She* does not weep; Jesus Mary, no. She feels no grief for her poor father. You had better take her away with you to England, had you not?'

Mrs Gresham, who had travelled so much that she talked practically all European languages adequately, replied in the purest Castilian that this was precisely what she hoped to do.

Denham stared at her, looking like a child about to cry, her underlip pushed out, her face red.

'Vairy well,' said Mrs Dobie, in English, which she believed that she spoke well. 'Oh, yes, cairtainly. She is mooch too good for Andorra. She had bettaire go to England and be a fine lady like her mothaire. By God,' she broke into Catalan, 'she looks a fine lady, indeed! Do me the favour to look at her.' She waved a hand at Denham, who lounged sullenly in the window, in a brown cotton dress which needed washing, bare legs, and broken shoes.

The English looked at her, with sympathy and no scorn.

Meeting two pairs of kindly eyes, clear green and candid grey, Denham turned redder and her underlip stuck out farther.

A cool, smooth hand was in hers. A pleasant girl's voice said, 'You *will* come to England with us, won't you, Denham? We want you.'

Denham blinked. She saw Audrey, fair-faced and kind, and beyond her Evelyn, a dazzling figure in scarlet, white and black. These two against the dreary litter of the parlour, and, as a foil to them, Mrs Dobie, surging out of a black dress, her mauve face blotched with crying.

Anger and some other feeling fought blindly in Denham's soul. Anger that these people should have come, cool and lovely and exquisite, to stare at and despise her father's family and home.

'Yes, darling child,' said her Aunt Evelyn's clear, loud voice. 'Of course you'll come. It's all quite settled. Of course you'll come.

Exquisite, fascinating, forward; which were they? Had her mother been like that? Denham's memory, leaping back, believed that she had. That clear, staccato voice – it called her across the years. Darling child; darling child. Oh, yes, mother. Yes, Aunt Evelyn. Of course I'll come.

'Dunno,' Denham mumbled, and awkwardly pulled her brown hand out of Audrey's white one. 'Dunno yet.'

'Oh, yes, cairtainly,' said Mrs Dobie. 'To be sure she go with you. Why no? She don't like the people 'ere; she spik to nobody; she 'ide from all our friends when they come. Perhaps in Inglaterra there will be peoples good enough for 'er. Oh, yes, cairtainly she go with you, señoras, if you will 'ave 'er.

'Oh, we *want* to have her, Mrs Dobie. That's just it, do you see? We *want* to have her, terribly. That's quite settled, then. We're starting back today week, Denham. Can you be ready by then?'

Denham said nothing, not yet sure whether she could be ready ever to start with strangers to a strange land. No; on the whole she was sure she could not; but nevertheless, ready or unready, she seemed to be going to do so.

The ladies said good-bye. They went. They took the steep hill path down to Andorra in the afternoon sunshine.

Denham stared after them, frowning, from a rock above the house. All this going with people, or, alternatively, staying behind with other people . . . was it necessary? Why not go with oneself, stay with oneself? Of course, there was the money question; she knew she had a little, left her by her father, and she would jolly well see she got it, too; but it probably wasn't much. And then there was Aunt Evelyn's odd, absurd, familiar grace, and her 'darling child', and Audrey, cool and fair, like a flower with kind eyes. Denham felt dazed, dazzled, helpless. These people dragged at her, with their kind chatter and their grace. Oh, yes, certainly she'd go with them; in the end she'd go, whatever fight she put up. A rabbit might as well say it would not go with a snake.

2

There passed Denham a dishevelled, bare-headed and pale young man, running down the hill, fleeing ineffectually from his passions and his doom. A tormented young man, who could not even go for a holiday in Andorra without finding trouble there, trouble in beauteous female shape, to be hated and desired. He was cultured; he was intellectual; he knew about architecture, cathedrals, pictures and beauty; but these did not guard his soul from the assaults of love and hate when he met a handsome female peasant. He ran down the hill path, from the peasant's home to Andorra town; he ran, but he could not shake it off. How she disgusted him! How she was vulgar, stupid, gross! How extreme was his distaste for her mind, her soul, her insipid, silly chatter! How he was bored when she threw her arms round his neck! And how, with what intensity, what craving ardour, he desired her!

'My God,' said Denham, in mild surprise, seeing him rush by. 'This sun has touched his head.' But she knew that he was also keeping company with Paquita Jaime up at Las Escaldas, for all Andorra knew that.

'How it vexes him,' Denham reflected. 'I don't wonder. She would vex me, Paquita Jaime. What does he do it for, then? Very probably he is not quite right in his mind,' she indifferently concluded, as she moodily climbed the hill, to be out of earshot of the house in case she should be called.

22

She sat down on a rock and reflected. Was there, then, in all these mountains, a-glitter with blue and gold flowers in the sun, no place for her, no spot where she could stay, unmolested and alone, and go her own way? Not, of course, in Andorra town. There one would be pursued by the amenities of people one knew, and by the loud importunities of a nagging step-mother. Besides, how could one live?

Beyond the frowning mountains there was Spain on two sides, France on the other two; beyond Spain and France the rest of the world. To see the rest of the world was, after all, an adventure. To see England, her father's home, her mother's . . .

The infant Denham had loved her mother. The girl Denham had been mildly fond of her father. These two English persons in a foreign family had accepted and understood one another, in a tolerant, undemonstrative way. Two selfish, idle, unsociable people, they had neither desired one another's companionship, nor offered their own; they had each gone their ways, aloof and content so long as no one bothered them. They had understood one another, without intimacy. Denham missed her father.

Denham, who accepted life as it came, did not reflect how strange it was that her father, a solitary man, one of the world's recluses, should have married her mother, a talking woman, a civilised, cultured woman, a woman of the world. Nor how strange it was again, that, having fled to a Pyrenean republic for remoteness and freedom, he should have taken yet another wife, tied himself up again with obligations, with perpetual companionship. Denham was right not to think this strange, for it was not strange at all. It was merely life. Neither was it strange that she, who loved freedom and aloneness, was going to England with relations who knew neither. Nothing, perhaps, is strange, once you have accepted life itself, the great strange business which includes all lesser strangenesses.

There was a scrambling in the fir copse, and a small, solid brown boy climbed on to the rock. It was Pepe.

'She sent me to find you,' he remarked. 'She says you're to come in, and not go out till after the funeral.'

'Oh, go away.'

'She said you were to come in at once. She is angry.'

'I said, go away.'

'Am I, then, to tell her you won't come?'

'If you like. I'm not coming in yet.'

'Well,' said Pepe, indifferently, 'I shan't go home myself, then, yet. She'll be angry. I shall go and play in the town.'

He slithered off the rock.

Peace descended again; that peace which is the reward of competent dealing with relations.

CHAPTER V

Trapped

I

The motor diligence from the Andorran republic to the wider world started from Las Escaldas. It contained the Greshams, a few Andorrans going about their business to neighbouring towns, one Spaniard going to Spain, two Americans, and a great quantity of English. You would not believe, did you not see it, the number of English who were apparently visiting this small country.

'Andorre is being opened up,' Evelyn explained brightly to no one in particular. She always gave the republic its French name, for she had been brought up in France, and greatly admired Gallic civilisation. 'Yes; opened up.'

'Mon Dieu!' Guy gently murmured to Denham, as they dashed off down the steep road. 'The Hidden Republic is hidden no more from God's own tourist. It has become a resort of fashion. We search the world for loneliness and find only the British. One never feels such distaste for one's countrymen and countrywomen as when one meets them abroad. No?'

Denham looked round at their fellow travellers.

'I don't know,' she answered, literally. 'I've never seen them anywhere else, I suppose.'

His pleasant dark eyes smiled at her.

'No more you have! You've yet to meet the lion in his native lair. But don't tell me you don't detest tourists.'

'Not,' said Denham, considering it, 'more than natives. Less than natives, really, because I don't usually know them, and they don't stay so long.'

'True. Two excellent points in our favour. But you'll admit we mar the landscape, wherever we are. You'll grant that we're not exactly aesthetic ornaments in a countryside. Anyhow, I can assure you that we detest meeting one another; it irritates the nobler types among us to frenzy. Partly because it reminds us that, however noble, we too are tourists, partly because it spoils that abroad feeling, and gently speaks of England, home and duty. Of course there *are* tourists who flock together and like it, but those are the baser types, and we despise them ... Poor Humphrey is looking quite sick and wan, either with turismo, the motion of Andorran diligences, or *l'amour.*'

Denham, looking back at Andorra la Vieja, from which they so quickly ran, thought, what a lot he talks. Does he go on like this all the time?

She soon found that he did. She decided that it was less trouble to make no attempt to answer.

Swinging round the hairpin bends of the shocking road, Humphrey grew all the way gloomier and gloomier. They entered Spain, through Seo d'Urgel, and dismounted at the French frontier for lunch and the customs.

'Nothing to declare,' said Humphrey, bored, in Italian, the language he always spoke abroad. 'Nothing. Nothing at all. All these cigars are in process of being smoked. You do not think so? You are quite right. But I shall not pay, for I shall not cross your frontier today. I am returning to Andorra. I have left something behind which I must fetch.'

'What in the world are you talking about, darling?' asked Evelyn, at his elbow. 'What have you left behind?'

'My watch,' said Humphrey, gloomily. 'I left it at the inn. I shall go back and fetch it, and follow you in a few days.'

'You're going all the way back to Andorre! But, darling, how silly. They'll send it all right, if you write.'

'I don't think so. I shall go myself ... Anyhow, I don't like the look of the French weather, and there are these cigars ... Take my portmanteau with you. I shall walk back by the bridle path.' He drew out his watch. Guy gently pressed it back into its pocket.

'There is a clock,' he said, just above us. It would look better were you to consult it.'

2

The rest of the party slept that night at Ax-les-Thermes. Guy went in the evening to a cabaret, where, said Audrey, he hoped he might see something improper.

'Well,' said Evelyn, 'I wish Humphrey was here, to go with him. Mind you, I don't like that kind of thing myself, it's so stupid, but it cheers the boys up. It would cheer up poor old Humphrey terribly, and take his mind off that girl. Now in Andorre there's not so much as a cinema. It's funny, but being terribly intellectual and all that doesn't seem to prevent men enjoying themselves in that way. It's funny.'

Her daughter Noel looked as if it was not. Noel, fastidious, Oxford, and nineteen, turned a deaf ear to some of her family's conversation. Audrey sometimes called her a prig, and possibly she was. She could not, however, help it. When her reticence or her taste was offended, she withdrew as into a shell.

Guy came in late, and said next morning that the cabaret had been dull and poor.

'The Pyrenees are altogether too primitive. No grace or wit or elegance. I nearly asked for my money back.'

'What did you see, darling?' Evelyn asked.

'Oh, well, it wasn't quite so dull as all that,' said Guy. 'What time is that train?'

'I'm really vexed with Humphrey,' said Evelyn, when they were seated in the Midi express. 'It's too bad of him. Goodness knows how long he'll stay in that place now.'

'Long enough for his purposes, no doubt,' said Guy.

'That,' said Evelyn, 'is the worst of his having no job to do, only writing. Now if it were you, you would have to be back at the Foreign Office on a given day. Humphrey can stay in Andorre for ever. He may marry her.'

'He's never married them yet,' Audrey consoled her.

'Well, I don't know that it's not as bad ... ' Evelyn glanced towards Denham and Noel and the other occupants of the compartment, and dropped her voice a fraction of a tone. 'He may bring her home with him. Back to London, like that girl from Thermopylae, and the one from San Gimignano. Mind you, I'm not prudish, but I do say it's too many. It's not fair on the girls, for one thing. And, too, it's extravagant. It's not even as if they made him happy, either. They all get on his nerves after a bit, and of course this one will too. I do call it tiresome of Humphrey. His father'll be so annoyed. I wish he'd marry some nice girl and have done.'

'He'll never have done,' said Guy, 'however many nice girls he marries. He wouldn't go on thinking them nice for more than about a week. Humphrey's an idealist; that's what ails him. He won't be happy till he gets her – and he never will get her.' He yawned, lit a cigarette, and began to read *Le Rire*.

Denham thought what a very sociable young man her cousin Humphrey must be. Thermopylae, San Gimignano, and now Andorra. Did Thermopylae, San Gimignano, and Humphrey live all together, she wondered, in one house? And would Paquita from Las Escaldas live there too? Of course, an idealist in the matter of human companionship has to be very sociable, or else not sociable at all; he must either try every one in turn, or try no one. Denham thought she would rather try no one; it would save trouble.

'Well,' said Evelyn, settling in her corner, 'father'll be terribly disgusted. Terribly. Give me a cigarette, darling, will you. Are you comfortable, Denham dear? Really, quite?'

No, Denham was not comfortable, though she did not say so. She disliked sitting still, and her aunt and cousins, being English gentlewomen, always when they travelled in trains opened a window wide and admitted a current of cold air. Denham, though reared in cold air, disliked currents of it in trains. Also, she wore a thin cotton dress and only a waterproof over it. The Greshams had tweed coats and skirts; it was all very well for them; besides, English gentlewomen are hardy as to cold air, though hot air or close air routs them at once.

As to their mania for admitting cold air into rooms, it is shared by no one; even their brothers, English gentlemen, know better than that. Gentlemen know that fresh air should be kept in its proper place – out of doors – and that, God having given us indoors and out-of-doors, we should not attempt to do away with this distinction. But ladies will have meals out and fresh air in, and generally confuse the universe. Denham, though in no sense a lady, liked meals out, too; but she did not like cold air in. Also, she felt train-sick and home-sick and cooped up, and gloomily uncertain as to whither life was taking her. Gloomily conscious, too, of inferiority, of poor clothes and manners and ungentle outlook. This bright, finished, gay, polite family, so merry, so chattering, so friendly, so kind, so expensively neat – what was she among them? A cold kind of wary doubt, like an animal's, fought in her with adventurous desire. One was trapped by such desires into intimacies closer than one's sober self approved.

3

Interesting it was, thought Denham, to be in France; flying along at what seemed to her, knowing few trains, a tremendous pace towards Toulouse. To be in Spain one moment, to be in France the next – it made the heart stir and flutter like a goldfinch wakened from sleep. Frontiers; what romance! Not all the nagging *douanes* and impatient queues of passengers could spoil it. Say frontier, frontier, frontier, ten times, and the word unlike most words so treated, still retains a meaning. Love, hate, friendship, virtue, vice, God – these become as sounding brass and tinkling cymbals, but frontiers remain.

Outside the dashing train, now descended from the Pyrenees, was the neat Aude country, rivers and small hills and little old towns and farms. English people in the trains, but on the stations French people, the French of the south. Farther north they would become squat and plain and Gallic, but here were Latins. Bright, vivacious, charming people, gayer than Andorrans.

The Greshams weren't interested in the journey, because they knew it already. A travelled family. It was wonderful how much they knew about abroad. They glanced at Carcassonne in passing, only to complain of Viollet-le-Duc's towers. All the way Guy and his mother bought and read French newspapers. Sometimes Guy bought a funny one, but he only pretended to be amused by it; comic papers did not actually amuse him, in any language, for they were not clever enough, and continental pictorial humour seemed to him very naïve. However, since he was cosmopolitan, and a man of the world, he read and chuckled over foreign comic papers, though not English ones. Evelyn thought them terribly dull, Audrey found them crude, and Noel was bored by the large proportion of jokes about men and women in love.

The Gresham ladies (or, anyhow, Evelyn and Audrey) read the more serious French press, and understood, apparently, all they read, and had a lot to say about the *lois laïques*, M. Heriot, and so on. There was nothing, thought Denham, even in foreign newspapers, but provided food for intelligent comment from this well-instructed family, nothing at which they gaped and said, 'Never heard of it,' which she said herself when they tried to include her in their conversation. What lives they must have led, mugging things up! Hardly worth it, really;

they could scarcely have known an hour's leisure in their lives, not one hour when they were being merely stupid and idle and taking in nothing at all. For a time Denham hoped that Noel was, perhaps, stupid, because she did not talk so much as the others; but she soon discovered that Noel made entirely apposite and shrewd remarks from time to time, in her clear, dry little voice, and understood everything that was said, and was not stupid at all. So no one in the compartment was stupid except Denham, unless it was the German lady in the corner, who looked it.

Denham went to sleep.

4

Rain began, as it does in central and northern France. The skies were overcast; the south lay behind. The people at the stations were no longer Latins, happy and idle, but Gauls, worried and industrious, the world's busiest workers, thriftiest savers, hardest haters, and best bureaucrats. Their talk was sharp and quick; they would stand no nonsense; one could imagine that it was they who had first conceived passports, to prevent the world's denizens from moving about their planet as they chose.

Evelyn, looking with her green stare beneath long curled lashes at her sleeping niece in the corner, thought kindly, What shall we make of her, the gawky child? Will she shape? What in the world shall we make of her in London? ... Anyhow, I couldn't do anything else. She's not a bit like Sylvia. Not one little bit. I suppose she takes after her father's people in Devonshire. What can we train her to do? Of course, she may marry ... Some men like that barbaric style; it makes a change ... I can't imagine her learning to be a doctor, or a lawyer, or a teacher, or a secretary, or any of the usual jobs. She might play some instrument – the 'cello, perhaps. She looks like that, rather – that heavy face with high cheekbones that musicians have, often from being Slavs, I suppose. But I don't think she knows a thing about music; not a thing. The question is, what *does* she know anything about? We haven't struck it yet. I don't suppose that Andorre school taught her anything ... Those fearful clothes; we must see to that the very day after we get home. Either she's terribly shy, or she hasn't an idea in her head. She never says anything – not anything to count. I suppose she's sure to be right in her head, poor child? That awful woman did say something ... What nonsense, the child's only paralysed; simply paralysed with shyness. Audrey must take her in hand. The idea of her and Audrey being the same age! It's ridiculous. She's like a child of twelve.

Denham opened her eyes and, meeting her aunt's, coloured. Evelyn smiled at her, and thought, I believe she likes me a little already. Touching, poor child. Then she stared out of the window at her darling France, which she adored, and which always fleeted by so quickly in the rain. She had a French grandmother, and had been to school in France. She was a quarter French by blood, and more by sympathies.

PART TWO

THE HIGHER LIFE

CHAPTER I

Seeing London

I

Peter Gresham was a bland, gay and shrewd little publisher. He knew everyone worth knowing, as the phrase goes; he ran hither and thither about London, talking, dining, appraising, collecting pictures, furniture and good stories, witnessing the drama (nearly always on first nights, in someone's box), and yet not forgetting or omitting to publish books which brought him kudos or cash, or both, as well, of course, as the necessary number of those other books which bring neither, and which publishers, it is thought, publish out of kindness. He was a happy little man; his hospitality, his dinners, his cigars and his drinks were well spoken of among his friends. His town house, in Chelsea, was a centre of social life and entertainment; his country house, in Surrey, was a weekend resort of many. Since his family, like himself, was sociable and friendly, none of them found it too many, either in country or town. The world *is* many; the Greshams accepted that fact, and liked it. So many was it already that they could add a new cousin to it and scarcely notice the addition. A new and strange resident upsets some households, makes them creak and strain uneasily, causes irritation, throws a blight. To the Greshams it was but one more person in their already thickly populated world; there was a pretty little bedroom empty which had been Catherine's before her marriage, and into it Denham went. The Gresham hospitality was extraordinary. Peter beamed on his wife's niece through his rimless glasses, and told her she would enjoy London. Nothing like London, said Peter. Denham quite agreed. Nothing she had ever seen before was in the least like London.

2

London. The problem was, why did so many people live in it? Millions and millions of people, swarming over the streets, as thick as flies over a dead goat, as buzzing and as busy. Why? Did they all agree with Uncle Peter that nothing was like London and that they must, therefore, be in London, this unique spot? Did they all *have* to be here? Had they been adopted by relations and brought here, or did they do something here which they couldn't do elsewhere? Shops, factories, offices, newspapers – millions of people, it seemed, worked in these; presumably they would starve if they didn't. Uncle Peter had to go to his publishing office, of course; that kept him in London. Audrey attended the publishing office too, Guy the Foreign Office, and Humphrey various newspaper offices. Catherine was married to a Member of Parliament. But why did Aunt Evelyn, who did not attend offices and could have lived all the time in a house in the country, elect to live all the week in

London? To be with the others, possibly – Uncle Peter and the rest. Some people had that idea – that people mattered, that it was important to be with the people one liked. Denham hadn't it. She thought that the thing was to be happy and comfortable, in a nice place.

Denham, with her customary sweeping dismissal of what she did not understand, presumed that Londoners were mostly mad. Obviously, quite obviously mad. They walked along the streets even on the coldest, most disagreeable days, with the slow, halting gait of persons who followed a hearse.

'Why do they all walk so slowly?' Denham asked Audrey, as they picked their way along Oxford Street.

'There's such a crowd,' Audrey replied, as if this were an answer. But it was no answer. Why should many people walk more slowly than one? If they all wanted to move fast, why should the fact that there were many prevent them?

It was the same on the moving stairways at the underground stations. People crawled slowly down them, even when their trains were just coming in. Of course, if they preferred slow movement, it was all right; but it seemed queer that so many apparently able-bodied people should enjoy moving like invalids. Surely it was more fun on a moving stairway to run?

And then the streets. Thousands and thousands of omnibuses, taxis, vans and cars, all roaring down the streets together, like an army going into battle, mowing down with angry trumpetings such human life as crossed their path. Were they all necessary? Was human life in London so cheap? Denham, after the first, had no personal anxieties on this head, for she felt competent to evade the assaults of these monsters, neither had she much pity for the victims, for they could probably well be spared, and certainly the population needed thinning; but it seemed a curious way of doing it.

They went shopping for clothes. Evelyn took Denham to a dressmaker, and had her clad. Audrey took Denham to a hairdresser, and had her shingled. Shingled and clad, Denham had a certain distinction of style, with her long, strong, straight body, broad dark head, narrow dark eyes sunk deep under low black brows (Audrey said she ought to have these thinned, but at this she rebelled), square jaw, and the thrust-out underlip of an arguing child. A fine-looking young woman, people called her, though not pretty. The peasant type. A foreign or Celtic peasant, not Anglo-Saxon. Evelyn was rather proud of her. She looked more interesting than most nieces, if she said less. Chiefly she said 'Why?' The Greshams, intelligent but busy, sometimes had time and inclination to tell her, sometimes not. She said 'Why?' when her Uncle Peter took her to his office, and she saw rooms stacked from floor to ceiling with books.

Peter could tell her that.

'In the hope that people will buy them, of course.'

'Why should people buy them?'

'Oh, to read, I suppose.'

Denham's eyes wandered over the incredible piles, catching a title here and there. *Studies of Contemporary Drama* – hundreds of them, lying in a great heap. Would anyone in the world read a book called that? Drama was surely to be looked at, not read about. Then she saw the author's name,

'Humphrey Gresham.' Of course; that would be why Uncle Peter was publishing it.

'Humphrey's book of collected dramatic criticisms,' Uncle Peter said, seeing her look at it. 'It's coming out in a week.' He looked annoyed because Humphrey was still in the Pyrenees with some absurd woman, and he thought this very silly. Denham too thought Humphrey silly, but more because he thought it worth while to write and publish criticism of plays than because he was staying in the Pyrenees, which had sense. Denham had been taken to several plays in London, and she could not understand what there was to do about plays except see them, or why anyone should want to read or hear what anyone else thought of them. Did anyone's opinion of anything matter, except one's own, she wondered. And, even if you hadn't seen a play yourself, you wouldn't be any nearer knowing whether you would like it from reading anyone else's views of it. Denham knew this, for she had tried, and been badly deceived. Most plays, she had discovered, were tedious stuff, about people sitting in drawing-rooms and talking, and getting excited about love, and so on; but what the critics wrote of them was much stupider still.

The same with books. Books were mostly dull enough, but criticisms of books were quite unreadable. The Greshams all read them, but then they appeared to be so constituted as to be able to read anything. It was nearly a disease with them.

'Here,' said Peter, opening a door, 'is where Audrey works.'

Audrey sat at a table, surrounded with papers and books, the sunshine striking a dusty beam on her fair head and neat white silk shirt. She was dictating to a shorthand typist. She looked cool and pretty and competent and clean. She smiled at her father and cousin, and finished dictating her letter, which was to tell someone that Mr Gresham would be happy to consider his novel should he curtail and amend it. What a good letter, thought Denham, admiring Audrey. What a good choice of words. 'Consider' was just right; it committed you to nothing.

Peter quickly turned over press notices of a new book of memoirs.

'Bad,' he grunted, flicking through them. 'Good. Moderate. Oh, of course, the *Era's* sure to crab him, since they had that row. Who does it in the *World*? Jimmy Metcalf – good; he'll be all right about it; I dined him well last week. Sidney Bendish in the *Period*: spiteful fellow, crabs it, of course. Gregson in the *Comet*; heavy, but useful. That the lot? Now I must leave you, Denham. Audrey'll look after you. Miss Watkins, send someone to find Mr Chapel and ask him to come to my room at once.'

He hurried away, bustling through the office like a plump little whirlwind.

'There's so much fuss and work suddenly created in the office when father comes,' said Audrey. 'It's like stirring up dust. It doesn't subside till he goes out to lunch. Would you care to sit and look at some of the books, Denham, till I'm through? Then we'll go to lunch.'

She indicated a bookshelf stacked with volumes in paper jackets. Denham looked at them, without appreciation. *Comparative Psychology*, *Some Literary Movements*, *The Nineties in Perspective*, *Mildew* (someone's poems), *Borax and Honey* (someone else's poems), *Verse of Today* (everyone's poems), *Shortbread* (someone's novel), *The Wheels Go Round* (someone's play), *Maunderings* (someone's essays), *The Greenhouse*, *The*

Greenfinch, *Midnight and Morning* (novels), *An Edwardian's Past* (memoirs), *The Dalmatian Coast* (with maps). This last Denham condescended to take out and inspect. It seemed sensible, and had nine maps. One could read a book like that. She sat down and did so. All books should have maps. If Uncle Peter didn't know that, he ought to be told. Maps attracted readers. If *Shortbread* had a map on its cover instead of a black young man with nothing on, dancing a foxtrot beneath a black sun, someone might buy it. Having done so, the purchaser would no doubt be disappointed, but it might then be too late to return it. What incomprehensible rot most books were. But this Dalmatian coast book seemed all right.

'The sea at this point is very shallow, and care should be taken between points A and B (see chart).' Whether this author was right or wrong, this was a subject worth writing on, unlike most subjects written on in books.

'There,' said Audrey. 'Let's come out. Early July's a dreadful time in the office – such a hustle to clear off everything before the slack time.'

But early July was all right out of doors. The young ladies walked across Green Park. The sun shone slightly but truly, and the park was bland and bright, and full of midsummer greenery, gentlemen and ladies poised for flight to country places, lower persons, paper bags, lovers, racing children, and dogs. Audrey chattered away; they met friends; all was gaiety. They visited a bookshop in Chandos Street and discussed where they would lunch. Denham perceived and indicated a ham and beef shop with marble tables which they passed in St Martin's Lane, and Audrey said, 'Good gracious, no – it's filthy.'

'Is it? How do you know?'

'Well, it's obvious from a mile off. Here's the St George's; that'll do.'

But Denham, used to Pyrenean cafes, could not see that the ham and beef shop was filthy. She lacked standards. Would there be dirt in the food, she speculated, or on the tables and chairs? A lot of people seemed to be putting up with it all right. But probably not ladies and gentlemen. Ladies would rather not lunch at all than lunch filthily. They preferred hunger to dirt, and they detected dirt in such odd places, where the vulgar eye could perceive none.

4

After lunch Audrey returned to the office, and Denham strolled about the streets alone. When alone she felt relieved from strain; she dropped down to her natural level. With these Greshams life was like walking on a tight-rope. The things you mustn't do, mustn't wear. You must, for instance, spend a great deal of money on silk stockings, when, for much less you could have got artificial silk or lisle thread. Why? Did not these meaner fabrics equally clothe the leg? Why had people agreed that one material was the right wear and that others did not do? Why did not anything do?

The same with gloves, with shoes, with frocks, with garments underneath frocks. In all these things people had set up a standard, and if you did not conform to it you were not right, you were left. You wore thick stockings and brogues in the country, thin stockings and high-heeled shoes in the town. You wore a hat if you gave a lunch party, a sleeveless dress in the evening. You had, somehow or other, to conform to a ritual, to be like the people you knew. You had to have, when you ate, one food brought in after another, each with fresh plates and different kinds of instruments to eat them with, as if on purpose to take time and trouble the servants. Trouble, indeed, to others and to oneself, seemed to be one the greatest objects of this strange human life.

Denham sometimes dreamed of a life in which one took practically no trouble at all. One would be alone; one would have no standards; there would be a warm climate and few clothes, and all food off the same plate, if a plate at all. And no conversation ... It would be a very low-class, lazy, common life; it was better not to think about it while one was trying to be civilised and high-class. Thinking about it might cause a lapse, such as savages make from time to time when missionaries have captured and trained them. Denham, a savage captured by life, was trying to grasp its principles. She enquired continually why one thing was better than another, and tried to understand the answers, which were vague, or careless, or cynical, according to the occasion and the answerer.

'Because we've agreed that it shall be done like that,' Guy said once about something, and added, 'And if you want to know why we all have to do things in the same way, you had better go and watch sheep in a field or monkeys at the Zoo. You want to know a great deal too much, Denham. You had better join my Church, which doesn't encourage questions.' For Guy, incongruously, was a Roman Catholic. 'You see, he's in the Foreign Office,' Evelyn had vaguely explained, and Denham had accepted this reason without surprise, supposing that, since many foreigners were Roman Catholics, those who had to correspond with them and consider their affairs found it convenient to be Roman Catholic too.

'Not,' Audrey had put in, 'that Guy really believes anything of the sort, I'm sure. He couldn't however hard he tried. Any more than I could. Could you, Denham?'

'I don't know,' Denham had said. 'I've never tried.' But what she really felt was that one might perhaps succeed in believing almost anything, if one tried hard and long. Almost any kind of life you might enter. Putting on Roman Catholicism was probably no more difficult than putting on culture. But there would always be a part of you, a secret, hidden part, which would never put on anything, but would stay as it was born, naked, savage, sceptical and untutored.

Denham, lounging along Charing Cross Road, jingled the coins in her pocket and decided to go again to the Zoo. She was luckier, she felt, than Audrey, wasting a fine afternoon among those awful books. What a trade it was, increasing the number of books in a world already overstocked with them! As bad as parents, who increased the number of people. There must be millions of books already that people hadn't read. If they must read, let them read those. Yet Uncle Peter poured forth books all the time, as pleased as a cat having kittens, and half the people who came about the Greshams' house seemed to have a hand in writing them. It was obviously part of the higher life. Perhaps they'd try to make her do it sometime. Audrey was writing a novel, and Evelyn had written, and wrote, short stories, and Noel poetry, and Guy articles and biographies and light verse, and Catherine political tracts, and Humphrey every kind of thing, even a play of the kind that is acted on Sundays. Yes, they would be sure to try and make

46

her write, sometime. It was like going to picture-shows, a thing cultured people had agreed among themselves to do. If she ever had to write a book, it would be nearly all maps. Large-scale maps of country paths and roads. The reading would say what the paths and roads were like; nothing else. She would like to do Andorra, which had never been properly mapped, because Andorrans are a backward people. Would that kind of book count as a real book, like a clever, noble book about politics, or love, or contemporary drama, or millionaires found murdered in their libraries? Would it make Catherine stop despising her?

'Damn Catherine,' muttered Denham, and bought a bag of animal food and forgot the higher life.

CHAPTER II

Going to the Play

I

Humphrey came home. He was sick of love. Disillusioned young man, he had left his Paquita abruptly, having found her out in treacheries with another, nay, with many others. Denham could have told him from the first that those were Paquita's habits. He would have found no difficulty in believing her, for he knew all women to be liars and cheats; but, until he had found her out himself, he had endured it for love's sake. Now he was through with her; she was as bad as all the rest, as all the frail female creatures of Thermopylae, San Gimignano and London. Base, common, vulgar cheats; alas that man, a rational and spiritual being, should be chained by his desires to these earthen vessels. Humphrey returned to his bachelor chambers in Half Moon Street and resumed the pen, with a vain gesture of repudiation towards an entire sex. He meant to write another play for Sundays, more bitter and ironic than ever. And, since it was only for Sundays, he need not be squeamish as to what he said.

He went round to Mulberry Square the evening after his arrival, looking gloomy and pale. Families are like midges, invented to annoy one.

'Well, darling,' said Evelyn, kissing him. 'You look terribly ill. Was the crossing shocking?' She did not like to ask whether he had come to England alone or with a woman.

'Did you find your watch?' asked Guy, who was also there for the evening. 'You had quite a long hunt for it, anyhow.'

'Yes,' said Humphrey. 'I've got it. When I got back there I thought I might as well stay on a little. I knew it would be vile weather here.'

'Oh, don't apologise,' said Guy.

Peter bustled in.

'Well, Humphrey, well, well. You're only just in time for your book.' His eyes, through their round glasses, telegraphed to his wife: 'Has he brought her back with him?'

'What book?' said Humphrey, bored. 'Oh, I remember. I remember. I rather wish it had come out while I was away. Now I shall have to see the reviews.'

'Oh, they'll be all right,' said Peter. 'Got to be, since you write for half the papers that will review you.'

'They'll be just as usual, no doubt,' Humphrey replied. 'Praise from one's friends and blame from one's enemies, both equally stupid. I don't care to see them. I'd have stayed away, only my money ran out.'

Catherine dashed in. She was dining with them, between two Liberal meetings. She looked dashing and chic, in her short, swinging skirts and small smart hat, her shingled head well poised, her soft, dimpled face full of vivacity and politics.

She was twenty-four, and had been married for two years to a Liberal Member of Parliament.

'Hallo, dear boy. Find your watch?' – for Guy had told her that.

Humphrey was tired of this question. Families are very stupid. But Catherine did not make him answer; she cascaded on about her meetings, and about Tim, the Liberal Member, who, it seemed, was to speak in the House that night. It was obvious that any husband of Catherine's would have to speak in the House fairly often.

Speaking in the House, thought Humphrey gloomily. What an occupation. For his part, he would rather be a clown in a pantomime.

Denham came in from the Zoo, with dusty shoes and grimy hands, and a smudge across her cheek. She had spent too long with animals, and forgotten about the higher life; so, seeing Humphrey, she asked, with simplicity and because she wanted to know, the question no one else had asked:

'Did you bring Paquita to London?'

Struck dumb for an instant by this ill-bred impudence, they all stared at Denham and at Humphrey. Then Catherine swept on again, glibly liberal, well supported by Peter and Guy. Humphrey, white in the face, turned his back on Denham, and said sulkily to his mother that he must go, for he was dining with a man. He was furious with her and with the rest for having gossiped to Denham about the girls he had brought home from Thermopylae and San Gimignano. Was it anyone's business but his own whom he brought home from abroad? And this damned girl, rapping out her damned question at him, with everyone standing around ... God, what a thing was family life!

Evelyn said, in her cheerful staccato, 'Oh, can't you stay and dine, darling? What a pity. Can you come in later, then?'

Humphrey said he could not, for he and the man were going on somewhere. He went, like a sullen child.

Denham came back to her senses, stood in the middle of the room, red-faced. She had said one of the things which are not said. She had offended Humphrey and shocked the family. Certainly she had been too long with the animals.

'Poor Humphrey,' said Evelyn. 'You embarrassed him terribly, Denham. What in the world made you ask him a thing like that, child?'

'Wanted to know,' Denham mumbled, ashamed but accurate, and left the room for she felt uncomfortable in it.

'Lord, what a fool,' remarked Catherine, who disliked fools.

Audrey defended her. 'She's only clumsy and gauche, and blurts out things other people only think. I don't believe she's really a fool.'

'She doesn't know Humphrey, you see,' Evelyn explained. 'She doesn't know him a bit. So she couldn't know how he'd mind having a thing like that said. She doesn't know how terribly sensitive and reserved he is about love.'

'My dear mother, anyone would mind being asked in a room full of people whether he'd brought a mistress home from the Pyrenees. Anyone would. That is, if he'd ever thought of doing it. If Denham doesn't know that she's a fool ... Of course, I think it was a mistake to let her hear about those other women; she wouldn't have thought of it if you hadn't.'

'My dear Catherine' – Guy's air was fatigued – 'you surely haven't lived all these years in London without discovering that everyone in it knows everything, and a little more, about

51

everyone else's affairs. If Denham hadn't heard that tale from us, she would from someone else. You can't hide your mistresses under a bushel in this town. Not in Half Moon Street. Especially such handsome ones as those two women were. And I say that if Humphrey chooses to do such spectacular things, he's no right to object to fair comment.'

'Oh, well, I dare say the girl meant no harm. But I can't stick a fool.'

'I should have thought that, with all your experience of listening to them in the House ...'

'Quite. The more I see and hear them, the less patience I have with them. But the fools outside the House can do more damage, you'll admit.'

'I dare say. Yes, I suppose they are better shut up in a certified house together than loose.'

'Well, I must say,' said Evelyn, 'that, as Denham *did* ask Humphrey that, I wish he had answered her. Now we're no wiser than we were about it. That girl may be in Half Moon Street, or she may not. He may be dining with her now. He said a man, but men always say that. Yes. They always call them that. We simply don't know.'

'Exactly,' said Peter, fidgeting about 'Well, suppose we have dinner, as we have all to go out.'

'In a minute, darling. Arnold Chapel is coming, you know. He's coming with us to the theatre.'

2

Arnold Chapel, who faced Denham across the table, was a tall, dark young man, with eyeglasses and a nice smile. He was a junior partner in the Gresham publishing house, and, though not in the Foreign Office, a Roman Catholic. Denham was not surprised to see so many of these about, for there were, of course, more in Andorra. Mr Chapel was a lively and pleasant talker, and had, Denham observed, no doubt about his knives or forks or anything. She was still looking in vain for someone who, like herself, seemed unsound on those small points which mark the lady or the gentleman. Mr Chapel also suffered, obviously, from this curious desire which people had to eat meals in houses other than their own.

'Don't see what they *get* out of it,' Denham pondered. 'Unless it's more food. And this one looks as if he could afford plenty at home. Anyhow, it can't be that, because Aunt Evelyn and Uncle Peter and the rest are always eating at other people's houses, and they get lots at home. And the servants do the washing up, so it can't be that either. Must be something else about it.' She was up, as usual, against this mysterious secret that other people had. She wished she had it too, since it was obviously part of the good life. These people were, no doubt, right. They were strange, but attractive. Their minds moved along paths she knew not, their hearts were set on objects that she too must learn to desire.

Chatter, chatter, chatter – how they talked! The Greshams and their friends assembled together had no flashes of silence. Just as well, thought Denham, that she didn't talk too; she didn't see how she could have got in, anyhow. They could scarcely all get in themselves. At one end of the table was Peter, pouring out story after story, with eyes that twinkled through beaming glasses. Peter didn't keep his good stories for company; he presented them to his family too. At the other end was Evelyn, talking without a pause, with her wide, bright, childish stare that perceived so much more than anyone would have thought. Down the sides were Catherine, whose clear, resonant voice and laugh sounded above all the others, Guy, making gentler sounds, but the most fluent of them all, and really the most amusing, Audrey, making intelligent remarks in her fresh girl's tone, Arnold Chapel, being pleasantly absurd in his soft, literary Cambridge voice. The two quiet ones, Humphrey and Noel, were not there; Noel was on a reading party and Humphrey dining with a man.

Arnold Chapel was sparring with Catherine about something. Behind the friendly argument was something real – a slight but defined distaste on both sides. Catherine could not really take seriously persons who were so superstitious as to have become Roman Catholics. Of course, if they were in the Foreign Office, like Guy, it was different; that might be just following a fashion, or a step towards promotion. Guy one might condemn as frivolous, or cynical, or insincere, but not as weak in the head. But Arnold, who was only publishing, must be somewhat superstitious, very religious – it was the same thing. Unless he had sacrificed his intelligence merely to be able to say to people, 'You see, I'm a papist—' In either case, one could not think of him as an intellectual equal. Catherine did not even try to do so. Arnold perceived that she did not, and resented it. He thought her conceited and bigoted, with her political preoccupations and her anti-religious bias – quite different from his friend Audrey, who, though not bitten by religion herself, tolerated it in others.

Peter, a kind man, cut across the conversation to ask Denham what she had seen at the Zoo. She began telling him, animal by animal. Arnold broke in. Had she seen the aquarium?

No, Denham had not seen the aquarium yet. They were all off then about fishes, and about a new bear there was. It seemed that they only cared much for the new animals. Denham did not even know which were the new animals; they were all new to her. So the talk slipped away over her head again. Guy left off exchanging funny and scandalous stories with Catherine about Members of Parliament, and told funny and scandalous stories about the Zoo. Even fishes, it seemed, led, when in London, those odd, amusing lives that were common to all Guy's acquaintances. Indeed, the whole world, when Guy surveyed it, assumed the air of an agreeable and diverting Zoo.

Arnold Chapel thought, 'A queer, silent girl. Picturesque, though. And what a splendid head. She can't be stupid, with that head.' For though twenty-eight, he was still young enough to judge by appearances.

Guy was telling a story about Mr Hamar Greenwood and family prayers; Catherine about Mr David Kirkwood in the House; Evelyn was talking of Polish dancers, and Peter of someone's Sunday play; Denham had never heard of Messrs Hamar Greenwood and David Kirkwood, never seen the Polish dancers or the Sunday play. No one could blame her for sitting silent. It was so much less trouble . . .

Nor could anyone blame Catherine for thinking her cousin the stupidest girl she had ever seen. Not only did she know nothing to start with, but she seemed to have no faculty for picking anything up. Ordinary social education was wasted on her. She had much better, thought Catherine, go to her father's relations in Devonshire.

They all, except Catherine, went on to a theatre. It was the first night of a play by someone they knew. Their box was opposite that of the embarrassed author, who veiled himself and his voluminous correspondence behind a curtain. It was a small theatre, and the Greshams appeared to know everyone in it.

'I can't see how it matters who's here,' Denham thought. (Many of her reflections at this time took the form of puzzled statements as to what she failed to see.) 'The play's what matters. I wonder why they care who else is seeing it.'

'There's Angela and Cyril,' said Audrey, waving a hand to the stalls. 'And Andrew Blair. A pity the *Beacon* sent him instead of Tony; it won't be his kind of play at all.'

'Angela looks terribly plain,' said Evelyn, after inspecting her through opera glasses. 'What's she done to her hair? And she's got two spots on her chin. She looks terribly plain; really she does.'

'She does, sometimes,' said Audrey. 'She looked lovely in court at her decree nisi on Wednesday. You never know, with Angela. Would you call her pretty, Denham?'

'Which?'

'Third from the end of the fourth row, in a blue cloak, with light hair. She's funny, she's so changeable. She's not a bit pretty tonight, somehow.'

Since that was settled, Denham did not feel called upon to pronounce an opinion. Evelyn and Audrey, she knew, felt a queer interest in whether people were pretty or not, and how, and why, and when.

The curtain rose, and the female Greshams laid aside their femininities and became intelligent. They were, and so were the gentlemen, a good deal more intelligent than the play. If they had written the play, it would have been much better; that was obvious. As it was, it was not very good. It was, however, well received. At the end of the first act there was a great clapping and many ejaculations of applause.

'I'm afraid it's a failure,' said Audrey.

'People seem to like it all right,' said Denham.

'Oh, that's nothing. They're mostly his friends and the critics. They always make a noise. He's a critic himself, you know. I must say, it's not much good.'

'I give it a fortnight,' said Peter, a practised judge.

'I wouldn't give it a week if I were the manager,' said Guy. 'Poor Leonard, he ought never to have tried.'

'What do you think of it, Miss Dobie?' Arnold Chapel asked.

'Rotten,' said Denham, concisely, for once agreeing with the rest. And Arnold thought her a girl of sound judgment.

'They're all going out to have drinks and agree what to say about it,' said Audrey, of the critics. 'Leonard's fate will be settled by the time the curtain goes up. He's gone behind, poor Leonard.'

Peter, Guy and Arnold went down to drink with the critics, and people came in and out of the box, including that Angela who was not pretty tonight, but had looked lovely at her decree nisi on Wednesday. They all said they were afraid it was no good. The gentlemen came back, reporting the play damned in the bar.

'Jimmie Barton's not coming in again; he says he can't stick it,' said Arnold.

'Jimmie scarcely ever can stick more than the first act,' said Audrey. 'He oughtn't to be a critic at all if he dislikes all plays so much. It's not fair.'

'Well, he's afraid of being sick. As he's got a middle seat, that wouldn't do. He says he can imagine the rest, and write a less unkind notice than if he'd seen it.'

'The question is, how unkind any of them will dare to be,' Guy said. 'They talk like this in their cups, but their words in the morning press will be smoother than butter and sweeter than honey. Snobbism and terror will save the unhappy Leonard from execution.'

'After all,' said Evelyn kindly, 'he's done his best. Yes. I'm sure he's done his best.'

'That's what *I'm* afraid of, too. Poor old man. Critics oughtn't to write plays. However, of course they always will.'

'Of course it may be a fearfully strong second act,' said Audrey hopefully, as the curtain rose.

'The third act may still pull it up,' she said, as the curtain fell on a cordially clapping house.

At the end the author was called by his enthusiastic friends, and made a little speech, thanking the audience for their appreciative reception.

'Doesn't he know it's a failure, then?' asked Denham clearly, just above the author's head. His face flickered for a second.

'Sh.' Audrey nudged Denham, and Arnold suppressed a giggle.

Guy whispered, 'He is buoyed up with liquor and inflated with the plaudits of his friends. And now you've spoilt his one happy night, poor devil.'

It seemed that the theatre was near the rooms of Mr Chapel, so he asked the party in to have drinks and sandwiches with him. Invitations to visit, on any pretext, the rooms of others were seldom refused by the Greshams; it was obviously an important part of the higher life to end the day in some such social fashion, so to Mr Chapel's rooms they all adjourned, and sat there, refreshed by conversation, food and drink, until one o'clock. Denham, who had a corner of a sofa, went to sleep, and had to be woken when the Greshams decided, for some reason, that it was time to go home.

'It seems absurd,' declared Evelyn. 'I could sit up till morning talking. Till breakfast time, you know. I never feel tired in the night. In the day I do, but not in the night. Except in bed. Bed's terribly exhausting. I wake feeling a rag if I've been in bed too long. So does Peter, don't you, darling? But I can dance or talk all night. Why, that child's gone to sleep. Wake her up, Audrey. Fancy going to sleep, with all the noise we were making. I hope she's not caught anything. Good night, Arnold; I'm sorry we have to go so early, but Peter has to catch an early train to Oxford. He's got some quarrel with the Clarendon Press, or something silly.'

They streamed, like a merry and bickering brook, into the summer night, and into their car, which Audrey drove home, while Guy walked off to his rooms in Bruton Street.

Audrey said, 'How absurd to go home a night like this. Let's go a spin to Richmond, instead.'

'No, darling.' Evelyn was firm. 'You've had enough for tonight. You'll come in and go to bed. Denham's asleep already.'

But Denham was no longer asleep. A spin to Richmond she thought a good idea, not like sitting about and talking. She would have liked a spin to Richmond.

'Let's go,' she said.

But Evelyn refused. 'I can't have you looking like a ghost tomorrow at the Selwyns' dance, Audrey. You must get some sleep before you go to the office. Really, darling, I mean it.'

Denham wished they had gone to Richmond straight after the play. This family was apt to spend the night doing the wrong things. Then, when, as now, one of the right things came into their heads, there wasn't time to do it. On the whole, Denham considered, they led misspent lives. That was to say, by her natural standards. Of course, by the standards she had now set before her, their lives were all but perfect.

As they went in, Evelyn said, 'We might ask Arnold to come down to World's End with us some weekend soon. And another thing – we must really decide on the date for our party. We've put it off too long already, waiting for those lamas. Let's sit down here for a bit before we go up, then we can talk about it … I do think Angela was looking plain tonight. I expect it was partly that divorce business; it's always such an upset. And partly, you know, that cloak she had was the wrong blue. Wrong for her skin, do you see; it brought out the blemishes.'

Denham, since she might not go to Richmond, went to bed, leaving the Greshams thus discussing the date of their party.

CHAPTER III

Giving a Party

I

'What kind of party?' Denham asked Audrey.

'Oh, the usual kind. Just standing about and talking.'

'Oh.' Denham had been to some of these, and did not care for them. She pondered for a minute.

'Why do people like them?' she enquired, anxious to learn, and to conduct herself well at the party.

'Oh, well, they're just a way of meeting people,' Audrey explained.

A way of meeting people. Of course that was what it was. Like so many other occupations. It is so difficult to meet people in this life that one must contrive all kinds of ways of doing so.

'And you wear your nicest clothes, and see other people's and all that.'

Denham took this in. She was trying to be intelligent about clothes.

'How jolly,' she commented soberly.

'One always,' Audrey went on, 'feels more alive in the evenings. Don't you think so? It's the time for doing things.'

'Perhaps,' said Denham, and wondered, then why not do them, why not go out somewhere, have a picnic or an adventure, instead of standing about and talking? She suppressed this thought, knowing it to be second-rate, and asked, 'What shall you wear?'

Audrey, pleased that Denham was coming on, said, 'My pale green, I think,' and added other details interesting to young females. Then she discussed Denham's costume. Denham followed panting after her. It was fine to be talked to like an equal about abstruse matters such as these. In Andorra she had refused to join in conversations about what to put on, regarding them as dull, but with the Greshams it was different; the Greshams threw a glamour even over clothes. They talked about whether Guy looked well in a frilled shirt, and whether Humphrey could be made to get his hair cut. Encouraged by all this, Audrey mentioned a new novel which Greshams had just published, and which, it seemed (fond delusion of publishers!) 'everyone' was talking about. But here Denham got left. Novels were still above her. Clothes you can speak of a little, whether you understand them or not, but, unless you are more adept than Denham in the social arts, you must have read a page or two of the book mentioned, or have read or written a review of it, or at least have heard others discussing it, before you can acquit yourself creditably on the subject. Her crude, 'I've not read it,' led nowhere.

'Oh, but you must,' Audrey said. 'It's really good. Frightfully clever and alive. I thought I'd given it you to read last week.'

'Yes. But I've not had time yet . . . I began it.'

'Well, didn't you think the beginning was very funny?'

'Yes,' said Denham heavily. Audrey gave it up. Denham was coming on, but she hadn't much humour, and didn't care for novels. Audrey went off to the office.

Denham went out too. She took a bus to Trafalgar Square, and stood outside Foster Groome's shop in Whitehall, looking at the maps in the window. They gave her a pleasant feeling of ease; you could relax over maps; you didn't have to live up to them, as you did to novels, clothes, and people. With maps you could be merely yourself; a low self, but your own. It was not really right or wise to look at maps too long; to do so was to be like a drunkard who hangs continually about a public house.

2

The Greshams' party was, after all, not quite like other parties, for they had lamas at it, fresh from Tibet. The lamas sat in an alcove in the drawing-room, with incense burning before them, and every guest presented the Grand Lama with a little gift as he was introduced. It was a really good idea, and made the party quite distinctive, and everyone enjoyed it very much. It had been Guy's idea; Guy knew everybody, even lamas, and being in the Foreign Office, knew how to establish relations with them.

'Rather wonderful, aren't they,' said Arnold Chapel to Denham, who stood looking big and brown and rather fine in a gold tunic.

Denham turned over the adjective, in her literal way.

'I don't know ... I suppose they're quite ordinary where they belong. Just clergymen, aren't they?'

63

'Yes, that's all, I suppose. But they're striking in a London drawing-room, you'll admit. Or don't you admit that any human beings are striking? You have the air, do you know, of being sublimely indifferent to the whole human race.'

'Have I?' Denham wished people wouldn't make personal remarks, but would mind their own business. Still, she knew she must talk to the people who talked to her; this is done, at parties, and Aunt Evelyn was quite close, looking towards her. She pulled herself together and said that probably there was a fog tonight.

'A fog? No; why?'

'Well, there often is. Then it's a clear night.' That did as well.

'A perfectly clear night ... Will you eat or drink?'

'Yes. Both.'

They made their way to the refreshment table, and ate and drank.

'I am to have the pleasure of spending this weekend with you, I believe. Mrs Gresham has asked me down to World's End. Do you know it yet?'

'No. Is it nice?'

'Delightful. The house is in a pine-wood on a hill, looking over the weald. Are you fond of the country? I should imagine you were.'

'Well, I don't know much of it, except in Andorra. I like it better than towns. There's more room and fewer people, and more things one wants to do.'

'You don't much care for London, I expect?'

'Oh, yes.' Denham recollected herself. 'London's very nice. All the plays, and concerts, and shops, and picture shows, and parties, and people.'

The young man looked at her with some interest. She was a strange girl, he thought, and hard to understand. She talked oddly. But he was attracted by her brown, brooding face.

Denham was beginning to enjoy the evening. It was exhilarating to be talking like a real person at a party, looking like the others, and drinking claret cup. She liked this young man, though he was rather a strain. Doing difficult things well is gratifying, and she was succeeding, anyhow, in conducting a perfectly rational and ordinary polite conversation with someone at a party.

3

The Grand Lama began to chant aloud. He seemed to be uttering a blessing.

'Aren't they wonderful,' people said, pleased. Some of them thought it would be very nice to visit Tibet and be asked to parties there and given presents and admired. Others opined that this was not what happened to you if you visited Tibet.

Humphrey thought, what a lot of idiots they were, all gathered together like this. How pleased his mother and the rest were that they had thought of the lamas before anyone else did. What a hollow business social life, and indeed, all life was. Yet he talked away to his friends, as if life were not hollow but solid, and led about a young Italian literary friend of his and introduced him to English literary people, and talked very cleverly about music to a Polish musician, and about radium to a Hungarian scientist, and was generally intelligent, as if the bodies of women did not for ever trouble and undo the souls of men, and as if life were a rational and logical business after all.

Catherine dashed brightly from friend to friend, like a bee from flower to flower, full of spirit, politics and joy. She laughed at the lamas, for she laughed at everything and everyone, and, too, she did not understand about religion and clergymen. She and her liberal friends made little liberal groups about the room; they made you feel as if to be a liberal was great fun, and as if even a liberal might be Prime Minister some day. And *then* he'd show the world. Tories were fat-heads, and socialists were muddle-headed fools; to liberals the sceptre had been given. Catherine was attractive; she carried her politics lightly, as a joke, yet ardently, like a sword. She was a chic blue-stocking, a political wife who was yet independent and not her husband's chorus; indeed, it was far more likely that he would be hers. She enjoyed her mother's party, though she found at it too many non-politicals, and an excessive number of idle women, second-rate literary persons of both sexes, and people who, for one reason or another, did not count. Catherine liked people to count. In her view, people ought either to count, or to stay in their own homes. Of course there were plenty of ways of counting. You could count by merely being a personable and brilliant member of society, or by standing in the liberal interest for some constituency, even if you failed to prevail on anyone to vote for you. But, if you did not count somehow, Catherine had nothing to say to you. In her opinion, her cousin Denham did not count, and should have stayed in Andorra, where it perhaps matters less if you count or not. But once or twice this evening Catherine's darting glance lit for a moment on her cousin, and she wondered whether some day it might be possible to revise one's opinion of her. For Denham seemed to have absorbed and held the attention of Arnold Chapel (who did, after all, papist or not, count a little, for he was a rising young publisher) for quite a long time. Odd, Catherine had time to think, if the stupid, gauche, silent Denham should prove to have the faculty of attracting men ... It was certainly one up to Denham, the way Arnold Chapel stayed at her side. For he knew everyone, and could have no trouble in finding someone to leave her for, which is one's difficulty at those parties at which one knows few.

4

Evelyn enjoyed her party. This high, happy hum and buzz of people talking on a top note, neither rising, falling, nor pausing, was very musical to her. Nice people chattering together, all in their good clothes, enjoying themselves, refreshing themselves with her well-arranged foods and drinks, looking charming (those who could), talking cleverly (again those who could), chitter chattering like a turning mill stream, greeting one another with ejaculations of pleasure, admiring the lamas in their alcove (who were now being fed with foods carefully designed as suitable to lamas) – one's friends thus gathered together were really the meaning and the heart of life. Evelyn felt graceful, felt young, felt in tune with her friends, liked herself in her old green dress. She talked to everyone; she felt she was being a good wife to Peter, for she talked to his young literary aspirants, who didn't count yet, but who, Peter hoped, would some day. She introduced these to those who did already count; for she too, like Catherine, distinguished between counting and not counting; and indeed to do this is one of the first social lessons; one of the next is to be kind to those who do not count, and this Evelyn had never needed to learn, for she was of a very kind nature. She too noticed (though she never seemed to notice anything, with her wide, strange, elfin stare and unceasing chatter) Denham and Arnold Chapel. Having noticed them, she looked round to see where Audrey was, and saw her being, as usual, charming and capable and nice, and, thought her mother, looking a dear. Noel was there too, exquisite and childish and rather quiet, with a long-legged college friend. These two young girls seemed (as the universities will) in London yet not altogether of it; their hearts and minds were elsewhere.

5

But Audrey and Guy were wholly of London. Guy moved from person to person, being agreeable, amusing himself and others, liking to hear himself talk, entertaining his friends with well-found tales which had neither foundation nor coating of truth. Guy as a dinner-table raconteur would go far. He could tell good stories in four languages, and in none of them needed the assistance of fact. Guy would make his mark in diplomatic circles.

Audrey, in the intervals between being a good hostess, was being happy with a brilliant young French actress who had her heart. Audrey, in her composed and cheerful way, was subject to these admirations. The stage, in particular, had glamour for her; she went, like her father, to every first night imaginable, and cultivated actors and actresses, introducing them to such of her friends as were dramatic critics. She was an intelligent girl, and could discuss drama quite as well as was necessary, that is to say, as well as other people could discuss drama. Denham, listening to her, would sigh, for she knew that however far she got along the road of culture, she would never get as far as that.

6

A crowd of handsome, chocolate-coloured men and women ran into the room, with loud ejaculations of politeness. Humphrey had invited them; they came from a Soho dancing cabaret, and, before that, from the Sudan. They had fuzzy hair and noble features and happy expressions and splendid bodies only slightly clad. Humphrey went forward to receive them.

'Dear me,' said Evelyn. 'Humphrey really should have warned us. They look terribly hungry, but I don't know what they like to eat. That's the awkward part of it; I don't know what they eat. And the lamas aren't a bit pleased; I'm sure they can't be. You can't tell, with lamas, because their faces aren't expressive, but I'm sure they're terribly hurt. It's making them like part of a Barnum show, instead of distinguished guests. Humphrey shouldn't have done it.'

'Humphrey's always in with natives,' said Audrey. 'They look a little like Denham, don't they. But they smile more. I like them.'

Humphrey was introducing the Sudanese to his parents; he called them all by their names, like the stars.

'We're so delighted to see you,' said Evelyn. 'Yes. It was terribly nice of you to come.' But still she was worried, thinking of the lamas. And she was right, for the lamas, led by their chief, were rising in offended silence and collecting all their presents in a large basket which they had brought for the purpose. Peter, through the interpreter, begged them to remain.

'The Grand Lama says,' the interpreter reported, in some embarrassment, 'that it is time they went home.'

'My dear fellow, you've left out the gist of it,' said Peter. 'They don't care for the fuzzies, isn't that it?'

'Well, Asiatics and Africans, of course—'

'You must tell them,' said Peter, 'that the Africans are a mistake. They've mistaken the house, come to the wrong party, d'you see.'

The interpreter passed this on.

'The Grand Lama says, in that case, would it not be advisable to tell them of their mistake, that they may find their right destination?'

'Well' – Peter helplessly fingered his glasses and fidgeted – 'now they *are* here, don't you know, one can't well turn them from the doors. So deucedly inhospitable, and all that. At least, I suppose one can't . . . Humphrey, come here a moment. Those infernal fuzzies of yours have upset the lamas; can't you take them away to some night-club, and give them drinks?'

'They've just come from a night-club,' said Humphrey. 'And I should say they've had quite enough drinks. They're going to dance now. What's the matter with the lamas about them? What snobs Tibetans are! If they aren't pleased let them go. We're all going to dance.'

'Oh well, it can't be helped. Le Mesurier, you tell them we're very sorry and all that, but we can't turn our guests out, even when they're uninvited. Tell 'em the fuzzies are charming fellows, very important and distinguished and religious and all that.'

'Oh, they know all about fuzzies, I'm afraid. But I'll tell them.'

'It's no use,' said Guy. 'They've taken offence. They're going home to bed. Or wherever lamas do go when they leave parties. Well, they've done their turn; it's the fuzzies' number now.'

The lamas filed out, with the grave courtesy for which lamas! are noticeable, even when offended. The Sudanese took the floor, lithe and handsome as panthers, with gesticulations and ejaculations of happiness. They danced alone and with one another, twirling, whirling, leaping, and snapping the fingers. They infected the rest of the party, and the Europeans took to the floor too, footing it in the sober walking movements of the modern dance.

'Shall we?' Arnold Chapel asked of Denham.

'All right.'

Someone was playing dance music. The chocolate people spun and leaped to it, and the white people walked to it, holding one another close.

English dancing was stupid, thought Denham, for, if you dance at all, why not dance quickly, why not spin and leap like an African, and get some fun out of it? English people had done so before the war, Evelyn had told her, before the terrible war which had sobered us all so. When she was young, dancing was freer and gayer and more rowdy. So was everything else, including boys and girls. Anyhow, since this was now the way one danced in England, one had to conform to it, and one wandered about the room with one's partner, keeping step, keeping time, glad not to have to talk and to be using, in however demure and ladylike a way, one's body.

Arnold was a good partner, easy and light-footed. He held

the strong firm body of this unknown girl, and clasped her strong firm hand.

Unknown: that was what they were one to the other, and strangeness grew in both, the breathless strangeness of a mystery. She was not what he was familiar with, not one of the jolly, knowledgeable, companionable girls who made his world; she was strange, like a clergyman from Tibet or a fuzzy from the Sudan. Strange, like beauty and adventure and far countries ...

To her, he too was strange and admirable; he embodied the grace and the culture of the life into which she had been swept, of the civilisation in which she was a stumbling débutante. He stood high above her on the road on which her feet were set. Further, he was graceful and lithe and strong, and his dark eyes smiled at her as they danced.

The brown people suddenly stopped, and bowed to the white, as if they had been performing at a cabaret. They wiped their glistening faces, and their hosts gave them to eat. The white people stopped dancing too, and gathered round the brown, watching them eat.

'They like *foie gras*,' said Humphrey, and gave it them.

It was a ridiculous party; one felt that anything might happen, and any person of any colour come in. It was more like a variety entertainment at the Coliseum than a party. Denham thought better of parties than she had before, especially when the chief Sudanese, after his food, began to spin round and round like a top. Anyone would think they had been paid to perform at the Greshams' party, but they had not, they had merely come as Humphrey's friends, and these were their ordinary evening habits.

'I wonder how soon he'll be sick,' thought Denham, interested, watching the spinning chief.

'The boys are too absurd,' said Evelyn. 'I can't imagine where they pick their friends up. I hope Humphrey isn't really intimate with all those brown women. He carries his friendships with women too far. And they're the type he likes; he doesn't care for ordinary English girls, they bore him. Bore him, you know. Humphrey's terribly easily bored.'

'Good-bye, my dear: such a lovely party.'

The white guests began to go home to bed, or wherever white guests go when they leave parties. It is less easy to rid yourself of brown guests, and at last Humphrey had to take them away himself, to the nearest night-club, where they settled down to play mah-jong.

7

The Greshams sat round their dining-room and consumed such food as their brown and white guests had left them, and talked, which is what hosts and hostesses do when their parties go. Denham noticed that even they seemed glad that the party was over.

They talked about their guests of both colours. They agreed that it was a pity about the lamas having been offended, but that lamas were obviously offended too easily. Guy told stories of other things which had offended lamas, and of action taken by them in consequence. They all thought he had better go round in the morning and placate the lamas. They wondered if Humphrey had yet got rid of his Sudanese. Peter wondered what impression had been made by the young lady whom he

73

had been introducing to reviewers and editors as the author of a brilliant first novel he had just published. Guy feared that the impression had been one of such plainness of feature that the young lady had been better unintroduced and left to the editors' and reviewers' imagination. Peter agreed that it was certainly unfortunate that intelligence and beauty in young females were so often found divorced. No oftener, Noel's friend put in, than in young males. Peter dared say not, but then who cared about beauty in young males? It seemed that all the ladies present did so. However, Peter believed that editors and reviewers did not agree with them. He liked his women authors to have looks; when, as in this case, they had few, and those of the wrong kind, the personal introduction might well be damaging.

Then they began to gossip about the love affairs of others, and the latest quarrels, literary, political and personal, between people they knew, and Audrey and Evelyn, as ladies sometimes will late at night, mentioned various acquaintances who were, so they said, victims to drugs. Young Oxford, who did not think the nourishment consumed by others an interesting topic of discussion, went to bed, and Denham went too.

Denham's room was next that of Noel and her friend, and long after she was in bed she heard them talking. For even Noel talked late, could not, it seemed, cease from this so fascinating exercise of the tongue. She and her friend might talk about different things from the others; they might not discuss other people's love affairs or vices, or retail amusing stories which had been imparted to them in confidence; but certainly they talked. How wonderful, thought Denham, it must be to be able to think of all those things to say. In Andorra and

Mallorca it had been precisely the same; nearly everyone had talked all the time. Talking is one of the creative arts, for by it you build up things that have, until talked about, no existence, such as scandals, secrets, quarrels, literary and artistic standards, all kinds of points of view about persons and things. Let us talk, we say, meaning, let us see what we can create, or in what way we can transmute the facts that are into facts that are not yet. It is one of the magic arts. The trouble about it is that, even more than the other arts, it is practised by the stupid, who can create nothing worth creating.

The Greshams, however, were not stupid. At the hour of 2.30 a.m. Peter was getting into bed, wishing that Evelyn would come up, because he had a great many more things he wanted to say before morning, Catherine, in her little study in Smith Square, was hearing from her husband the story of the evening in the House, Evelyn, Audrey, and Guy were gossiping round the broken meats in their dining-room, Noel and her friend were lying in bed, talking about the problematic careers of such of their friends as had gone down that term, and Humphrey, with a score of chocolate men and women, was joining in the loquacious life of London's night-clubs.

Only Denham, having nothing to say, was sleeping the sleep of the stupid, of the lower animals, who eat and drink and play and lie down to rest, and say nothing about it.

CHAPTER IV

Country Weekend

You might think, if you were inadequately informed as to country weekends, that they would be an intellectual rest for Londoners tired of being clever all the time. Denham supposed this, and that down at World's End (which sounded like the name of a pub) the Greshams would, as she vaguely put it, stop. That is, Peter would stop booking and going to first nights and talking about authors, Evelyn would stop going out to dine and having others to lunch, Audrey being intelligent and not coming home at nights till two o'clock, Guy telling funny stories of which the point was as often as not in a foreign language, and all of them being sociable. For surely World's End must be a quiet place, away from people.

But it was not. The Greshams, a host in themselves, had others to stay with them. They crowded up; they squeezed in clever guests as tightly as one packs a suit-case, and then, when quite full, billeted more clever guests in neighbouring cottages and inns. In short, far from stopping, they accelerated.

Arnold Chapel was there, and a distinguished gentleman novelist, an eminent and liberal politician with brilliant wife, and an idle middle-aged lady, and two or three nice young friends of Guy and Audrey. They all had very high spirits, except possibly Noel, who was naturally quiet, the politician who was weighted with the cares of not being in office, and having only a shadow cabinet to mind, and the idle middle-aged lady, who had, instead of high spirits, that kind of bland, twinkling, urbane detachment only to be found in bachelors and spinsters who are at once well-bred, worldly, and past middle life, for they grew up in a more civilised and worldly age than this earnest period and also have never committed themselves to those serious and permanent connections with life which must needs anchor and sober the soul. They are the world's dandies, walking delicately and blandly through it like spectators at the Zoo. Thus, anyhow, was Miss Rome Garden, whom Peter Gresham was always urging, quite in vain, to write books, an undertaking she regarded as rather common, like getting married, or standing for Parliament, or otherwise entering the world's bustling lists. The only thing Miss Garden would do in this line was cross-word puzzles; for these she had a somewhat morbid and degrading penchant, they were a vice and a snare to her. She had already won by them a hundred and fifty pounds. A degrading vice, she admitted, for it meant entering into the minds of the puzzle-makers, and these showed every evidence of that loose thinking and illiterate imbecility which characterises popular journalism.

These puzzles were among the occupations practised at World's End this weekend (which, it is surely unnecessary to remark, was largely wet). Not satisfied with solving all they could lay hands on, they even made new ones for themselves.

Evelyn had unlimited pencils and paper in the house, and with these they played the most frightful games. Reviews, one was called. As if it wasn't enough to read, write and talk about books and their reviews half the time in London, without playing games about them in the country.

Denham wouldn't play reviews. She found, instead, an out-house in the garden, where gardener's tools were stored, and amused herself with these.

Here Arnold Chapel found her, after tea on Saturday, seated on a pile of faggots and making a whistle. His face, as he looked in at her, had a pleased, soft look, as if he had found a puppy playing and would have liked to caress it.

'Aren't you coming in?' he said. 'Reviews are over.'

'Well,' said Denham cautiously, 'I expect it's something else now, isn't it?'

'Charades.'

'I thought it would be something like that. I like it better here, I think. There's lots to do here.'

'You're not very sociable, are you?'

Denham considered. 'Don't know. Perhaps not. It's chiefly that it's nicer out here than in there – more to do that I like.' She waved a comprehensive hand at the attractive jumble round her. 'I'm making a whistle. Then I thought I'd make a boat and try it on that stream below the house.'

'How old are you? Thirteen?'

'What rot you talk. Twenty-two, of course. How old are you?'

'Twenty-eight. Have you always hated indoor games?'

'I like some of them all right. Billiards, and some card games. I don't like pencil games or talking games. Do you?'

'Why yes, I think I do. They've an attractive silliness that

78

appeals to me. I like talking, I'm afraid. I expect I talk a lot too much.'

'One can't do the things one likes too much, can one?'

'I'm afraid so. You, for instance, might sit in here alone too much, and make too many whistles.'

'Too much for what?' Denham had the persistent literalness of a child.

'Well, more than is good for you. And more than your friends like, too.'

'Oh well.' Denham's tone dismissed one's friends from any share in the ordering of one's life. 'People shouldn't care what other people do. Why should they? I never care what anyone else does, so long as they don't do it to me.'

'You're an individualist. And perhaps you don't care much for anyone?'

'Yes, I think I do.' Denham frowned over the baffling, teasing, bewildering Greshams who swung into her mind. 'Yes, I do. But I shouldn't care a bit what any of them did. I don't care if they play with pencils and paper all day, so long as I don't have to.' She put the whistle to her mouth, and blew a shrill blast.

'Not bad. Now I think I shall make a boat.'

'I'll help, may I?'

'Are you any good?' Denham glanced doubtfully at his white, indoor hands.

'I used to be, when I was thirteen too. You make yours, and I'll make another, then we'll race them.'

'Don't they want you for the charades?'

'Oh, blow the charades. I'd rather make a boat. Only I haven't a knife.'

'Have you lost it?' Denham carefully selected a chunk of wood. 'There might be one about here somewhere. Only it'd probably be a rotten one. One's own knife is the only good knife, as a rule. You can use mine when I've done.'

It rained and rained. Through the open door the wet yard sang and gurgled at them. The grey afternoon crept about the dim corners of the shed, coldly touching the two close-cut dark heads, the big brown girl in her red jersey stooping intent over her task, her black brows drawn down, the boat cleverly taking shape in her strong, practised hands, the loose-limbed young man standing by her, his narrow eyes merry and soft, straying from her hands at work to the solid curve of her head against the red row of pots behind it.

'Here.' She passed him the knife, critically examining her handiwork.

He sat down and picked up a chunk of wood and got to work. He was on his mettle. He wanted Denham to see that he could make a boat as well as she could. More than boats seemed to hang on it. Though she was no good at his things, he would show her that he could do hers.

'There,' he said presently, and held it out.

'A bit narrow in the beam, isn't it,' she commented.

'I don't think so. We'll try them presently, when it clears.'

'It's nearly stopped now.'

He faced round to the door.

'Well – not very nearly.'

Denham stood up.

'Come on. This won't hurt us. We'll go down to the brook.'

'Let me fetch you a coat.'

'No, I don't want it.'

They went out into the soft tail of the rain. The puddles in the yard splashed with fine drops. The hillside was sodden and bright green, and squelched beneath their feet; the fir copse dripped silver. Beyond it fled the stream, full and merry with the rain.

'Here's a good regatta starting point.' Arnold selected a reach where the stream ran gay and smooth for some yards before tumbling over rocks. They placed the boats together, released them, watched them flee together to the rocky fall, over the fall to the pool below, down the pool to its hurrying outlet, and so on between grassy banks. Then one of them was caught in an eddy, spun round and round, flung into a patch of reeds and held. The other sped neatly on.

'Mine's done,' said Denham. She fished it out of mud and reeds. 'Let's see how far yours will get.'

It got to a gravel shore ten yards below, where it lay beached.

'Jolly good,' said Denham. 'Shall we try them again?'

He came up to her, his retrieved boat in his hand. He felt pleased, as if he had satisfied a small boy.

The rain stopped, and the west was suddenly a sheet of yellow. The young man saw the young woman standing against it, the short ends of her damp black hair caught with light, her bare wet arms golden brown. His heart turned in him, for she was no small boy, but a woman. Their eyes met, and the look in his filled hers, childishly absorbed till now, with consciousness of him.

'I want to kiss you,' he said simply. 'You don't mind?'

'No.'

They came together; his face was hard and prickly against

hers; the face of a man who has shaved closely ten hours ago. He held her from him and looked into her grave brown face.

'You adorable darling.'

Steps and voices came down through the copse. They had discovered in the house that the rain had stopped, and had burst rejoicing into the open.

Arnold stepped away and picked up his boat. 'Shall we race them again?'

'Hallo, you two!' It was Audrey calling out.

'Hallo, you house-fuggers. We're racing boats.'

'Please don't let us interrupt you.' That was Guy, a smile behind his eyes, as he perceived in theirs their secret joy that they had embraced.

But he spoke too late; they had been interrupted. They knelt by the brook with their boats.

With Guy and Audrey were a gay group, all come out to take the air after the rain. They went on down the hill, their cheerful nonsense trailing after them on the still air. Arnold, who enjoyed being one of such a party, had no wish to join them now. He wanted to stay with Denham, who never talked nonsense, who did not know how, whose talk, when any, was of concrete, literal things. He wanted to kiss Denham again. Soon he did so. Why not, since they both liked it?

'There's no one the least like you,' he said. 'Do you know that?'

'Lots of people, I should think. Why not?'

'No, no one. No one. No one.' At each no one he kissed her; he was working up to more and more feeling about her, and she about him. Both touched the edges of passion as they clung together in the wet yellow evening. They loved to embrace one another; thrills of joy shivered through them as their lips and hands touched. They were savouring one of the elementary human pleasures. Both had savoured it before, with others, for both were young creatures susceptible to the elementary passions; but neither so keenly before as now. As far as you may, on so slight acquaintance, love, this young man and woman loved now. Neither looked ahead, for to love, to play together and to embrace was, for the time, enough.

2

They had to do charades after dinner. Even Denham had to play. They assigned to her inarticulate parts, such as the tree in the Garden of Eden, and she did not mind much, though it seemed waste of time. She was happy and at peace, with Arnold in the room. He was happy, but not at peace; he was excited and strung up; he vented himself in gaiety and laughter.

'Arnold was very brilliant tonight,' said Evelyn, when the evening was over and the inn guests had gone across, conducted by Audrey and others, to the inn. 'I never saw him in such good form. I thought he was terribly brilliant.'

'Denham was a bit keyed up too, wasn't she,' Guy commented. 'I heard her speak several times.'

Evelyn stared at him out of her big eyes. 'D'you mean anything, Guy? You don't think there is anything, do you? Of course they were out together after tea—'

Guy yawned. 'Well, there you are. Obviously they both enjoyed being out together after tea. That's all I say.'

Evelyn's thoughts leaped on.

'Of course, he'd have to get a dispensation. Still, that's easy ... Of course, it would be terribly unsuitable, they're so different. I always thought Arnold and Audrey might one day think of each other like that. Audrey's got no religion, so that would be unsuitable too in one way, but they're keen on the same things, do you see. Now Arnold and Denham belong to different worlds. Mind you, I don't think they'd be happy together, not for long.'

'My dear mother, how lightly and incurably your thoughts run to wedlock. That's the last thing Humphrey or I think of when we hear of love. The point is that they *are* happy together, this moment. It doesn't need to be for long. God forbid that we should always marry where we love. There are quite enough marriages already, without adding all those. And God also forbid that Arnold and Denham should ever marry!'

'As to that,' put in Miss Rome Garden, 'he has already forbidden it, by making them of different churches.'

'Of course,' Evelyn continued to muse, for as the night got later the more she mused and spoke of love, 'I expect Denham could become a Catholic quite easily, if that were all. I'm sure she wouldn't be particular about that. She'd never grasp the difference. She hasn't got a theological mind, I'm sure. Should you say she had, Miss Garden?'

'Pray don't ask me. The mind of Miss Denham Dobie is a sealed book to me. But I should imagine you are right that theology is not one of its natural tendencies.'

'Really, darling Eve,' Peter remonstrated, 'Guy is right, you run on too fast. Too fast and too far. You can't go converting Denham to popery and marrying her off merely because she and a young man both seem in good spirits the same evening. You mustn't do it, my love, really you mustn't. You talk too much, that's your weakness. So do I; we all talk a great deal too much. We must leave people to arrange their own affairs. All this tittle tattle—'

'Now papa's off,' murmured Guy, who thought it went with his side whiskers and his Victorian chairs to call his father that.

The others came in.

3

The night was now clear and full of stars. Denham, who had neither been to the inn nor taught not to eavesdrop, had heard through her open bedroom window the talk about Arnold and herself. It did not make much impression on her. Evelyn was always talking like that about someone or other, discussing people's relations together, and so on. Denham dismissed it briefly as 'cheek.' She did not see what it had to do with anyone else how much she and Arnold liked one another and what they meant to do about it. So far as she was concerned, they meant to do nothing about it, except go on liking each other, sailing boats, walking about, kissing when they wanted to kiss. Marriage? Indifferently, Denham dismissed it. Not a satisfactory arrangement, in her view; it asked altogether too much. She had seen married life in Andorra and in London; an exacting, industrious business. What had marriage to do with kissing and sailing boats? Neither she nor Arnold had thought of it. And what was all that rot about theology? How people did chatter about what did not concern them. However,

Denham philosophically supposed, they had to chatter about something, they couldn't help it. It pleased them and didn't hurt anyone else.

She still hung out of the open window, after the conversation was over, for she liked the smell of this place. She sniffed up the piney air and found it good. It was better than London down here; more to do.

Someone leant out of the next window. It was Miss Garden, examining the night before she retired. Denham saw the neat grey head, the incisive, eye-glassed profile, poised for a moment against the yellow light from the bedroom. What had she said? 'The mind of Miss Denham Dobie is a sealed book to me.' How queer, to be a sealed book to anyone. Yet everyone was. All these people, their minds and motives were too strange to be understood. What were they all after? Denham found them disconcerting, wished she knew. Miss Garden was attractive; you could love her if she let you, only she probably wouldn't. They were all attractive. Arnold was attractive. Well, Arnold was more than that ... Denham's heart turned within her when she thought of Arnold.

She saw Miss Garden draw her curtains, heard her say, 'Well, child, what?' and knew that Audrey or Noel had come into her room. They would talk, then; they would continue that endless game which Denham did not know how to play. For a moment Denham felt lonely, to be perhaps the only person not talking that night at World's End. It was low, uncivilised, like an animal. If she was going to be Arnold's friend, she must learn to talk more. You could not expect Arnold to be sailing boats all the time, or even kissing; she must try to be intelligent, and to play at charades and even reviews if he

86

wanted to. And talk more, yes. Why not begin at once? Since talking in the night was part of the higher life, she would talk in the night. To whom? Why not to Miss Garden, next door, whose room some other talker had just left?

Before she had time to repent, Denham flung on her kimono and made for the door.

4

'Come in,' said Miss Garden's clear, cool voice.

Denham opened the door and shut it behind her, standing against it, big and awkward. Miss Garden too was in a kimono; she sat in an arm-chair, plaiting her grey hair and reading a French novel. She looked up at Denham, surprised but agreeable, waiting for her to speak.

Denham said, 'May I come in? I want to – I want to talk.'

'By all means,' said Miss Garden, who was used, at any hour, to the confidences of young women, though she had not expected them from this young woman. 'Sit down.'

Denham sat down, on a prim little bedroom chair by the window. Now she was for it; she must talk or fail. But she repented her precipitance. She ought first to have thought of something to say. It was not so easy as walking through a door, this talking business. Especially with a person who gave you no help, but sat and waited, her finger in her novel, her enigmatic regard (was it amused, ironic, or merely expectant?) coolly upon you. What in the world *do* people talk about in bedrooms in the small hours?

'A fine evening after the rain,' said Miss Garden, after a moment.

Denham took the cue with relief. So this was what they talked about. Good: she could manage that all right.

'Yes,' she agreed. 'The glass was going up when I came upstairs. The temperature in the porch was sixty. That's four degrees higher than last night. I should say tomorrow would be fine. The wind's from the north-east. The gardener told me that was a good wind for fine weather down here.'

'That,' said Miss Garden, 'is the sort of thing gardeners do say. It means nothing. Fine weather is like the spirit; it bloweth where it listeth. I'm older than the gardener, so I know.'

'The question of winds,' said Denham, 'is rather difficult. In Andorra—' She talked for a minute and a half of Andorra winds and their relation to various types of weather. She forgot that she was talking, forgot herself in her subject. Miss Garden listened, with half a smile. An odd young woman, she was perhaps reflecting, to enter the bedroom of an only slightly known elderly lady at this hour in order to talk about Andorra winds. The winds, doubtless, were a smoke-screen put up to conceal an advance into some more pithy topic. She waited, and did not yawn, though she was, in truth, sleepy.

Denham concluded the Andorra winds. She sat silent for a minute, brooding, her thoughts, it seemed, turned inwards. She made as if to speak again, paused.

'Now,' thought Miss Garden, 'we shall have it ... Yes?' she blandly encouraged.

'But,' said Denham, 'once you get the other side of the mountains it's all different. *There* you get the west wind bringing rain, as often as not. Because, of course—' She explained why, at some length. Talking was easy, after all, on interesting subjects.

'Well,' said Miss Garden presently, 'weather is certainly very exciting.'

'Isn't it,' said Denham. 'And isn't it done badly in the newspapers.'

'Most things,' said Miss Garden, 'are done badly in the newspapers.'

'Are they? I don't read anything but the weather. They're nearly always wrong about that, when they look ahead. Of course, it's difficult.'

'Very difficult, I'm sure.' Miss Garden suppressed a little yawn.

'What do you think is the best kind of barometer?' Denham asked after a moment, leaning forward, her elbows on her knees.

'I don't know.' Miss Garden's yawn broke into a laugh. 'I've never looked deeply into the subject. You have, I expect?'

'Well, I've looked at a good many kinds. I'm not sure, between two, which is the best one—'

'Are you going to tell me about them? Will it take long, because, if so, isn't it perhaps a little early in the morning to begin? I mean, there's all the day—'

'Oh, all right.' Denham fell silent. Perhaps the talk had been long enough, though it had not been so long, she thought, as most night talks. She got up.

'Good-night, Miss Garden.'

'Good-night. That is, if you must go? I didn't mean, you know, to stop our conversation, only I thought possibly barometers might prove too large a subject to enter on. There's nothing else you wanted to say, I suppose?'

'No, that's all tonight, thanks very much.'

Denham returned to her room, rather pleased with herself. She had talked for quite a time. And it had not been really difficult, either. She was certainly coming on.

Miss Garden, getting into bed, thought, 'A curious episode. Will she get it out, whatever it is, tomorrow, I wonder? But why to me?' She chuckled at the memory of the earnest face.

'You'd think her whole heart was in winds and weather and barometers.'

She arranged herself comfortably in bed, with her novel at her side, for a last read, before the curious thought crossed, for a moment, her mind, 'What if it really is?'

5

Sunday was fine, and the younger members of the house party took sandwiches and walked out for the day. A queer walk, Denham found it; one of those sociable walks, when people talk all the time. At first they all kept more or less together, but after lunch Denham and Arnold detached themselves, and enjoyed the afternoon more than the morning. The others strolled over wood and hill amiably chattering, except Noel, who was feeling cross with Audrey, having by accident seen a sentence in a letter Audrey had been writing in the train yesterday to a friend, and it was about her, how she was extravagant in her expenditure and Audrey couldn't think what she did with all her allowance. Noel had not known that Audrey would write about her like that while professing friendliness. Audrey sometimes gave her these small shocks. She digested them in silence, turning them over and over, brooding and resentful, unable to forget. Audrey forgot offences much more quickly, and inflicted them more often. She was fond of Noel, though faintly jealous of the classic precision of her features, and more often irritated by the fastidiousness of her mind. Noel felt Audrey deficient at times in a sense of honour. Her mother, too ... They said things, they sometimes did things, that jarred. And now it seemed to Noel that she must be tarred with the same brush, for she had read that sentence about herself in Audrey's letter to the end. Of course if you see your own name, you do want to see what about it. You read it almost before you know what you're doing. Anyhow, Noel supposed bitterly, if you are a Gresham. Why write, talk or think about each other's private concerns, anyhow? Why not leave one another alone?

We never do, thought Noel. We're always talking each other over. All of us but Denham, and she doesn't talk at all. She's an owl, but she's got some sense about that ... This sort of thing, between Audrey and me, wants thinking out. It means we aren't really, at the bottom, friends—

It was the sort of psychological problem she could have discussed with a Somerville friend, only she would have to make it impersonal – a kind of 'What should Miss A. do?'

Audrey was finding the day rather tiresome. Her especial friend, Arnold, was off with Denham; Noel was moody and in the sulks about something; Guy was being affected and monopolising the conversation and flirting with two girls at once. This having to go out for the day just because it was Sunday was a bit of a bore really; there was such a thing as being too conventional. The older people, who had stayed about near home, were better off. Evelyn and Peter and Miss Garden and the gentleman novelist and the Liberal politician and the Liberal politician's wife were, no doubt, sitting about in the garden and being amusing and comfortable, having what Audrey called 'good talk.' Arnold and Denham were – well, goodness alone knew what Arnold and Denham were doing. What would he find to talk to her about? Weather – animals – trees – food – the map – these were not Arnold's subjects. Audrey shrugged her shoulders, and supposed that Arnold must think Denham handsome. As, of course, so she was, in a big, queer way.

It would be funny if they should really fall in love. Funny and rather sad, because of course they weren't suited in the least . . .

In front, Daphne and Joan, the two pretty girls, were mocking Guy's stories, laughing and sceptical. Audrey turned round to Noel, who was behind her on the path, and said amicably, 'How badly Daphne's done her eyebrows. The shape doesn't go with her nose.' Noel winced. She thought such comments in the worst of form. One's eyebrows were, like one's expenditure, one's own, and it was low of other people to comment on them.

'Has she? I've not noticed,' she returned, and Audrey thought, 'Sulky little prig.'

Kenneth Allen, Guy's friend, caught up Audrey, and talked about the training of mice. Audrey pulled herself together and became social, merry and alert.

6

Arnold and Denham strode along in silence and talk. The silence was Denham's (she had perhaps exhausted her powers

of loquacity in the small hours of the morning) and the talk
Arnold's. Denham didn't mind Arnold talking if he wanted
to. Sometimes she listened, sometimes she was busy looking
at the tilings they passed, and didn't listen. Occasionally she
raised a topic herself, such as wasps' nests, moles, squirrels,
ants, or how many miles one walked an hour. Whatever the
topic, Arnold always said more on it than she did; his speech
was at a ratio to hers of about a hundred to one. Even when
she wasn't listening, she liked to hear his nice, soft, easy voice
drifting along, liked him to be playing happily at the world's
favourite game, undeterred by her inability to play too. She did
not know that he was nervous. When there was a little silence,
she said, doing her bit, 'What's your favourite food?' and they
talked about that for quite a long time.

But really he had been silent because he had been wondering whether he should kiss her again, or whether that would
be a fool's game. He wanted to kiss her very badly, but he was
a young man of very decent feelings, and felt that he ought to
think this thing out before he went on with it. How did she
regard him, and how he her? Was this to be a solid love affair,
or merely a weekend pastime? He felt that it might become,
for him, if he went on kissing her, quite a solid love affair, and
he was not sure if either of them wanted that ... So, after
his night's reflection, he had started the day meaning to be
impersonal and prosaic. However, he had succumbed to the
temptation of going off alone with her, and now he badly
wanted to make love again.

So, after a brief hesitation, he made love again, and the
afternoon passed very enjoyably for them both. By tea-time
they both perceived that they were in love. The usual kind

of strong attraction netted them firmly about, and it would have been of no use to struggle against it, even had they endeavoured to do so. They knew that they must meet very frequently in London and continue this thing. They made engagements to lunch together this week, to play tennis in Regent's Park, and to go to kennel shows. The affair, in short, promised well.

7

At dinner that night everyone knew that it was an affair. Even male creatures could scarcely miss it.

Arnold joined in conversation about the Diaghilev ballet, and compared Woizikovsky with Idzikovsky, and discussed the pictorial values of Massine, but rather absently, as if some force were dragging him downwards from civilisation towards the level of Denham, who, being asked by the politician's wife, who did not know her, whether the combination of Massine and Pruna was not the most delicious thing in the world, replied, supposing it to be some kind of fruit salad, that she had not tasted it. It was obvious that this force, with its downward drag at one lover, was, as yet, exerting no effective upward pull at the other. Denham's aspirations towards the higher life were earnest but fitful, and meals were, for her, off times. She ate stolidly through them, an indifferent Philistine within the gates, gay, informed chatter frothing round her like a play to which she was not listening.

'Denham behaves,' Evelyn said to Audrey, later, just a rather stupid child of twelve. I wonder if I should have her examined. Perhaps an osteopath ... They say it's all the spine, and I dare say hers wants loosening up. It did wonders for Clara Elton's girl, cured her of stooping and breathing—'

'Denham doesn't stoop or breathe,' said Audrey shortly.

'Well, no. Physically, she's magnificent. Nothing seems to tire her. It's her head that seems weak, poor girl. It's probably a case of arrested development. I really think I must have her seen to.'

CHAPTER V

Getting Engaged

I

From the beginning to the end of their acquaintance, Denham never discovered what Arnold's parents were busy about. Certainly they were busy with something, and Denham supposed that, like other Londoners, they were writing a book, or possibly a book apiece. But what kind of a book or books she never knew. All that filtered through of their avocations to her comprehension was expressed in loud, continuous and argumentative conversation. Mrs Chapel, a stout, vivacious, and apparently learned lady, was the loudest and the most constant talker; Mr Chapel was lean and comparatively quiet, but also learned, and joined issue with his wife at considerable length. Sometimes Denham thought they were writing a history of Great Britain, or of the world, which, she gathered, was quite the fashion nowadays among Londoners. At the other times she thought it must be a natural history book, or a dictionary, or a book about art. Mrs Chapel would say things like 'Cro-Magnon art ...

Obviously Atlantean . . . And what about the Amphisbaena? They didn't swim across the sea!' Mr Chapel would say things like, 'You go a great deal too fast. You jump to conclusions. And you eliminate the human agency in dealing with these small reptiles. Sailors have always carried them about from land to land.'

Or Mrs Chapel would say, 'They dyed themselves with whortleberry juice,' and Mr Chapel would reply, 'That is extremely doubtful, at that late date. By that time they were having free intercourse with the Phoenicians, who used purple shell-fish.' Or they would discuss the soul; moths flying into candles, soularies, a-souling, not having seen a soul, and other aspects of the spirit of man and human beliefs about it. There was someone called Frazer, whom they both seemed to quote a lot.

Arnold joined brightly in these conversations, but he did not know nearly as much as his parents did. Sometimes he would try to draw Denham into the simpler parts of the talk, but he presently gave this up. Denham had no objection to this kind of conversation; it seemed to her more sensible than many other kinds, as it was not about people, who were the dullest of subjects. But, naturally, she was able to make no contribution to it. Mr and Mrs Chapel did not require or desire her to do so; they did not expect young women to know anything worth knowing, and they soon learnt that this particular young woman was an untutored savage. Arnold felt that they regarded her as Cro-Magnon, or Atlantean, or neanderthal, or something of that kind, and were interested in the shape of her skull and in whether she would prefer to dye herself with whortleberry juice or purple shell-fish. They scarcely regarded her, anyhow, as their son's young lady friend.

Yet Arnold and Denham went everywhere together, entranced one with the other, walking in that state of mutual intoxication which blinds the eyes and befogs the brain. They went to dog shows, horse shows, theatres, cinemas, Richmond Park and the Zoo. In Richmond Park Arnold proposed marriage.

Denham said, 'Don't think so. I should be no good at that,' and they argued it. Ardently he wanted her and she him, and her will wavered beneath their joint desire. But still she repeated it. 'I should be no good at marriage.'

'What do you mean, darling idiot? Marriage is nothing but being always together.'

'No. There'd be a house to look after – meals, and servants, and people calling, and all that. I should disgrace you. Hate it myself, too.'

'Rubbish, *that* isn't marriage. Marriage is just you and me.'

'Might be babies, too.'

'Well, that'd be fun. I'd like that, wouldn't you?'

'No,' said Denham. 'They'd be a bother.'

'Oh, well, forget them. Marriage is just you and me. If you loved me the way I loved you you'd want it more than anything in the world.'

'I do want it. But I think we'd both be fools to do it.'

'Let's be fools, then. Darling heart, let's be fools ...'

He stifled her mouth with kisses, her breathing with his hard embrace that was like a trap closing on her. Her wisdom slipped away in the dappled sunlight of the oak copse, and she mumbled, 'All right, then. Let's be fools.'

'What,' said Arnold, next day, as they walked to the park for tennis, 'do you believe, my love? Religiously, I mean. Are you Anglican, agnostic, or what?'

'Church of England,' Denham replied, glibly and without interest.

'What a funny thing to be. Why are you?'

'Well, father was. He was a clergyman, you see. Being Church of England saved a lot of trouble, because there was no English church in Andorra.'

'You don't sound as if you much cared what you were. I wish you'd become a Catholic. I'd like us to belong to the same church. Suppose you look into it?'

'Why? I mean, what's the point of belonging to the same church?'

'Well, I'd like it. Wouldn't you? And it makes things easier, rather. The authorities prefer it. Of course mixed marriages can be arranged quite easily, but there have to be special provisions about the children and so on.'

'Well, I hope there won't be any of those, but of course you never know. All right, darling, I'll join any church you like. But I won't *go* to church much, you know. I don't like it.'

'You can settle about that later. All I want you to do now is to go under instruction. I'll introduce you to Father Gilbert, of Mount Street, before you leave town. Then you can read up some things about it while you're away, and begin instruction in October.'

'I don't want to read anything. I know all about it. Everyone in Andorra was Catholic except father and me. I used to have to go to church too when I was at school.'

'Well, if they find you know all about it you can be baptised quite soon. It will be ripping your being a Catholic too. Toss for courts.'

'I don't care what I am. Rough.'

3

In Mount Street Denham was interviewed by a small, intelligent priest, to whom, thinking to save him and herself trouble, she professed herself quite willing to be admitted into his church forthwith. But it seemed that this did not do. She must first have instruction, in order that she might know what she was doing.

'I do know,' she said. 'I was at a Catholic school, and I lived with Catholics. I know all the things they do.'

'But it is possible,' he replied, gentle but firm, 'that you don't know why they did them.'

'Yes, I do. They had to.'

'But why had they to? What was the sanction behind it?'

Denham, bored, sighed a little, and he gave her three little books to take away and read. A great bother about nothing, she thought, when she was quite willing to be baptised straight away.

She tried to read the books that evening after dinner. One of them began about the Bible. 'How Protestants regard the Bible.' What did it matter how Protestants regarded the Bible? Apparently they regarded it as 'the sole and adequate Rule of Faith.' Denham had never thought of regarding the Bible like that. The book went on about Socinians and what they argued. Then came 'How Catholics regard the Bible', and then 'How the Apostles regarded the New Testament'. All this regarding – was it really necessary for her to enquire into?

A little further on the book said that an enquirer must begin by studying the Penny Catechism; obviously Denham had begun with the wrong book. 'The enquirer's further questions would be answered by reading, or by instruction from a priest.' Well, there wouldn't be any further questions from her. It was a rash subject to ask questions about; one would probably get answered.

'It is not essential that the enquirer should be a master of theology before entering the Church; a sound knowledge of the substantial doctrines is sufficient. The important thing is to be thoroughly imbued with the principle of belief in the authority of the Church, and to be ready to accept, in general, whatever the Church teaches as belonging to the deposit of faith.'

Denham sighed, and turned over the pages, to find the deposit of faith. Infallibility; Particular Doctrines an Obstacle to entering the Church; Predestination; Reprobation; Justification; Final Perseverance; Sanctification and Merit; Number and Meaning of the Sacraments; Indulgences; the Immaculate Conception.

It all seemed very complicated. Did Arnold really understand and believe all that? Denham did not think that anyone in Andorra, except (one presumed) the priests, had bothered about it much. Why couldn't one join a church without going into all the odd things that churches believed? It only put one off.

She turned to the Catechism, which shot at her a running fire of questions. 'Who made you? Why did God make you? In whose image and likeness did God make you?'

'Well,' thought Denham, 'he can't have made us *all* like him, as we're all quite different from each other.'

Many of the questions were of the leading variety, such as, 'Is it a great evil to fall into mortal sin?' and 'Do those pray well who at their prayers think neither of God nor of what they say?' Easy ones, but hardly worth asking, thought Denham; they were like the interrogations of which bus conductors deliver themselves when given farthings – 'Do you believe that these are of any use to me?' There were so many questions to ask to which one didn't know the answers beforehand.

Denham turned to the end of the Catechism. There was a piece about going to bed, how you must undress modestly, thinking about death. How could one, when undressing alone, do it modestly or otherwise? Of course, one might forget to draw the curtains when the light was on.

Denham closed the Catechism. She found such spiritual chit-chat tasteless and embarrassing. Definitely, she did not care about it. It was a pity Arnold wanted her to be a Roman Catholic (as everyone in England except Roman Catholics themselves seemed to call it). Perhaps she would tell him she couldn't manage it after all. But then he would be disappointed. In thinking of Arnold she forgot the Catholic Church, and slipped into an ecstasy of love. Oh, yes, she would be a Mohammedan if Arnold wished it. For Arnold she would be a Roman Catholic, learn to talk, read books, be intelligent, sociable, and like other people. She would eat off as many plates as he liked – hundreds and thousands of plates, and a fresh knife and fork with each of them. She would have meals cooked and laid in courses, and not snatch things out of the larder when hungry. She would, in brief, fully embrace the higher life, and, if to join Arnold's church were part of this, Arnold's church she would join. She would be ready to accept whatever the Church taught as belonging to the deposit of faith. She would learn, if necessary, to answer all those foolish questions in the Catechism. She would even undress modestly, thinking about death.

Guy came in and saw her sitting in the window seat, the pamphlets of his faith spread about her. He smiled.

It's not,' he told her, 'so bad as you would gather from its literature, the Church. Probably no church is. All the same, I don't advise you to join it. I don't think it's your line of country, exactly.'

Her line of country. But it didn't do to begin to think of that. Her line of country ... possibly it didn't lead to matrimony at all, let alone joining churches.

'It's all right,' she answered Guy. 'I can manage it, I think.'

'Don't discourage her, Guy,' Evelyn put in, looking up from the proofs she was correcting, staring through horn-rimmed reading glasses. 'It'll be much more comfortable for her to be a Catholic, the same as Arnold. More harmonious. Mixed marriages are terribly depressing. They say the Pope hates them. Of course, you must go over if you honestly can, Denham. But not unless, mind you. You can think it all out at Torquay, can't you.'

'Dear mother,' Guy remonstrated, 'one can't think out the Catholic Church. You have either to shut your eyes and go for it blind, or stay where you are. Of course, you may *think* you're thinking it out – that's another matter. But it only wastes time. Don't try to do that, Denham, pray.'

'Wasn't going to.' Unnecessary advice people gave. It wasn't likely she would waste her time thinking about something she had already decided on. Especially so dull a thing as this.

'Have you packed, Denham?'

'No. I don't know what to take.'

'Well, you'll want stout walking shoes, of course, and knitted stockings, as well as light ones. And a woollen suit, and a coat and skirt, and some cotton frocks, and waterproof, and some hat that stands rain. And something for the evening.

Here Evelyn broke off, doubtful. What *would* Denham want for the evening, staying with her father's married sister at Torquay? What did that kind of person put on in the evenings? They probably had high tea, or some kind of supper with cold meat and pink or white shape and stewed prunes. High necks and long sleeves went with that.

'Some kind of afternoon frock,' said Evelyn.

5

The Greshams spent August each in a separate place. Peter was in Cromer, for golf, Evelyn in Normandy, for a rest, Guy in Vienna, for amusement, Audrey in Czechoslovakia, for adventure, Humphrey in Italy, for art, Noel in Sunderland, for the North Sea, Denham in Torquay, with a paternal aunt and cousins. The aunt was married to a Torquay dentist, a very thriving man. The aunt too throve, so did her sons and daughters. They were not shy or retired, they were not bored by people. Denham concluded that her father had been a freak or sport in his family. His Torquay relatives chattered away, saw people, consumed meals in the houses of others, gave others to eat and drink in their house, like the rest of the world. This made Denham feel lonely. She had imagined that possibly her father's family might resemble her father in this matter, but quite the contrary. Indeed, her aunt deplored to her this unfortunate quality of her father's which had induced him to seek out for his life so lonely and remote a spot.

'Why, you can never have *seen* anyone out there,' she ejaculated. 'Oh yes,' said Denham, with regret. 'I did. There were lots of people about.'

'But no English, my dear.'

'They came sometimes. More and more lately.'

'Well, it was high time you left that odd place and came home. What I say is, no one wants to spend their time gadding about and gossiping with their neighbours, but a little human intercourse we all do require. I daresay you've led quite a smart, gay life in the West End this summer, haven't you.'

'S.W.3, Aunt Evelyn lives in,' said Denham, always geographically accurate. 'Not west.' Had it been a smart, gay life? She supposed it had.

'Well, we can't offer you *that* down here,' said her aunt, who was a little touchy about the family into which her brother had married. 'But we've plenty to do in Torquay. Lots of life going on, and you'll meet plenty of pleasant people. Do you enjoy whist?'

'No.'

'That's a pity. We have very nice progressive drives on Wednesday nights. The girls go. Perhaps you enjoy tennis and golf more. And are you fond of bathing?'

'Yes. All those things. And boating, and fishing, and walking. I shall have lots to do.'

'Well, you must come out in the evenings with us too. We have some very bright evenings. There's a nice reading circle, too.'

'A what?' Denham was apprehensive.

'A reading circle. You all study some book together, and meet and talk about it.'

'What for?'

'What funny questions you do ask, to be sure. Study should be a part of life, shouldn't it, as well as play. Pardon me.'

The Bartletts asked for pardon when they sneezed or yawned or hiccupped, or made some other inadvertent bodily ejaculation. And when others craved their pardon for stepping on their toes, their reply was, 'Granted.'

'Yes,' said Denham, meaning that she would pardon her aunt for hiccupping, but Mrs Bartlett understood her to be agreeing that study should be a part of life.

'And then,' she added, 'the girls help in theatricals and concerts, they've quite a lot of talent really. I think we can manage to give you quite a cheerful time down here.'

Out of the frying-pan into the fire. Gloomily Denham perceived that Torquay was much like London. In Torquay, as in London, people obeyed the Christian precept and loved one another, and forsook not the assembling of themselves together.

But the people were different. The Bartletts were not the same as the Greshams. They said, 'pardon me', and 'granted', and their jokes were different jokes, and they did not discuss books and pictures, though they talked about the drama, which flourished in Torquay. Their interest in books was, as Denham observed with relief, apparently confined exclusively to the circles in which they studied them. They were a lively family, and all right to go fishing and boating with, though they talked too much.

Torquay wasn't bad. One could shrimp and prawn and fish, and bathe, and wade, and boat, and play tennis, and golf. The Bartletts and their friends were full of activities, and, like the people in London, preferred to perform these in company with others rather than alone. They thought Denham rather a dull dog, because she said little or nothing, and had an odd habit of sneaking off by herself; still, she was good at sports, though idiotic at book teas. Also she carried with her, from her associations with the fabulous Greshams in London, the aroma of a social level higher than that of the Bartletts in Torquay. Not that she herself had much style. Rough, they said, and queer, and manners so blunt as to be almost common.

6

Denham left Torquay to go to Arnold and his people at Fowey. They had a cottage in the town and a fishing boat in the harbour. All day Arnold and Denham fished and sailed and cruised along the coast, landing in creeks and caves, bathing and wading and exploring. It was the perfect life. If life with Arnold were to be like this, marriage would be a happy lot.

Denham said one day, as they sat on the sea wall at Polperro, having lunch, 'Why shouldn't we live somewhere about here, Arnold? It's better than London.'

'I should say it was. Oh, lord, why can't we always have it?'

'Well,' said Denham, 'we can.'

'Earn our livings fishing, you mean?'

'Yes. Or some other way. We shan't need much.'

'Good. Let's do it.'

But he did not mean it. Denham, looking at him, saw that he did not. He was not regarding it as a practical proposal at all.

'But I mean really,' she explained, taking the last sandwich. 'We don't need more money than these fishermen do.'

'The trouble is, we mightn't earn so much,' he lightly answered her.

'I don't see why we shouldn't, after a little practice. Anyhow living here would be worth it, even if we didn't. I've got a little, you know, of my own. Haven't you?'

'Only my hard-earned wages, I'm afraid. The very thought of London, down here and in this weather, is appalling.'

Denham pondered. They all said that, all the people like him. But somehow or other they all went back to London when the time came, and didn't seem to find it so appalling when they got there.

'Arnold,' she enquired, puzzled and literal, 'do you *want* to live in London?'

'Denham,' he returned, 'I certainly don't. But my job's there and I've got to.'

But all the time he did want to. Denham perceived that.

'They,' were so odd. (By 'they,' Denham meant almost everyone but herself.) They were for ever saying, for no apparent reason, what was not precisely the case. A lie to gain an end is one thing, and anyone can understand that. But all these objectless misstatements as to desires and feelings – where was the sense in these? Denham sighed, gave it up, and finished the last sandwich.

The thing was to make the most of the present. Here they were together, sticky with salt water and burnt with sun and air, with no duties or obligations, cruising from bay to bay. Perhaps, before the holidays were over, Arnold would realise, and not merely say, that it really was better than living in London, and would remain.

But no; when the appointed time was arrived, back to London Arnold went, sighing and groaning, but shouldering the white man's burden as if it were an inevitable fate. Back to London, to publish more books. Back to London, to finish his own book and prepare it for the press. (For it goes without saying that Arnold too wrote books.) Back to London, as Arnold reminded Denham, to get married very soon. They thought of the end of November, just before Advent came to stop weddings. Back to London, as Denham, rather bored, remembered, that she might proceed with her instruction in Roman Catholic tenets and be presently admitted into that Church.

She got out the horrid little pamphlets again and tried to read them in the train up to Paddington, but, after six weeks of shore loafing, they made less sense to her than ever. Why should she bother with them? She was quite ready to be admitted into the Church without further ado. Her object was to get through with it as quickly and easily as might be, without any more fuss or talk.

Ten more days of September, all October, nearly all November – then marriage and Arnold. As if he had been thinking the same thought, Arnold, sitting by her in the train, slid his arm unobtrusively behind her, a cautious eye on the newspaper-reading man opposite. She took his brown hand in both her own and held it tightly, and thrills of the familiar kind shivered through them both. Even heading towards London, leaving Cornwall and the sea behind, life was violently exciting.

7

Early in November Denham was received into the Roman branch of the Catholic Church. Her instruction had been rapid and easy, for she had given no trouble and asked no questions, on the excellent grounds that, were she to do so, she would have to listen to the answers. Her only demur was when she was told that the necessity of re-baptism was based on the presumption that her last and Anglican baptism had not been well performed. She saw in this a loophole of escape from this ceremony, and protested that, since her father had been a clergyman, he would doubtless have seen to it that all was correctly done. However, the opinion of authority was against this view. The priest said that in all probability the water had failed to flow, and, in view of such a contingency, she would have to be re-baptised.

'Why should they think it didn't flow?' she asked Arnold afterwards. 'They've no reason to think so.'

'Anglican parsons are so casual,' Arnold replied. 'They don't think it matters.'

'Well, no more it does. How could it? ... No, never mind, I remember now why it does, don't tell me.'

So Denham was baptised. The day before that she had made

a general confession of her life, which was much more difficult. In fact, she found it so difficult that, after her unaided efforts had brought her no nearer thinking of anything to say, she had asked Arnold to help her.

'What did *you* say?' she asked him.

'Well, I tried to remember the things I'd done.'

'But I don't know which of them were wrong. How can I?'

'Oh, well, one can just go through the Commandments or the Catechism or something, and see where they fit in . . . It's not so difficult, really. You might get Father Gilbert to help you.'

Denham sighed and sucked her pencil.

'Shall I say I've undressed every night without thinking about death? I have.'

'No. Ask Father Gilbert. He's quite sensible, really.'

'It's a bother asking people. I'd rather do it myself. I dare say I'll think of some things presently.'

Two days later she said to Arnold, 'I find I've done nearly everything. Almost all the sins in the Catechism and Commandments. My list has got quite long.'

'Well, one has actually done most of them,' Arnold agreed.

'Not quite all, though,' Denham said, turning over the pages of the Catechism. 'I've not been to non-Catholic schools or taken part in the services of a false religion, or made idols, or consulted spiritualists or fortune tellers, or trusted to charms, omens, dreams, and such like fooleries, or done simony . . . at least, I may have, I don't quite know what that is, really – or given divine honour to the angels and saints, or belonged to a secret society, or killed anyone, or committed adultery, or seen immodest plays and dances – have I, at least? – or married within certain degrees of kindred or at forbidden times ... But most of the others, I think ... It says one needn't make a confession after this more than once a year.'

'I say, darling.' Arnold was a little uncomfortable. 'You really are keen on the Church, aren't you? I mean, you aren't just doing it because of getting married?'

Denham stared at him, puzzled.

'Of course it's because of getting married. How do you mean? What else could it be, Arnold?'

'Well, of course, I know it began because of that – only I hoped by now you were perhaps getting keen on it for its own sake – getting to see its fineness, you know, and that it really is the truth.'

'Well' – she frowned, impatient of discussion – 'I don't understand about religions, you know. But I expect it's the best one, as you belong to it. Anyhow, I'm joining it.'

So Denham put on Catholicism with the same dogged determination with which she endeavoured to adopt the other practices and tenets of the Higher Life.

Soon after she had done so Arnold and she were married in Brompton Oratory.

CHAPTER VI

Getting Married

I

For their honeymoon they went to the Balearic Islands. The exquisite loveliness of Mallorca, its gentle airs and mild winter suns, its great sweet oranges, little deep-streeted Moorish towns, ancient inns and blue bays, its olive-grown mountains, straying, jingling goats and beautiful and amiable inhabitants, combined with the excessive love which this couple bore one another to make the weeks they spent on this island a period of complete and unmarred bliss, culminating in an exquisite and smiling Christmas in the little orange-gardened town of Soller. In the new year they visited Minorca and Iviza, less attractive islands, and Arnold became interested in Iviza in Phoenician remains, which greatly abound there. To such remains as these Denham, being uneducated, was indifferent, but she enjoyed exploring the island, in spite of the ill weather which beat on it in early January, and which made their passage to and from it a sorry business for Arnold, who was a poor sailor. They then returned for a few more days to Mallorca, staying in Palma, and skilfully evading the other English who abounded there, for Palma had by then (January 1924) become a favourite resort for those who sought refuge from the rigours of the British climate. Denham, though buildings left her cold, consented to examine with Arnold the cathedral, the Franciscan monastery, the Arab baths, and the other architectural features of the capital, though, for her part, she preferred loafing about the narrow cobbled streets, and peering into the old shops.

As to Arnold, he liked everything he saw and did; rapt in love, the two spent radiant days; drowned in passion, they sank deeply into blissful nights. Nothing marred or jarred their joy.

'No one before ever loved as we do,' cried Arnold, the articulate one of the pair.

'I expect,' said Denham, as deeply enamoured but more literal, 'that everyone loves in much the same way.'

So excessive, though by no means unique, was this way, that it was undisturbed by the argument which arose as to whether they should return to Mallorca to live, or stay in London.

'It's for holidays, an island like this,' Arnold maintained. 'It would spoil it to live in it. Besides, I couldn't publish books here.'

'You could write them,' said Denham, humouring this morbid and incomprehensible desire to increase the number of books in the world.

'That's true,' he agreed. 'It would be a glorious place for writing. But I can't, unfortunately, at present live by writing. That's the public's fault, not mine, but there it is. So I shall have to publish other people's books for the time being. Besides, it's not really an uninteresting job, you know; it brings one up against all kinds of more or less amusing people. As well as plenty of fools, of course. And the mere technique of book production is rather fun – type, and so on. And the gamble of it is exciting, too. It's really not a bad job, as jobs go.'

'Well,' Denham amicably accepted his peculiar tastes, 'I'd rather have less money and less work and live somewhere decent. But so long as you like it—'

'You'll like it too, sweetheart. I'll make you like London yet.'

'I'm sure,' Denham granted, 'it must be the best place, as you all think so. Perhaps when I've lived in it longer I shall find out why. Anyhow, it's the biggest,' she allowed him, kindly and justly. 'And the most crowded. And it has the most buses and trams and things.'

'One's right at the heart of things there,' Arnold tried to explain. 'In the centre, not on the circumference. One's more alive than in other places. One sharpens one's mind on other people's. It's a hell of a place in lots of ways, but a live hell, not a mortuary. You can't stagnate in London. It's galvanic.'

Denham vaguely gathered that London was good as a restorative for half-dead persons, or as a preservative of life in those who were in danger of decay.

'But everyone doesn't need all that,' she demurred. 'You might be quite alive in yourself already.'

'You might, you certainly might,' he answered her, with an embrace. 'As for you, you'd be alive in Tibetan snows, or at Peckham Rye.'

But Denham hadn't meant herself, whom she knew, indeed, to be not alive in his sense at all, but mentally stagnant even unto inertia. Probably she did need London . . .

'Where's Peckham Rye, Arnold?' she asked, changing the subject from the personal issue.

'Oh, it's a beastly suburb.'

Denham had heard suburbs mentioned before by Londoners with derision or distaste, and sometimes wondered why.

'Aren't people who live in suburbs alive?'

'No. Dead as mutton, it is believed.'

'Why are they? And how is it known?'

'No one knows why. It's their own dark secret. I expect they spend too much of their time in trains and buses. Now, don't waste time arguing about the accepted premises of life, of which one is that suburbans are dull. Heaven knows what you'll be trying to upset next.'

'I don't try to upset things. I only want to know why.'

2

To London they returned, in mid-January, and plunged into fog, frost, and darkness. They had decided to live for the present in the top flat of a large house in Tavistock Square, where the occupants of the other floors were already known to Arnold. Arnold, with his easy sociability, had thought this rather a pleasant arrangement, since the people were cheerful, agreeable people enough, and wielded pens, pencils and paint brushes, so that the hall and passages were decorated with their studies. To be sure they were, some of them, a little fond of free love, but, after all, as they weren't religious, what could one expect? And there was no need to see much of any of them.

Arnold's novel was coming out in February, with his own firm. Though this has the drawback that the public may think no one else would take your book, it has the advantage that you can see that it is well advertised. Arnold cared very much for this book, which probed very deeply into human psychology, recording thought and emotion in that particular fashionable medium which some consider an accurate transcription and others do not. Arnold hoped that it would make a good deal of stir, even create that 'discussion,' which is the publisher's ideal for a book, but which no one has ever actually heard, and establish his name among the highbrow novelists, for no one wants to be thought only a publisher.

Meanwhile, his daily work interested him, and Denham was to him breathless wonder and delight, and settling into the flat most amusing.

The choice of furniture and decoration had been his own, assisted by his married sister and the Greshams. His parents had gone to explore in Egypt for a year. Denham seemed to have an erroneous idea that it didn't matter what the inside of houses looked like, so long as they were reasonably comfortable, and contained the things one was likely to want ready to one's hand. She insisted on pinning maps on the walls, and these, with a barometer and thermometer, were the only mural decorations she cared to hang, though she made no objection to anything Arnold liked to put up. She had no feeling against overcrowding on walls, since pictures didn't get in one's way, like too much furniture standing about the floor. In the end, what with Arnold's rather promiscuous artistic taste, which ranged from early Cretan to Dadaism, what with the graceful Second Empirism of his sister, the Russian ballet decor of Evelyn Gresham, and the potting-shed and gunroom notions of Denham, the flat was a queer hotchpotch. It was further deranged by Denham's small dog, who, like other dogs, was a mistake in flats, and by Arnold's bullfinch, who would sit on his shoulder, and to whom he would cry 'tweet'.

Denham, safely now back from the disintegrating influences of travel and holidays, set herself to lead the good life, with an earnestness even greater than the earnestness with which she had, on first coming to London, laboured to live up to the Greshams. Living up to Arnold was far more important. She must now be a hostess, a guest, a giver and receiver of visits, an eater in the houses of others, a preparer of food and drink to be consumed by others in her house.

As Arnold and Denham drank their morning tea, they would read their post, which was thick with invitations. Arnold was for accepting them all, except those which clashed with each other. Though every now and then he would say, 'Tuesday evening – that fills up every night next week, doesn't it? No, I'm hanged if we will; we must have one evening alone together. Say no.' Denham would say, 'What about two evenings alone together, Arnold? Or three? We might say no to the Fosters' dinner on Wednesday.' But there was some reason why this would be a pity: the Fosters' dinners were amusing; Denham would enjoy it; they would meet jolly people, it would be better to go, nuisance as it was getting so many nights filled up.

At first Denham said sometimes, 'What about your going without me? I'd rather like the evening at home,' but on no account would Arnold go without her. He would not, he said, enjoy it; he wanted his friends to meet her and her to meet his friends; he liked to see her in the room at parties, looking so much more wonderful than anyone else. Denham would sigh a little.

'I'm no good at them, you know. I don't talk as much as the others do. Not nearly.'

'What does that matter? The others gabble away; you *are* . . . Though, of course,' Arnold added, 'I think you ought to talk as much as you can, because the things you say are so adorable.'

The young husband's point of view. Denham had in mind her Aunt Evelyn's.

'If you go out to dinner, my dear child, you've got to talk. It's not fair on your hostess if you don't. It's not fair, either, on the men next you. Not fair, do you see. They've got to keep it up, and if you don't help they can't. Besides, it spoils a dinner to have a dead spot. If you can't talk, you mustn't go out. Women who can't or won't speak when they're out are a public nuisance. We've all got a duty to society, do you see. You'll try to remember that when you're married, won't you; it's terribly important and true.'

Denham did try to remember it. She must keep on talking when she went out. If she didn't, it let Arnold down. It didn't matter what one talked about, but one must utter something, or one was a public nuisance. A fantastic fact, but terribly important and true.

She would consult Arnold before a dinner party. 'What shall I talk about, Arnold?'

'Oh, anything that turns up, I suppose. Anything that's happened, or that you've read or heard or thought or seen. Honestly, old thing, I don't see the difficulty – if you want to talk.'

'The only thing I've read lately,' Denham said, 'is that book on dog diseases. I could talk quite a lot about Isaac, I think. His coat's coming out.'

At dinner that night, when her neighbour said to her, 'Did you see the Guitrys last week?' she replied in the manner of Ollendorf, 'No, but the hair of my dog is coming out. Do you know the best treatment for it?'

The young man (whose name was Sitwell) did not, so she told him. She also furnished other information about dogs. He thought it was rather a good game, and when she said, 'Have you ever had a dog with kidney disease?' he replied, 'No, but I have a goldfish with acute neurosis.'

But after a time he grew bored with animals, for whom he had no great affection, and endeavoured to lead the conversation into other paths. Denham, however, did not follow him along these, for she had nothing to say about his subjects. He spoke of Spain, believing her to have come from this country, and mentioned Moorish edifices in –Andalusia and Gothic in Castile. He asked her, when she said she had lived in Andorra, of what type was the architecture in this republic, observing that he hoped to pay it a visit the following Easter. She replied, briefly that, the buildings were mainly houses, castles, and churches, and that at Easter he would find it deeply under snow. Which, he asked, did she consider the most interesting town to stay in there? Towns, she answered, were not, in her view, interesting to stay in at all, either in Andorra or elsewhere.

After this the conversation languished, and finally lapsed. Arnold's wife was certainly rather a dull dog, the young man decided, though of striking appearance.

Conversation twinkled briskly about the table, the Guitrys, whoever these might be, seeming to Denham to absorb more than their fair share of it. She gave it up, and consumed food.

While duck was being eaten, her right-hand neighbour turned to her and mentioned some film which he had seen which had pleased him, inquiring if she had chanced to see it, and if she did not think it good. Denham settled the matter promptly with the statement that she had seen it and had thought it not bad. This was the point at which she always stuck. The affirmative which was, for others, the beginning of a flow of comment and exchange of ideas was to her merely a bald affirmation of a fact, the shutting, not the opening, of a door. People desired to know if she had seen a film, a play, a book, or a Guitry; she satisfied their curiosity, and left it at that. What was there more to say? Any amount, obviously, for all about her people were saying it.

She caught Arnold's horn-rimmed eyes on her from across the table, in a fond and fleeting look, a swift caress. Yet she knew that she was letting Arnold down, by not talking. In the glance of her hostess, a little later, she perceived no caress, and she recollected how her aunt Evelyn had said that hostesses did not like dead spots at their dinner tables.

Audrey was there, next to Arnold, talking away, happy, intelligent, competent, amusing and amused. Audrey was never a dead spot. She and Arnold enjoyed themselves talking together, though one might think they would have got through all they had to say in the mornings at the office. But that was about work; this was evening conversation, bright and dinnerish.

Well, anyhow the duck was good. And now trifle approached.

'What's your favourite pudding?' Denham asked her right-hand neighbour, as questions seemed to be the fashion.

And, since her neighbour did not make his answers closed doors, they really did converse about that. Being what is called a highbrow, he liked to talk about puddings, films and music-halls. On puddings the high and the low of brow can meet.

'One might always talk about the food at dinner,' thought Denham, rather pleased with herself. 'It would make a new subject for each course.'

After dinner Audrey talked to Denham, telling her, among other things, how well she looked in her new dress. Denham, who took the melancholy view of clothes, said, 'It's hellish to get into,' and brooding over that, neglected to comment on the new dress of Audrey. In fact, she did not know it was new, or that Audrey looked pretty in it; she never knew how anyone looked in anything.

At half past ten she told Arnold that she must go home to perform some office for Isaac. Arnold said, 'Can't Winifred see to him?' and Denham gave him a morose glance, such as one gives to those who endeavour to knock from under one's feet one's reasons for doing what one desires to do.

So they both went home together at half past ten, while the rest of the party settled in for a night's entertainment.

'Why so early, my best?' Arnold asked of her, with his affectionate mockery, as they walked to their bus.

'I wanted to be at home,' Denham adequately replied. 'And it's not so early. Aunt Evelyn says one *can* go away after dinner at halfpast ten.'

But to Arnold the question had always been how late after dinner one could stay.

Presently they gave little dinners themselves.

Denham said, 'Wouldn't it save a lot of time and trouble and plates and things if we put all the food on the table at once and let them all take what they wanted?'

'Too much of a scramble,' replied Arnold, who always had some sensible man's reason why the accepted way of doing things was also the best way.

But Evelyn gave Denham the true reason why they must not put all the food on the table at once.

'You mustn't try to be original yet, Denham dear. You don't know well enough yet how to keep the rules to break them safely. You must wait a bit, and meanwhile do things like other people. You see, when you break social rules, you should always seem to be *ahead* of fashion and convention, not lagging behind them, do you see what I mean?'

'I can't,' said Denham, 'see that it matters whether one's ahead or behind, so long as one saves time and trouble and plates and things . . . I call the way we have our meals silly.'

For Denham even now had moments of barbarian revolt, in which she forgot herself and blasphemed against the Polite Life. But she settled down again to it, with a wistful sigh. Six courses, then, and coffee afterwards. And port with dessert, not before – but Arnold, fortunately, saw to the drinks, and Winifred, their competent young maid, whom Denham addressed in gruff, embarrassed tones, to the table arrangements. So their dinner parties went off all right, and the diners enjoyed themselves, talking and eating away, as diners will. So far as was apparent, no one was bored by them except the hostess. And she was getting used to it, becoming broken in to life, which consisted, she was discovering, largely in one boring occupation after another. Housekeeping, social functions, talking; seeing people, being intelligent, walking in the streets. Beyond the horizon of these doings, gleamed mistily the dream of some different life, some life in which she and Arnold should loaf in disreputable ease, in unsocial aloneness, beneath warm and radiant skies, eating, drinking and playing as they lounged on some hot beach, saying nothing but stupid things, such as, 'That's a big fish out there,' and 'Any chocolate left?' And fingers for forks and no plates. Would they be ahead of the social conventions, or behind them? Behind, no doubt; thousands of years behind; but, since there would be no one to observe them, it would not matter.

Conventions. An odd word. So were conventional and unconventional. Denham had heard the other occupants of the house in which they lived called unconventional. They even thought themselves so. 'If you don't mind a flat in a rather unconventional house,' one of them had said to her and Arnold. But now Denham knew that they weren't unconventional at all. They lived just like other people, and did things in the same way. They had lots of plates at meals, and they talked about painting, and their shoes and stockings were always pairs, and they never said, during the soup, 'Let's have the port at once.' To be sure, some of them were, apparently, what newspapers call intimate together, without having undergone marriage – but that cannot be considered unconventional, exactly, though, of course, thought Denham, remembering church teaching on this, matter, it was doubtless wrong.

No, the occupants of the downstairs flats were not in the least unconventional. None of them would have dreamed of going out into the streets with their shoes laced with string. Denham had not so much dreamed of this as done it, in her early days in London. She had not understood but had accepted her Aunt Evelyn's reasons why she must never do it again, and why the kind of laces sold with shoes are the only permissible way of tying shoes. Not to tie one's shoes with string; she had made a mental note of it. But did anyone else in this house need to make a note of it? They did not. They had pure instincts, where she had only information from outside. Their obedience was of the soul, hers an enforced, shallow thing. Their state was the more gracious.

CHAPTER VII

Publishing a Book

I

In February Arnold's novel was published. Arnold had seen to it that it was a volume of attractive appearance, with good type, paper and margins, and an artistic paper wrapper. He also saw to it that the review copies were sent out a fortnight before publication, with notes to editors suggesting appropriate reviewers, and presentation copies to various well-known literary persons who might be so good as to speak or write of it somewhere. How far these activities on the part of publishers and authors advantage their books is an open and often canvassed question. It is alleged that there are editors who are so much exasperated by such methods that they straightway hand the book in question to their poorest reviewer, bidding him make short work of it. But on the whole it would appear that most editors and reviewers are more responsive to treatment than this, and that, in this department of life, as in other, it pays to advertise. Arnold very much hoped that in his case it would do so. As to the reading public, they would be roped in by seeing the name of the novel written up large in tube lifts. He did not reflect that there is so very much literature provided on the walls of these small compartments that it is by no means certain that anyone item will be perused, and it is quite certain that anyone will read the advertisements of theatrical productions and tooth paste before they turn to anything so dull as the names of books. 'No recent novel has created so much heated discussion.' Arnold had decided that his advertisement should say this. 'Almost too hackneyed, don't you think,' Audrey suggested dubiously. 'Not a bit of it,' said Arnold. 'If other people's novels create heated discussion, I jolly well don't see why mine shouldn't.'

'I wonder,' said Audrey, 'if any novel really did ever create heated discussion? Did you ever hear any?'

'Of course not. But we'll go on telling the dear old public so, on the chance they'll believe it, and won't want to be left out.'

'The dear old public,' said Audrey, 'may be stupid, but they're not such gulls as we like to pretend. I only wish they were . . . I don't believe they're diddled by a word we say. But I do believe in letting them get used to the sight of the name of a book, then it may come into their heads at the right moment, at the library or the bookstall.'

2

Arnold gave Denham an early copy, and requested that she should read it and say how it struck her.

'How far have you got in it?' he asked her that evening when he came in from the office.

Denham showed him. 'Page thirty-one.'

He looked to see what part she was at.

'Jane alone in the wood. Do you like that?'

He had a particular wish that Denham should like Jane, who had, since he had become acquainted with Denham last summer, been increasingly identified with her.

'Yes,' said Denham loyally. 'But Jane's rather queer. The way she thinks, I mean.'

The page open before her transcribed some of Jane's thoughts, which ran thus:

'*A woodpecker, that's a woodpecker, because the woodpecker would peck her, why did the lobster blush, because it saw the salad dressing, no, because the table had cedar legs: can't remember the questions, only the answers. Answers, Tit-Bits, Pink'un, John Bull, other island, Shaw, getting married, why get married, ring, wedding dress, Mendelssohn, bridesmaids, babies, is marriage worth while, does one survive death? My religion, all the novelists, is marriage worth while? Love, dove, shove, glove, oh my love I love you so much it hurts, yes, marriage is worth while, oh yes, oh yes: oyez all round the town . . .*'

There were several pages of this.

'I suppose,' said Denham doubtfully, 'Jane did think like that. I suppose she was a little queer in the head.'

'If you'll think it over,' said Arnold, rather vexed, 'you'll discover it's the way we all think.'

Denham thought it over, then shook her head.

'No, I don't. I don't think glove when I've thought shove, just because it rhymes. I don't see why anyone should, unless they're trying to write a poem.'

'All the same,' said Arnold, 'if one tries to follow the maze of one's thoughts, one finds they're astonishingly incoherent.'

'But not like that,' Denham obstinately maintained.

'But, still,' she added, 'if you say Jane thought like that, no one can say she didn't, so it's quite safe. You can make people do anything you like; they're not like things, which have to be one way, and everyone knows what they're like. You've made a mistake about the moon, by the way, on page twenty-seven. If it was new, it wouldn't be in the east at ten p.m.'

'Good lord, no more it would. Never mind, practically all novelists slip up now and then over the moon; it would be rather priggish and pedantic not to. The literary moon doesn't really matter.'

But Denham believed the literary moon to matter a great deal more than literary human beings.

'I'd like you to like my book,' Arnold said wistfully. 'I hope you will, when you're farther on in it.'

'But you see,' Denham explained, looking at him with puckered brows and candid, serious eyes, 'they're the kind of thing I *don't* much like – not yet. Novels, I mean. I expect I shall get to them in time. But I haven't seen the idea of them yet. Aunt Evelyn and Audrey were always trying to make me read them. When I like any, I'll like yours. At least, I hope I shall,' she truthfully amended.

Arnold told himself that he would not have his Denham's naïf and devastating candour otherwise, but he wished, for all that, that his book could have taken her by storm and made her realise new worlds. He had put so much of himself into it, which meant, of course, so much of her ... Still, if you don't care for novels, you don't; it is a taste, like another. And, after all, most novels are by way of being domestic disasters, unappreciated on the hearthstone ... Anyhow, she would care for the way in which it was received, since she cared for him.

The way in which it was received began a few weeks later. On the Thursday morning after its publication Arnold opened his *Times Literary Supplement* in bed. He turned to the novel reviews; *Lone Jane* was not among them. It would be next week, then. He then turned to the short notices under the heading, 'New Books and Reprints,' as he always did, to see which of his firm's publications were there referred to. Archaeology, Architecture, Art, Biography, Drama, Fiction – Good God, what was this, under Fiction? '*Lone Jane*, by Arnold Chapel.' Under this heading was not inscribed, *See Review*, but a brief notice, which read as follows: 7¾ x 5¼, viii 319 pp. Gresham. 7s. 6d. net. A novel written partly in the rather hackneyed impressionist manner which makes a point of referring to its heroine in the second person instead of the third, partly in the more romantic vein of a still older tradition. Mr Chapel has a certain pleasant talent, but this story of an inarticulate, incoherent, yet passionate young woman would not suffer by considerable pruning.'

Such was Arnold's first review. He had not known how much he had cared that it should be a good one until his body told him, by turning first hot then cold, as if he were feeling faint.

'What's the matter?' Denham asked him sleepily, drinking her tea. 'You look rotten. Have your tea, you'll feel better.'

Arnold reached for his tea, drank it, and felt better, but not well.

'Here,' he said, and passed her the *Literary Supplement*. 'My first review. Read it.'

She read it.

'Not bad, is it,' she commented, having done so.

He stared at her, aghast at her ignorant optimism.

'*Not bad!* Which part of it isn't bad, I'd like to know? Except the first few words, down to 7s. 6d. net, it's all as bad as it could be.'

'It says a pleasant talent, Arnold.'

'It does not. It says a *certain* pleasant talent. That's entirely different.'

'Why? Isn't it better than an uncertain one?'

She was hopeless; she didn't understand words as used. He looked at her wrathfully.

'And anyhow, it's in the wrong part of the paper. It's not a review at all; they've fobbed me off with a snippet ... What's more, I believe I know who wrote it. I'd bet three guineas on its being that swine Paul Tarrant, whose book we turned down. It would be exactly like him to think he'd get even with me this way. He probably asked particularly for it.'

'Well,' said Denham, who was reading a letter from a veterinary surgeon, 'it's not so bad, really. I mean, it might have been worse, mightn't it?'

Arnold looked at her with bitter irony through the horn-rimmed glasses he had put on to read with. His dark hair was rumpled on end; he looked like a hurt little boy.

'A capital review,' he said. 'I am lauded to the skies. Let's leave it at that.'

She looked round at him, saw suddenly that he was unhappy. 'Arnold, you don't really mind, do you? What does it matter what reviews say? Will it mean people won't buy the book? But this is only one review – there'll be lots more, won't there? And anyhow, does it matter what people say about books?'

'It doesn't matter, of course,' he replied. 'I don't give a curse for reviews – I know too much about reviewers for that. It's only the silliness and unfairness of the thing that disgusts one. I don't care a hang really.'

'Then that's all right,' said Denham relieved. 'I expect it's just that you're feeling rotten this morning. Why not lie in for a bit, and have a day off the office?'

'I'm all right, thanks.' He got out of bed, whistling as he put on his dressing-gown.

'I've heard from Morgan about Isaac,' said Denham, taking up her letter again.

'Oh, damn Isaac,' Arnold replied, and left the room. To be brave and whistle was one thing, but to have the conversation changed to Isaac was another. Denham didn't care a curse about the review, nor the book, nor how he was treated, nor anything. She didn't understand in the least what one's first review meant, nor how disappointing it is to be among New Books and Reprints, when you have hoped to be among New Novels.

Well, he reflected, more philosophically, as he splashed about in hot water, how should she understand? She knew nothing of the literary world, nothing of reviews, nothing of books. It wasn't her sphere. She simply couldn't see that it mattered what other people wrote, said, or thought about one's books, or about anything else. The vanity of the creator, the most profound and the most sensitive vanity in the world, would never trouble her free and practical spirit.

Arnold dressed rapidly. He wanted to be at the office and to talk with Audrey, who understood all about reviews.

Audrey was nearly as much vexed as Arnold. She agreed that it was Paul Tarrant. Of course it was Tarrant; the malicious cat.

'He'll probably do mine too when it comes out,' she said. 'Can we send a note that he's not to have any more of our books, I wonder?'

'That won't help *Lone Jane* much,' said Arnold, sourly. And Audrey said, 'No, but it would be a way of getting back on Tarrant,' meaning really a way of saving her own book from Tarrant's claws.

One's bad reviews are written by one's enemies; this is one of the laws of die literary world. It is less fixed a law that the good ones are written by one's friends; after all, why shouldn't an impartial critic really admire one's book? If he should abuse it, he proves himself not impartial, but praise is another matter. On the other hand, praise not of oneself but of one's fellow writers is apt to be log-rolling, shamelessly administered by their friends. Arnold and Audrey, being both authors and publishers, were familiar with these simple literary laws, and their conversation was carried on strictly within them.

5

The weekend was better. A serious weekly periodical said that Mr Chapel's first novel was one of brilliant promise, and teemed with ideas. It devoted half a column to it, and depreciated another novel in comparison. Arnold read it to Denham at breakfast.

'Not bad, is it,' he said.

'Very good,' said Denham.

'The *Weekly Comment* review is important, of course,' he added.

'Is it? Good. Why?'

'Well, because ... Oh, well, it is. It's read by people who matter. It counts.'

'Who are the people who matter, Arnold?' Denham asked, curious to discover the meaning of this phrase, which she had frequently heard since coming to London. Probably in Andorra no one had mattered much, except to themselves. 'And how do they matter? And how is one paper more important than another? And what does important mean?'

Arnold, pleased with his review and his holiday morning, good-humouredly tried to explain.

'The people who matter, in an intellectual sense, are the intelligent readers and critics. And a paper is important, intellectually, if it's written and read by intelligent and thoughtful people. As to important ... well, of course, it's a relative word; it doesn't stand by itself. Important for some purpose, I suppose it means. More coffee, darling, please.'

'Is it more important that clever people should like your book than stupid ones?' Denham pursued, giving him more coffee.

'More important to me, certainly.'

'Why? Because there seem to be more stupid people. Isn't it important that a lot of people should buy the book? Guy says it's mostly stupid people who buy books or get them from libraries, because intelligent people can usually get hold of them, if they want to, some other way.'

'Oh, well, I don't aspire to be a best-seller among the

lowbrows. I should never be any good at that. My only chance is to make some kind of hit with the high-brows. I may not be much good, but at least I'm no worse than some of the people they praise up.'

'Well, I hope you'll make a hit with everyone,' said Denham kindly.

Next morning was a mixed bag. *Lone Jane* had a review in each of the two Sunday papers which Arnold took in. One of them said that it was a remarkable and arresting piece of work, the other that this was not the case, but that, on the contrary, Mr Chapel seemed singularly lacking in literary aptitude, and had better not try again. So it was a chequered morning. Arnold decided that the reviewer who thought he had better not try again was a man slightly known to him and disliked, and that the other was some person of sense and discrimination, who had judged *Lone Jane* on its merits.

'Well,' said Denham, changing the subject, 'let's go out to Elstree with our lunch and see how the ice is getting on. We'll take skates in case. If it's no use we'll have a walk.'

For Denham, after lounging about in contented laziness for hours, would suddenly be taken with a need for physical activity. Arnold and she were, when it came to games and activities, good companions. They skated together, played golf, tennis, and ping-pong, hit balls round the pocket garden of the house, or played parlour games with cards, draughts, and spillikins. And when some other inhabitant of the house drew them into one of those round games, 'with talking or writing in them,' as Denham put it, she set her teeth and nobly, if inefficiently, did her best.

It was more difficult when the game was conversation. In the friendly, light-hearted circle of Arnold's friends, with chaff flying brightly from speaker to speaker, with ridiculous wit alternating with sophisticated discussion or with personal gossip, Arnold's dark-browed wife would sit silent or monosyllabic. They liked her well enough, though she had acquired the reputation of being one of the Silent Women, who are, for all tradition may say to the contrary, more numerous and more silent than the silent men. It is commonly, and no doubt correctly supposed, that these persons are silent because there is nothing they desire to say. They are accepted, therefore, as features, so to speak, of the landscape, and the only trouble arises when they go out to meals at the tables of others and refuse to earn them with the prescribed coin of speech. Then hostesses and fellow guests look at them askance, as if they blamed them for leaving their own homes merely for the food.

Denham, having been warned against this form of crime by her aunt Evelyn, struggled manfully for speech, with uneven success. Perseveringly she strove for the gift of utterance, however little there might be that she desired to say. To speak: to form out of air by the contact of tongue, teeth and palate a flow of words, words, words – to this curious aim she doggedly applied herself, as to any other skilled and difficult craft. And forth, increasingly, the words came, and people began to have more hope for her, though she would never be nimble of tongue or of wits.

Winifred and Laura, the maids, were alarming. They would ask questions to which their mistress knew no answer, sometimes about food or drink, sometimes about household arrangements.

'I don't know,' Denham would gruffly say. 'Do whatever you like about it.' Or she would have a shot at the right answer, and see from the domestic's countenance that she was right off the target. Winifred and Laura did not think much of their mistress, and no wonder. She was so obviously not 'used to having things nice.' She saw no difference in merit between linen sheets and cotton, between pearls and glass beads, between silver and cheap plate. She refused, when she was alone, to have lunch laid for her, but would take a sausage roll or worse out of the larder and eat it as she stood. She was not, no, certainly she could not be a lady. She was a slattern, and idled about with toy soldiers or Plasticine or Meccano or something else ridiculous, all the morning, instead of doing something useful. And the mess she and her silly games made of the drawing-room – toys and puzzles and clay and litter of all kinds left about. And it was no use telling her about anything, for she didn't listen like most ladies, and make intelligent remarks; she shut you up with her abruptness and her gruff manner, and the inexpansiveness of her comments. Winifred and Laura couldn't think why a pleasant gentleman like Mr Chapel had gone and married one like that. Wherever had she come from, that was what Winifred and Laura would like to know. A funny thing, it seemed, too, when Mrs Gresham and the Miss Greshams, so nice and tidy and right, were her relations. But there, even the best people had queer relations, everyone knew that. Laura for her part opined that young Mrs Chapel was not quite right in her head; but Winifred thought she was probably only strange, and perhaps had some foreign blood in her, poor thing.

CHAPTER VIII

Being a Mother

I

April came, and at intervals the sun shone and warm breezes blew. Denham would go out into the country on her motor-bicycle, or by train, and walk about fields, woods, and lanes all day, and come back in the evening incredibly dirty, and laden with curious collections of animal, vegetable and mineral life. On Saturdays and Sundays Arnold went with her. But he sometimes expressed a desire that they should get back in time for some Sunday dinner, or play, or other urban entertainment. And without Denham he would not go to these; he was firm on that.

One day Denham, motor cycling between Missenden and Amersham, turned suddenly sick and faint. She got herself home as best she could, a horrid suspicion renewing itself in her. Next day she said gloomily to Arnold, 'I believe I've a baby coming on.'

They were sitting together after dinner. Arnold uttered ejaculations of applause, and sat on the arm of her chair and embraced her.

'Darling,' he continued, 'how fearfully exciting and jolly.'

'Jolly? I can't see anything jolly about it. I feel rotten, and the doctor says I shall probably go on feeling rotten, on and off, till it's born.'

'I know, sweetheart; it's too bad. I wish it could be me instead. But think what fun it will be when we have it.'

'Well, I don't care about them much myself. They're no use when they're quite young, and they're awfully in the way. You can't take them with you on days out, and they're always wanting something or other done for them. They seem to me silly.'

'They're quite idiotic, of course, for a bit. But they improve very quickly, I believe, and they're quite amusing in about a year.'

'Not very,' said Denham. 'Not if you have to look after them. I think it's a great nuisance, this happening. But of course it may pass off.'

'Pass off . . .'

'Yes; not come to anything. You never know, with babies . . . The doctor says I ought to keep quiet.'

'Well, then, you must keep quiet.'

'I don't think I shall. I expect I shall go on much as usual. I can't be bothered to think about the baby all the time. Anyhow, I don't want it.'

'But I do. I want it very much. I want it to be just like you. I shall adore it.'

'It will quite spoil our summer holidays.' Denham was pursuing her own line of bored reflection.

'It won't, really. It'll only mean we do rather less than we meant – lounge about more.'

'I feel simply rotten. Like nothing on earth. I've never felt like this before.'

'I suppose not, poor old darling. It's a rotten arrangement, that's a fact. It's an awful indictment of science that we've not invented a better one yet.'

But still, he thought, there it is, and babies must come somehow.

'It always seems to me extraordinary,' he added, reflecting on the wonders of nature, 'that they're born at all.'

'Seems to me natural enough,' said his wife, 'but a pity. However, it can't be helped now. We must just put up with it and see what happens. It may easily pass off.'

'You keep saying pass off, as if it was mumps or something. I don't believe babies pass off so easily as all that. Anyhow, I hope it won't.'

'Oh, well,' said Denham, 'don't let's bother, anyhow.' She extracted a wire and ball puzzle from a pile of such objects under the sofa, and concentrated on it. Arnold picked up another, and they worked at these for an hour. Denham strove with puzzles in the absorbed manner of a child, with intent brows and tongue between teeth.

Their drawing-room looked like an untidy nursery, with piles of games and modelling wax on the floor, toffee on the chimney-piece, and the small dog worrying an india-rubber bone on a Persian rug. It did not look like a proper drawing-room at all. The coming infant, if it should not pass off but arrive, would feel quite at home in it. But its mamma would have very little time to attend to it, with all the other occupations she had. You might as well expect a child of twelve to mind a baby.

This passed through Arnold's mind as he sat by his wife on the sofa doing puzzles. But then, he thought, when babies actually come they transform, he had heard, their mammas into new creatures – maternal creatures, with new instincts and devotions. Mammas do not go on being like small boys. That quality in Denham which he loved would make place for a new quality, of the kind commonly called deeper, which he would love even more. She would become feminised. Arnold regretted this in a way, for, in proportion as their child should gain a mother, he must lose a playmate; but still, life is like that, it marches on, and what you lose on the swings you gain (let us hope) on the roundabouts.

Meanwhile, it was very agreeable to be able to spend the evenings playing games together, undisturbed by the clamorous demands of young persons, who, whatever affection and pride of ownership they may inspire, are nevertheless often incontrovertibly in the way in homes.

Arnold put on a pair of ear-phones and prepared to listen to Mozart's Sonata in D Major, interpreted by Mr Norman O'Neill. He did not mind now many things he did at once, such as talking, doing puzzles, and listening to music. Denham seldom listened in; music bored her rather, and speeches more. She asked Arnold, however, to tell her when the weather bulletin came on; that was normally the only part of the programme to which she cared to listen. Arnold tried to make her listen to some of the news and speeches, because he found them funny, and wanted her to laugh at them with him, but it was no use, Denham lacked that kind of sense of humour. Perhaps she lacked every kind; she laughed neither at nor with things, was amused neither by P. G. Wodehouse, Paul Morand,

Charles Chaplin, nor sentimental solemnities. In a world uproariously amusing she remained gravely intent on her own businesses. Arnold had to smile at his jokes by himself when they were alone together. It was a pity.

2

Denham felt, and often was, sick in the mornings. It made her sulky; such a visitation had never overtaken her splendid constitution before.

Anyhow, she thought, I shall give up going to parties and things. I'll go to parties *or* have a baby, but I won't do both. So she renounced social engagements, and Arnold renounced some of them too, but not all.

'It's silly,' Denham logically pointed out, 'for you not to go to parties when you like them. Just as silly as for me to go when I don't like them.' Feeling sick had lowered her stamina, and caused her footholds on the crags of duty to slip, so that she often now forgot herself, and owned to the ignominious and low-class distastes against which she had striven. Tides of indifference to the good life often submerged her, and at such times she would baldly state the truth about her relation to it. They say that motherhood, at war with civilisation and artifice, often thus drags its victim down to her natural and native level.

Arnold, thus urged, would sometimes consent to perform social duties for the two of them. But more often he stayed at home with her, assisting at whatever ploy she had on hand at the moment, such as lead casting, table tennis, or naval battles in the bath. Sometimes he read fiction aloud to her, but she did not listen much, though he tried her with all kinds, comic, serious, and detective. He tried on her a depressed tale called *Andorra*, to which she listened for a little, then said she hadn't noticed it was like that there, and would prefer to hear a guide-book on the same subject, as books without people in them were nearly always better. These were, in fact, almost the only books which she read or listened to. Or, as she said, there might be people, but the people must do things and go to places, and not talk, except about what they saw and did. She liked *Robinson Crusoe*, and other books in which the characters employed themselves rather manually than mentally or emotionally (Crusoe's pious ruminations can always be skipped by those whom they do not entertain), but thrillers, in which the thrills were caused by chasings, kid-nappings, murders, Bolshevists, and international gangs, left her cold. She 'didn't believe things happened like that,' and usually detected flaws in the mechanism of the plot which spoilt it for her.

'He couldn't possibly have got there so quickly as that,' she would criticise, after pondering reflection or, 'I don't believe he could have kept a loose bit of broken glass in position long enough to saw through his ropes,' and, of course, if you worry about this in a story, where are you? She did not even believe that you could release yourself from bondage in a few minutes by rolling on a piece of cheese dropped by your jailer, and thus encouraging mice to gnaw their way through the ropes. As to the ordinary, non-sensational novel, mem-oirs, verse, or essays, she was hard put to it to conceal from Arnold how small reason she saw that they should ever have been penned. Arnold, as a publisher, was biased about books,

and thought that a certain number should be penned, in case
someone might like to buy them. He felt about books as doctors feel about medicines, or managers about plays – cynical,
but hopeful.

3

What with tennis, rowing, motor-bicycling, and other active
avocations, the Chapel baby did pass off in the course of the
summer. Arnold was disappointed, and when Denham said,
'That's all right,' they quarrelled for the first time. The differences between them cut sharp and deep. Arnold accused
Denham of having done it on purpose, and she said, 'Well, I
just went on as usual. I told you I should.'

Arnold said bitterly, 'The Church would say that it practically amounts to murder, the line you've taken.'

'The Church ...' Denham seemed to glance at it from far
off, as if she were trying to place it in her memory.

'Yes,' said Arnold disagreeably, 'the Church. The Catholic
Church. You belong to it, I believe. You joined it, if you
remember. Why, I don't know.'

'Because you belonged to it of course,' Denham reminded
him literally. 'You wanted me to, don't you remember. That
was why.'

'My wishes,' said Arnold, 'seemed to have weighed with you
rather more then than they do now.'

'No,' said Denham. 'It was that I didn't mind what church I
joined. I should mind having a baby. That's all.'

'I hope,' said Arnold, 'that we now have a family of four.
No, six.'

He would not have believed, a month ago, that he would ever be so disagreeable to Denham. But really she had hurt and annoyed him a good deal by her attitude. He had, as many persons have, a whim for a child or children; he thought they would be interesting to have and bring up, and he didn't see why Denham shouldn't have one like other people. It wasn't that she was frightened of pain, for she was neither cowardly nor highly strung, and bore the wounds of life with stoical calm. No; she had played the fool, and deliberately lost the baby because the idea of having it bored her. She couldn't, Arnold sorely felt, love him much, to have done that.

They made up that quarrel in a way, of course, in so far as quarrels are made up by bridging with embracings the rift between sundered wills. But the knowledge of the rift remained with both. It made Arnold sometimes irritable and Denham sulky. She wished the holidays would come, so that they could go away to the sea and be happy and peaceful, and forget London. If Arnold were sailing and fishing again, he would surely cease to brood over his child that might have been, and remember how much freer they were without it. A child. What an ambition! Denham simply could not understand anyone wanting such an encumbrance. It seemed as odd to her as wanting to write a novel.

CHAPTER IX

Exploring

I

The Chapels spent August on the south Cornish coast, staying with the Greshams, who had taken a house there. They boated, bathed, fished, and played games with balls, such as tennis, golf and rounders, on the beach, and Arnold became cheerful again and forgot his vexation about the baby. Talking always cheered him up, and with the Greshams talking was continuous. Cheerful, gossiping, sociable evenings followed out-door days.

Denham played games too, but her favourite occupation was rowing along the coast in an old fishing boat they had hired, taking soundings, and exploring for caves, and making a chart of the coast, which gave her peculiar pleasure. Sometimes Arnold went with her, but often she made off alone, leaving the rest of the party at their various pastimes, and spent absorbed and solitary hours paddling in and out of creeks, landing in sandy, fishy caverns, dropping the plummet deep into the green water and hauling it up, noting on the chart measurements, hidden rocks, inlets and, caves. 'Denham's chart' came to be a jest in the family, but to Denham it was the serious business of life, one of those grave and important avocations which are never pursued in the odd life of cities. Jolly good thing, she thought, that she felt and was all right again, that that interrupting attack of motherhood had passed off and left her none the worse. Now if only she had longer down here she might get quite a lot done; if only she had longer, and had not to leave it in September and return to the foolish life of London.

A deep, peaceful, sensuous pleasure in her surroundings held her. The chatter of the Greshams might disturb it a little, but for the main part of each day she could get away and be silent, lazy and alone. Arnold liked the chatter and the company; he was for ever trying to draw her into it, to make her join expeditions and parties of pleasure with the rest. Long hours of silent exploring and charting bored him a little; he wanted something livelier.

2

Then, one warm, still evening, Denham found a secret passage. It led from a hole high up in the wall of a cave, which looked from below merely a crevice. When she climbed to it, up the slimy green face of the rock and peered in, she looked into a well of darkness. Heaving herself up on to the ledge, she thrust head and shoulders into the crevice, and found that they could just get in. She dived into the slimy dark, and crawled on hands and knees; crawled, and crawled, and crawled, along a slippery rock floor, a wet roof just above her head, until the tunnel opened into rough steps. The steps dropped down into a cave; in this one could stand upright, and Denham turned on her pocket torch and looked round it. Not a bad cave. Fairly dry, and, as caves go, spacious. It had two outlets, the one by which she had just entered, and another at the opposite side. This also was a narrow crevice opening on to rocky steps, which climbed up. Denham climbed them, for about five minutes, then they fetched up abruptly against a wall not of rock but of bricks. On this she tapped and pushed, with no result. Apparently the entrance to the passage had been either recently or long ago bricked up. It would have to be seen to. The question was, what was on the other side? Denham calculated that the bricked entrance must be nearly, if not quite, on ground level. If that were so, it must surely be part of some building. What building, if any, stood there, on the cliff, say a quarter of a mile from the edge? Denham did not know, for she had come by boat. It was about two miles up the coast from the house where they were staying. It seemed absurd to be at the passage's very mouth, and yet to have to go all the way back along it to the other end, but there was nothing else for it, so she turned back, down the rock steps, into and through the commodious and agreeable cave (she must keep a lantern there, she decided, and some food) up the steps on the other side, and so into the long, slippery tunnel, until at last she peered out through the high crevice down into the shadowy cave, and saw beyond its mouth the swaying green sea.

Critically from her boat, having pulled a little way out, Denham examined the cliff face for a track that would take her up its face. There was nothing very good, but there seemed to be a kind of ridgy fissure, zig-zagging up to within about three-quarters of the way to the top, not far to the left of the cave. It looked worth trying, anyhow, though on a warm evening like this Denham, who was lazy, would have preferred something easier. However, she pulled in, tied the boat to a rock, and began to scramble up the fissure, hand over hand. It was tough and jagged going. Denham was, as usual, stockingless and in sandshoes, and her bare brown knees were cut and bruised by sharp rocks. The westering sun bathed her in its light and warmth; her jersey clung stickily to her damp shoulders and chest, and her bare head dripped. She must find a better way up for the future, she thought, rather bored. But the toughest proposition began when the gash in the rock petered out, with ten feet still to go. Ten feet of bare rock face, with, as seen from below, no aids to ascent beyond a few knobs, and an occasional tuft of thyme. Denham sat on the jutting end of the fissure and swung her legs and pondered. Was it possible or impossible? It is marvellous, she knew of old, what a few knobs of rock will do. Marvellous what one can climb when one has to.

'A pity,' she said, drawing her arm across her forehead, 'that it's so warm.'

She stood up, bracing herself for the last effort, calculating each foothold and handhold. Yes, on the whole, she decided, it could be done. A great bore if it couldn't, and if she had to climb all the way down and search for a better path farther off. She was inclined not to waste thus all the energy she had spent. She cautiously grasped a small rounded promontory with her right hand, flexed her toes against the rock's level face, and drew herself up until her left hand caught on a narrow shelf.

There followed in the next few minutes quite a creditable series of acrobatic feats, the success of which was exceedingly doubtful to the performer up to the moment when she was able to fling one leg on to the cliff's turfy top and heave her body after it. Having done this, she lay panting for a minute or two.

'I shan't,' she remarked, 'make that my usual way up here. It's a rotten one.'

The top of the cliff was rough turf and gorse, threaded by little aimless tracks of men and rabbits. Over it the gulls flapped and cried; here and there human beings walked, sat or lay. Some of these had seen, from a distance, Denham's arrival over the top, and had started forward to help her; now, perceiving that she needed no help, they were casting at her inquisitive glances. What ailed the young woman? She had not been fleeing from the tide, for the tide was ebbing; why, then, this perilous and arduous short cut from sea to cliff top?

Denham, indifferent to the speculations of others, was raking the landscape with observant eyes, trying to calculate the line pursued by the underground passage and the distance it covered. The only building in evidence was a tumble-down old coastguards' cottage standing a quarter of a mile from the cliff's edge. About the right position, Denham thought. She walked over the rough, choppy turf towards it, and, as she got nearer, saw that it was not lived in; it had large holes in its slate roof, and was no good as a house. All the better. But the door was locked; she could not get in. Unless through the holes in the roof . . . However, there were people looking, and, after all, there might be someone living in the cottage, and Denham regretfully admitted the necessity of drawing the line some-where. One couldn't climb into other people's houses through holes in their roofs; not with spectators standing about one couldn't, she amended.

She must find out about that house, who owned it, if anyone occupied it, and if the key was obtainable. Surely somewhere in that house must be the bricked-up end of the passage that came out in the sea cave. How long had it been bricked up, and how many people now knew about it? That was an important question. It was important, too, not to rouse curiosity by seeming over much interested in the house. It might be better to come after dark.

But the first thing was to make inquiries about it. Perhaps even some of the people on the cliff might know. Passing over two or three obvious visitors, Denham advanced on a couple who sat entwined in the silent ecstasy of love's young dream.

'Do you know,' she enquired of them, 'who that cottage belongs to?'

But the lovers only tittered. Perhaps they failed to understand her question; perhaps love had made them hysterical; or perhaps they felt such mirth at the sight of the big young woman with khaki breeches and bare, scratched brown legs, and straight dishevelled hair tossed over perspiring brow, that they must needs show it. Denham, who knew already that the poor have to laugh when they see people they think peculiar of form or garb (it is less mirth than a scornful comment on unconventionality) waited patiently for a minute, in case after laughter they found speech, then repeated her question. The titters were renewed, but, among them, the male was understood to reply in the negative.

Denham, now the observed of all observers on the cliff, turned away, too busy with the problem of the cottage to feel shy. She decided to sit down and wait, to give the other people time to depart. If they did, she would try the roof. It was becoming increasingly obvious that, anyhow, no one was inside the cottage at the moment. She lay down on the grass and waited. She calculated that she had an hour before the demands of the falling tide made it necessary to get back to her boat. Probably it was no use; people like the lovering couple usually stayed out, silent and contented, for long hours on end. The others might go, but these would remain.

But fortune was kind. The lovers, after ten minutes more of close and dumb embracing, and a certain amount more tittering, rose and went their way. Perhaps they had to get back for supper. One by one the other scattered groups also strolled away, towards the road that ran behind the cliffs to the next village. No one remained near enough to matter.

Elate, yet cautious, Denham made her cat-footed climb on to the ruinous roof, peered down through a gaping hole into an empty house, and in a trice had dropped down on to a boarded floor.

Empty; long empty and dismantled. The musty smell of empty houses pervaded the corners; long dead ashes fluffed about the hearth; grass and fennel pushed up through the flooring. There were two rooms, both on the ground floor. Denham examined the walls all round; they were of rough stone, not brick. Of course she might be on the wrong track; the passage might come up somewhere else. Yet this seemed likely enough ... Could there be a cellar? Hardly, for the vegetation of earth pushed up between the rough boards of the floor. Yet not between all of them; there were some boards unvegetated. Denham stamped on these, trying to evoke a hollow sound. At last one of them jumped loosely under her foot, and proved movable to her hand. She prised it up and peered through the gap; beneath her was a shallow cellar. Dropping down into this, she turned her torch light on to damp rough walls of brick. So far so good. Somewhere behind these walls, so closely bricked about, the passage must lie doggo. Exciting. Obviously the passage was not in use. For how long had it been bricked up? How many people knew of it? Did anyone know except she?

A deep, heady satisfaction surged in her. She felt like a person in love, or a religious who has found his vocation. Everything was panning out so marvellously, she had been so wonderfully led.

The next job was to discover the opening. The bricks, when tapped, should sound hollow. She tapped about a little, but nothing sounded very hollow. Presently she thought, it's time I went back to the boat. I shall come again tomorrow, and climbed up again, first through the floor, whose boards she carefully replaced, then out through the roof, whose slates were beyond her replacing, and so down on to the turfy cliff, still warm and fragrant with the dying golden end of day. To run to the cliff's edge and swarm dawn the long fissure to the rocks below was much quicker work than coming up, and she was pulling through the green evening sea for the home creek within a quarter of an hour of leaving the cellar.

3

Arnold and Audrey and Isaac the little dog were on the shore, wading in the rock pools and looking for prawns.

'Hallo, my dear,' said Arnold, 'you've been long away.'

'Yes,' said Denham. 'I had a lot to do. I climbed up the cliff beyond Polrew and looked at an old cottage there. I want to take it.'

'Take it? Instead of the Peewits?'

'No, as well. I like it. I should like to live in it, when it's been mended. It's got holes in the roof.'

'How many bed and recep.?'

'Two rooms. One to sleep in, one to sit in and cook in. I'm going to find out about it.'

'Rather fun,' said Arnold, 'to have a permanent Cornish cottage. Let's take it, if it's to be had.'

He helped her to haul up the boat over the bare, wet weed-strewn sands.

The sun was gone down, and the evening was quiet and dimly flushed. Arnold's old flannel trousers were rolled above his knees; his white, slim, long legs glistened saltily beside Denham's firm, brown ones. Isaac leaped round them with squeals of joy.

'Yes,' Denham agreed. 'It would be fun. It's a nice cottage.'

It has a secret door, she thought; a secret door bricked up, leading into a secret passage and two good caves. The secret door, the secret passage, the two good caves, rose to her lips for utterance, as Arnold, wet and salt and dear, tugged with her at the boat. Would he, could he, keep the secret passage a secret indeed?

Audrey, happy and freckled, and bare-legged, was stooping over a rock pool, crooning softly to herself. From the Peewits a bell rang, jingling merrily down over the sands to the ebbing sea's edge.

The secret door, the secret passage, the two good caves, ebbed back from Denham's lips like the sea. A selfish closeness locked them up in her.

'Bother; dinner,' said Audrey, and they went up the beach to eat it.

4

All the Greshams were staying just now at the Peewits. Into their gay, urbane civilisation Denham returned, like an explorer from solitary places, full of secret, savage joys and cares.

Denham, said Arnold, had seen a dilapidated cliff cottage two miles up the coast, and wanted to take it. After dinner they would go down to the village and make inquiries as to its ownership.

'My poor children,' Evelyn said, 'cottages on the Cornish coast are costly, however dilapidated.'

'I shouldn't think this could be,' said Denham. 'It's all over holes.'

Denham, with the instinct of primitive peoples, was deprecating what she loved, fearful lest others should covet it. The secret door was bricked up closely now below the threshold of her speech; the secret passage ran its tortuous course, dark and silent, through her soul. If they should be guessed at, who knew to what fantastic figure the price of the cottage might not soar, or what hordes of eager, acquisitive persons might rush up and take it by storm? Denham could see them all there. Guy, amused and debonair and conscious, writing poetry about it and making jokes; Humphrey, interested, behaving geologically in the caves, writing an article for a paper about smugglers; Audrey, all rational girlish delight and enthusiasm; Evelyn, picking her dainty way about the cellar, chattering like a pretty magpie, her high heels clicking on the stone floor, not caring really for the passage at all, but taking it all in like a picture, satiating her appetite for all kinds of life; Noel ... Noel, liking it so much and so silently that one would not really mind showing it her one day, when it wasn't quite so new.

And Arnold – well, of course, Arnold would like it; he would be pleased, excited, entertained; he would scramble up and down the passage with her, finding all sorts of new things ... But then, one wanted to do the finding oneself, in one's own secret passage. Little by little, day by day, new secrets would be revealed. If I were Lord of Tartary, myself and me alone ...

'It's rather damp,' said Denham.

'An undesirable residence, situate on wet earth. Water (c. but not h.) coming through the roof, no modern conveniences,' said Peter. He did not allude more closely than this to the sanitary arrangements of the cottage, because he was not of the generation which likes to say 'lavatory,' as often as may be. Humphrey, who was, roused himself from meditation to say, 'Where is the lavatory?' and Denham, who followed the conventions of no generation, but to whom one room was as natural a topic as another, replied, 'In an outside shed,' glad that this was so, and that the cottage sounded altogether so undesirable a residence.

5

After dinner Denham and Arnold went down into the village, and called on the policeman for information. The policeman directed them to the owner of the cottage, a retired sea captain, who had bought it some time ago from someone else, meaning to live there with his wife one day, but his wife had died and he was still lodging in the village, and, though he could have had the old cottage repaired and let or sold it, he had never done so. Yes, he was willing to let it, provided the tenants did the necessary repairs. He could let them have it for the summer for two guineas a week.

'I want it by the year,' said Denham; and that, he said, would be forty pounds.

'Twenty's enough,' said Denham, firmly.

Finally, they agreed on twenty-five, and the Chapels took it.

'We must find someone at once to do the roof,' Denham said, as they walked home up the cliff path through the warm dark.

She mentioned the things the house would need inside it. A bed, a table, two chairs, a stove, a plate, a knife, fork, and spoon, a cup, glass or mug.

'Two of each,' said Arnold. 'Where do I come in?'

Denham looked at him through the salt darkness.

'*Will* you live here, then? All the time? Do let's.'

If he would do that she would show him the secret passage and everything.

'Well, not all the time, of course. But we might run down often. I'd like to.'

'I'd rather,' said Denham, 'live here, and run *up* when necessary.'

'Darling, we can't. The office wouldn't let me.'

'Can't you give the office up?'

'You know I can't. We've had all this before, surely. The office is what we live on, after all.'

Yes, they had had it all before. Denham remembered.

'But I could be down here more than you,' she said.

'No,' he cried suddenly. 'No, no,' and turning on the path, he caught her to him and kissed her with violence and iteration. 'I want you, I want you. Don't you want me any more?'

She strained to him.

'Yes, I do. I do want you. I want you to live with me down here, always.'

The sea sighed below them, its murmuring a windy background to theirs.

'Darling; darling; my heart's love.'

If this were all, thought Arnold, later, as they climbed the path to the house. If this were all; if always they could love like this, want one another like this ... What is passion, he thought. A flame, a torch, leaping and sinking. But its flaming should light the day's march. Life and love should be, and were, intertwined. Separate them, and both are damned.

He thought this, not knowing why he should be thinking it, as he and his wife, hand in hand, walked to the house.

CHAPTER X

Householding

I

Every day Denham went to her cottage, by sea or land. She found a less direct and more commodious path up to it from the sea, and would moor the boat a little way away from the cave (her instinct was that of the bird who conceals its nest) and climb the cliff.

The first morning Arnold came with her. They had the key now, and could enter through the door.

'It'll want a good deal doing to it,' said Arnold, who was this morning inclined to be critical, distrustful, and obscurely jealous of the cottage.

'Not so much,' Denham said. 'The roof, of course . . .'

'And the floor, and the walls, and a few other things.'

'I don't think so. They're all right.'

'Look; the damp's coming through the wall in great patches.'

'I don't mind that.'

'Nonsense. It's awfully unhealthy.'

'Not so many things are unhealthy as people say. They make half of them up. I've noticed it.'

'I dare say. But damp on walls *is* unhealthy.'

'How do you know? You've never tried it, I expect.'

'Nor going to either. Nor are you. It must be seen to before anyone spends a night here.'

'Not so many things want seeing to as people think,' said Denham absently. Then, to end the discussion. 'Oh, all right, if you like.' But she expected that he would forget about it.

She showed him all the rooms, but did not indicate the cellar beneath the loose boards. After all, there was plenty of time for that later.

Every morning, while the roof was being mended, Denham went shopping in the village. She bought tin mugs and plates, some cheap white crockery ('Brown earthenware would be nicer,' said Audrey, 'more the old cottage style.' 'More *what*?' enquired Denham, uncomprehending, and went on buying white), two wicker lounge chairs, two camp stools, two camp beds, a deal table, an oil stove, a saucepan, a frying-pan, some dish cloths, and some disreputable-looking knives and forks.

'You *are* a rotten shopper,' the others told her. 'Why get such repulsive looking things? Nice ones cost very little more, and you might make it so jolly.'

'What's wrong with the things?' Denham asked, but did not care to know. This was her cottage, and the higher life should gain no admittance between its walls.

They gave her presents for it, which she accepted with pleasure, having no objection to their artistic, old-cottage ideas so long as the things were of use. Arnold provided an old dresser, which he picked up at a village sale.

'It would look jolly with blue willow cups and plates on it,' he said.

'It will look all right with the ones we've got,' said Denham, regarding her pile of mixed hardware with favour.

The family all seemed interested in the colour of her crockery; for her part she looked at it in a strictly utilitarian light. So long as the cups held drink and the plates food, well, there you were.

'One plate each for a meal,' she said, thinking it out.

'Only one?' said Arnold, meaning plates.

'Well, no, it can go on for several,' she replied, meaning meals. 'We can wash it in the evening, when there's nothing more to be done out of doors. Of course,' she added, 'plates aren't actually necessary at all. But they're easier, when it's eggs and bacon or sausages, or anything cooked.'

'Vim, darling,' said Evelyn, coming in with a basketful of shopping, looking lovely, like an anemone (wood, not sea), with cheeks pink from the wind.

Denham looked vaguely at the Vim.

'For the sink,' her aunt explained. 'And I've got you a terribly nice crescent-shaped brush. That's to scrub the Vim in with.'

'Thank you very much,' said Denham, doubtfully. 'I don't know how much I shall Vim the sink, though ...'

'Well, darling, you can't let it get messy and discoloured, you know you can't.'

Denham looked at her aunt in speculative surprise. Funny, knowing a person for over a year and still thinking she couldn't let the sink get messy and discoloured. Her attempts at the higher life must have been more successful than she had supposed.

'I shall be pretty busy there,' she said darkly. 'I shan't have a lot of time for the sink.'

'Indeed you won't. I know what camping in a cottage without servants is. The danger is that one does house chores from morning till night.'

Denham felt that danger to be remote.

'You'd much better come to the Peewits for all your meals, you know,' Evelyn added. 'Anyhow you must come to dinner every evening. That won't spoil your picnic.'

'Yes, I think we'll do that,' Arnold agreed. Denham said nothing. Arnold could do as he liked. For her part, it was dinner that bored her most at the Peewits. One had to get more or less tidy for it, and be sociable afterwards. Sausages in the frying-pan would better meet the case.

2

A week later a cart conveyed the Chapels' new household goods to the repaired cottage, and they transferred themselves thither, 'for a bit,' Arnold said. They rowed over in the afternoon of a fine warm day, accompanied by Guy and Audrey, who came to help to settle them in. After settling in, they all had tea together out of the thick white cups, sitting on the grass outside the cottage. They found it great fun. After tea they did some more settling in, though Denham thought all the settling necessary had already been done. They all stamped about the floor and the loose board, putting things in their places, but they did not know that the board was loose and that beneath it was a cellar. Audrey gave them household hints, about how to keep the kettle from furring, and the stove and the milk jar from smelling, and that kind of thing, for house management largely consists in trying to keep the tilings in the house from behaving as is natural to their species. Then they all climbed down the cliff and bathed, and after that Audrey and Guy walked back to the Peewits.

Denham and Arnold were alone in the cottage. It was the first evening they had spent alone together since they came to Cornwall. It was like getting married again, said Arnold, as they lay on the warm grass and watched the gulls swooping about them. Denham lay at ease, her chin on her folded arms. She was lazy and happy and at rest, and lit with happiness like that of a child on a picnic.

I shall tell him about the passage this evening, she thought, and was happy to think how pleased he would be, and how together they would go down into the cellar, and how she would find the loose bricks and take them out and reveal the passage.

'Well,' she said, 'I'm hungry. I shall do some sausages now.'

'Right. Shall I come and help?'

'Not unless you're keen to. I can manage.'

She went in, lit the stove, which smelt, got out the new frying-pan, the new lard, and the new sausages, combined them, and carried the result out to Arnold in the pan, with a loaf, some butter and two plates.

'May as well eat them out here,' she said, spreading the meal on the grass.

'This is jolly,' said Arnold. 'What else shall we have?'

'Tinned peaches?' Denham resembled a certain contemporary author in that she could eat anything so long as it came out of a tin. Arnold did not care for tins, and said he would stew some fresh apples over the stove. But when he went in to do so he found the stove was smelling disagreeably, so he turned it out and brought the apples out to eat raw.

'We must do something about that stove.'

'Oh, they always smell.'

'Not so loudly as that.'

'I expect it's because it's new.' Denham spoke indifferently, her thoughts elsewhere.

'What about going fishing?' she suggested. 'We might get some pollock for breakfast.'

They went fishing, but caught nothing. At ten o'clock they climbed the cliff again and let themselves into the cottage.

'It smells a bit mouldy,' said Arnold.

They were standing in the living-room. Denham thought, 'It's not fair not to tell him tonight,' and said, 'Now I'll show you something,' and pulled up the boards in the floor.

'Good lord, a cellar.'

'Come on.' Denham jumped down into it with her flashlight. He followed her. She pulled out the bricks and revealed the hole, and stood back from it with an air of a conjurer exhibiting the rabbit.

'A hole in the wall,' he commented. 'What's it all about?'

'Look down it.' She thrust the torchlight into the passage's black mouth. 'It's a passage. It comes out in a cave by the sea, and there's another cave, a better one, half-way along. It's a secret passage; it was bricked up, and I don't believe anyone now alive knows about it except us.'

He was peering down into the black tunnel.

'Well – this is really rather fun.'

'That's why I wanted the cottage,' said Denham. 'And that's why I got the camp stools and the small table. We'll put them in the cave, the near cave, and use it as a sitting-room. It will make a simply splendid room.'

'H'm.' Arnold sniffed the dank air that rose from the bowels of the earth. 'A little damp, probably ... All the same, the passage is thrilling all right. It must have been used by smugglers. Let's go down it the first thing in the morning. It's too late tonight, I suppose.'

'Oh, no, that doesn't matter. It's dark down there anyhow, so it makes no difference what o'clock it is. Come on.'

'No, the morning's better. We shall be fresher. Come to think of it, we've had a heavy day house-moving. We shall enjoy the passage more tomorrow.'

They climbed up through the floor again.

'The others will be awfully thrilled by this,' said Arnold. 'We must give an At Home in the cave.'

'But, Arnold, it's a secret, of course. What's the use of a secret passage that people know about? We mustn't tell anyone at all.'

'Oh, all right. But wouldn't that be selfish? They'd love it so.'

'It's a secret,' said Denham firmly. 'I found it first and it's mine, and I wouldn't have told you if I'd thought you were going to tell. It would spoil it all. We can't have the passage and cave crammed with people.'

'Very well, it's our secret, then. Just yours and mine. We *will* be selfish if we like.'

'Look here' – Denham regarded him suspiciously – 'mind you don't forget, and slip it out by mistake.'

'Oh, no; we won't either of us do that, unless we agree to.'

'I shan't. But you talk so much, you might forget. Let's both swear.'

'Cross my heart and hope to die. Now what about bed? I'm extraordinarily sleepy, with all this house-moving, and sausage, and sea air, and excitement. Let's make up the beds. Do you think they're comfortable?'

'We shall soon know,' said Denham.

They did.

Denham slept solidly, as usual, through the night. She had many limitations, but could always eat and sleep. Arnold, less good at both, was hampered by his sausage and apple supper, and by the narrowness of his bed, and lay awake a great while in the night, listening to his wife's regular breathing, the moaning of the sea against the cliff, and, after two of the morning, to the gusty squalls of rain that beat on their slate roof.

A rather silly idea, sleeping here. Why not dine properly, and have comfortable nights at the Peewits, and picnic up here, if Denham liked, by day? It was extraordinarily uncomfortable, and the night was becoming disagreeably cold and damp, and the rain came in at the window, and in the morning there would be only that beastly stove to get breakfast on, and no hot shaving water, and everything would be hugger-mugger. Camping out after twenty-five wasn't worth it. But, of course, Denham wasn't twenty-five yet. She might as well have been fourteen, from the way she went on. She and her passage and her caves . . . How soon would she get tired of it?

Arnold turned impatiently on his narrow bed . . . No, it *wasn't* good enough. He wasn't a sybarite, but there was no earthly reason, even on a holiday, why one shouldn't be comfortable. This should be their last night up here, while the Peewits was available. Later, of course, when they came down from London for weekends, they would sleep here. But the beds must be improved, and they must get the fire going.

Denham, of course, was sound asleep, as usual; so was the dog on her feet. Their impregnable sleep while he waked made him faintly resentful. If she had been awake too, they might at least have talked. Or, anyhow, he might ...

Talking. Why didn't she talk, just gabble along, like other people, answering his gabbling? Why did she never open her mouth unless she had something to say, and why had she so few things to say? A trivial, superficial matter, of course, but it counted in daily life. She was a good companion for playing games and exploring, but no use for conversation, were it either sense or nonsense.

He put out a half-impatient hand and touched the dark, ruffled head sunk in its pillow, letting his hand rest lightly on it, as if he would convey by the contact that message to his senses which the touch and feeling of her gave to him. That, at least, there was. She wouldn't talk, or bear his children, but he was her lover and she his.

The sea wind broke in a storm of tears on the roof.

3

They sat in pyjamas and coats by the smoky, gust-blown fire in the damp little room, and ate bacon, and looked through the rattling casement at the hopeless morning.

'A good day for the passage,' Denham said. 'We might furnish the cave this morning.'

Arnold sneezed.

'I caught a beastly cold in the night.'

'The folding table will just get through the hole,' said Denham. 'And the camp stools easily.'

'I suppose it's quite dark down there.'

'Not really quite. And I've got a lot of candles. I shan't bathe this morning. Shall you, or shall we get dressed right away and go down the passage?'

'I shall not bathe,' Arnold replied with irony, looking at the driving rain. 'As I told you just now I'm starting a cold. It feels like being a bad one.'

'Try Vapex. Oh, no, we haven't any here. There's whisky, though, and some lemons ... I shall dress now.'

'Oh, damn,' said Arnold, as a gust of smoke from the damp and smouldering fire was blown into the room.

'It'll be all right in the cave,' Denham said. 'We might take some sticks down and light a fire there and boil a kettle and have a drink. Rather fun, sitting and drinking down there ... You know, no one need find us for years if we stayed there and rowed over to the village to buy food and stored it down there. It's a perfect hiding place.'

'What's the use of a hiding place?' Arnold asked, trying to balance the kettle on the smouldering logs.

'Well, you never know when you mayn't want one. You might be wanted by the police or something. Or people might want you to go out to tea. Or they might come to call, and when we saw them in the distance we could get down into the cave and lie hid till they'd gone.'

Arnold grunted. He was not in the right mood this morning for caves and hiding places. He wanted comfort and warmth. It was the wrong weather for this kind of thing. Camping out is no good in the rain; in the rain what you want is a good fire and a chair by it and a book, or someone to play cheerful indoor games with.

'Look here, old thing,' he said, 'let's put this off till the sun shines. It will be twice as amusing then. Let's go back to the Peewits for lunch today, and stop there till it's fine.'

Denham stared at him.

'But why, Arnold?'

'Well, because this sort of thing is so jolly in nice weather, and so rotten in bad.'

'Everything's better in nice weather, of course. The Peewits is, too. As a matter of fact, the weather is more important there, because here there's more to do indoors. In the cave it doesn't matter if it's raining or not.'

'Oh, come, no doubt the cave's very splendid and all that, but we don't want to *squat* in it.'

'Why not? It'll be quite comfortable when we get the stools and some cushions and food into it. Besides, we can be up here as much as we like.' Denham looked with approval round the two rooms of the cottage, which already bore every appearance of habitation, with unmade beds, unwashed breakfast things, a greasy frying-pan on the hearth, and Isaac chewing bacon rind beside it.

'You'll feel different,' said Denham, 'when you've been along the passage. Do get dressed quick.' She pulled her jersey over her head and shoved her bare feet into sand shoes.

'I shall go down there now, and take one of the stools. I shall be back by the time you're ready.' She dived through the floor and disappeared.

A quarter of an hour later Arnold heard her calling from below his feet. 'Come on. Aren't you ready? Bring the other stool and pass me down the folding table. It will just get through the opening. We'll come back again for cigarettes and drink. Come on, Isaac, then. Isaac will like it, he'll think it's a rabbit hole.'

Arnold passed her the folding table, shoved Isaac through the floor, and, bearing a camp stool, dropped into the cellar and followed his wife into the bowels of the earth.

4

They sat in the cave, each on a camp stool, with two candles guttering between them, and smoked cigarettes, and sipped hot lemonade and whisky, for Denham had brought down a kettle of this brew and a small spirit lamp. They had been the length of the passage and come out into the sea cave and had then returned here. It was interesting, even thrilling; Arnold felt that. Having savoured its sensation, he now suggested getting back to the cottage to see what the weather was doing.

'I can hear what "it's doing",' Denham said; and so, for that matter, could he.

'But,' she added, 'we might go back and fetch down some cushions and a rug and something to eat.'

'To eat? We've only just had breakfast.'

'Toffee and apples, I mean,' explained his wife. She was reflecting with satisfaction that she now had access to her larder, hitherto barricaded by a respectful but observant cook and parlourmaid.

'And perhaps a little bread and cheese,' she added.

'Little pig,' said Arnold. 'The deadly sin of gluttony will be your undoing, my poor child. Look here, let's go a walk, rain or not. It's such waste of a good holiday morning to stop in. This soft sea rain won't hurt us. We'll take some lunch and walk over to the point.'

'All right.'

They climbed back into the cottage. The rain still drove against the windows and walls. Denham foraged in the larder.

'Bread, ham, cheese, doughnuts, apples, bananas, chocolate. That'll do.' She stuffed food into a waterproof satchel.

'Let's clean up a bit before we start,' Arnold suggested. 'Make the beds and wash up, anyhow.'

'Right.'

Denham made her bed in the simplest possible manner, by straightening and drawing back the dishevelled bedclothes over it. Arnold turned his hard mattress in the approved domestic style.

'I shall be more comfortable than you tonight,' he said.

'It doesn't really make any difference, turning the mattress,' she replied. 'It's just one of the things people say. There's no need to wash the cups and plates, they'll go on for tea.'

'Oh, we'd better. They'll be so sticky and nasty.'

With a faint sigh Denham held them under the tap and ran cold water over them. Arnold took some living up to, even in the cottage. Perfect freedom was never attained, never while you had a companion. Denham had a vague feeling that, since for all these months she had tried to live up to Arnold, he might now, in their private cottage, try to live down to her. Did one, then, *never* break down the prejudices of the well-bred about how to live? Did there never come a day when the well-bred said, 'Dash it all, we won't wash today, neither our persons nor the plates and cups?'

They walked in the rain to the point. Walking to the point: where would seaside life be without that entertainment? Supposing there were no points? At the point they ate their lunch damply in a slight cave. By this time Arnold's cold was worse. Denham regarded him pessimistically.

'It'll turn to bronchitis if you're not careful. Your colds do, don't they?'

'Apt to,' Arnold agreed. 'Seriously, Den, we won't sleep at the cottage tonight, if you don't mind. We'll go down and dine at the house and stay on there. It's no good being stupid about sticking to a plan when it's obviously better not.'

'All right, you go to the house. I dare say you'd better. I shan't, though. I've not got a cold, and it wouldn't hurt me if I had. I shall stay at the cottage.'

'Rot, darling. You can't stay alone.'

'Of course I can. Why not?'

'You can't. I should be awfully anxious about you.'

'What about? I mean, what do you think would happen?'

It was Denham's experience that people were always being anxious about other people for no cause shown. It was probably an inherited feeling, from the days when life was still more unsafe than it is now.

'What would you be afraid would happen?' she pressed him, desirous, as usual, for precise information.

'Well, it's pretty lonely up there.'

'Loneliness doesn't hurt people.'

'Someone might come about the place.'

Come about the place. Another of humanity's odd

anxieties. Denham's Andorran stepmother had been afraid of this occurring, too. A double anxiety, it seemed: solitude, and the marring of solitude. What were they supposed to do, those people who came about the place?

'They can't get into the cottage, if that's what you mean, because I shall lock the door, and the windows are too small. Anyhow, lots of people live alone all the time. And I've got Isaac.'

'It's so awfully uncomfortable there – draughty and damp, and no proper cooking arrangements.'

'It's not.' Denham was becoming sulky. 'It's very comfortable. I like it, and I shall stay. You go.'

'No; if you stay I shall. Absolutely.'

'It's such rot,' Denham protested, 'doing things we don't like doing because someone else does them.'

Thus casually she uttered her complete, disintegrating and shattering philosophy of living. Neither realised its repercussions on both their lives; the dialogue proceeded without so much as a pause of recognition.

'We'll both stay,' said Arnold crossly, 'if you really stick to it.'

They were walking back from the point to the cottage.

Arnold said presently, 'Look here, what about tossing for it? Heads the cottage, tails the house.'

Denham considered this. She thought it silly, when they could each do the thing they preferred without tossing.

'Toss for yourself,' she suggested, 'not for me.'

'No, for both of us. Are you on?'

'Oh, all right.' If Arnold was going to make a fuss, she supposed it had to be. It was a sporting chance for the cottage, anyhow.

'Best out of three.' He spun a penny and caught it; it fell tails, then heads. A sporting chance. Impassively Denham watched it spin and fall the third time. Tails.

'The house,' said Arnold, cheerful again. 'Our lives are saved. Come on and collect a few items for the night, and we'll get down there for tea.'

'There was nothing about tea in the toss. Nor dinner. It was only the night.' Denham, rigidly fair, accepted the decision of the coin without protest, but was not going beyond the letter of the bond.

Arnold conceded tea. 'All right. But we'll get down to dinner. What's the sense of walking all that way in the dark on a wet night, just for the sake of eating sausages off an oil stove?'

Denham had a feeling that she was being done, had, driven. She relapsed into sulky silence. She had lost this game.

6

In her comfortable room at the Peewits Denham lay awake, hearing the continued beating of the rain and Arnold's steady breathing. They had spent a gay, sociable evening, as usual, dined well, and gone to bed late. The family had thought it very sensible of them to come back; they had agreed that this kind of weather did not do for camping out, as they all persisted in calling the cottage. Only Noel had said, 'I don't see why not.' The others had all seen why not; all saw that odd something that other people did see, and to which Denham, alone among adult humanity, it sometimes seemed to her, was blind.

Well, they had won and she had lost. She had been an ass to agree to the tossing. She should have stuck to it that Arnold should decide for himself and she for herself. Instead, that coin, in league with the rest of the world, had forced her into the folly of doing what other people liked, not what she liked herself.

There must be an end of it. With the lucidity which the night watches bring even to inchoate minds, Denham saw that she must not sacrifice another night, or the game would be indeed lost. No more tossing. For the remaining week of the holidays she would firmly stay at the cottage, and Arnold could do as he liked about it. It would be jolly if he stayed there too and enjoyed it, but no fun if he didn't enjoy it. He'd better sleep at the house, and they could be together by day. He would have to give up the absurd idea that she mustn't sleep at the cottage alone. Why care what other people did? Why bother? Everyone should go their own way and be happy, not try to go other people's, to make other people go theirs. She wouldn't mind Arnold sleeping alone at a cottage if he wanted to; why should Arnold mind her doing it? Again there intruded one of those things that 'they,' that other people, saw, and that she could not see. This time it was something more than a question of convenience, or suitability, or doing things at the right time and in the right way. But Denham, since she did not see it, could not know what it was.

'I shall sleep there tomorrow,' she drowsily thought, and drifted into peace.

Evelyn too lay awake, talking to her husband. She often thus kept him awake by her speculations into the lives of others. These interested her so profoundly and intensely that she was for ever investigating them, dissecting and analysing, arranging them in her mind, weaving her clever imaginings about them. An incurable gossip, a sympathetic and intelligent scandal-monger, a skilled prober and revealer, an even more skilled creator. She could not help herself, not did she try. Her fireside chats about the characters and intimate histories of her friends and relations were famed in London. Women made the best listeners, and were more helpful than men, except Guy, who was all but as good at it as she was. Peter listened, amiable and mildly interested, but did not take her always seriously. He watched her as he might a charming child playing a game it is good at.

'Those two are drifting apart, Peter,' she was saying tonight. 'I never thought it could last; they're too terribly different.'

'Well, it's got to last, hasn't it? They're both Catholics; they can't have anyone else if they do drift apart.'

'Oh, Catholics have their ways ... But it mayn't get that far. Mind you, I don't say they're not still in love, in a way, though a lot of that's worn off too.'

'My dear, how can you tell that?'

'Oh, it's obvious. The way they look at each other. It's much calmer, more indifferent. And, when being in love wears off altogether, if it does, what have they in common?'

'Well, life, I suppose. Their home, amusements, holidays.'

'But look at them now. They want to spend their holidays in quite different ways. He's all for people, she's for going off alone. She likes the country all the time, he wants to live in London. He wants children, she won't have them.'

'How do you know, my dear woman?'

'Because I'm not blind. It was obvious what she felt in the summer. It's my belief she lost that baby on purpose. It's asking a lot of a man to ask him to stand that. That is, a man like Arnold, a Roman Catholic, who wants a child. Then, she scarcely ever talks, and he's such a chatterbox.'

'Well, he can do all the talking then.'

'My dear Peter, that's so dull. If you weren't a talker too I should be terribly bored with you . . . And she hates London, and parties, and everything of that kind; and she really does keep that house in a dreadful litter. Those maids of theirs have a bitter time trying to straighten it.'

'Well, my love, these little differences between man and wife aren't enough to break a marriage.'

'They mount up, Peter. They *nag* at love, d'you see.'

'You're a restless woman. When you're not making marriages you're breaking them.'

'It's only that I'm not blind. I see things. I don't want to; it hurts, the way I see things. But there it is. It's like looking into a clear pool and seeing all the fishes swimming about – that's the way I see people's thoughts and feelings all darting to and fro and in and out among each other. I see too much; I don't want to, but there it is.'

'Oh, you're an incurable woman.'

Being a woman *was* incurable, Evelyn's daughter Audrey sometimes thought, feeling connecting strains dragging at her soul. But when she said so to Noel, Noel, her delicate face slightly scornful, said, 'It's only a disease if you make it so. There's no need.'

One gathered that, at the Oxford College where Noel was receiving education, being a woman was not a disease, but a minor and by no means discreditable incident, well carried off. There was a fashion just now, Noel complained, of writing and talking about women as if they were some separate, peculiar and rather contemptible species, instead of ordinary human beings, with ordinary human qualities.

'They're not,' Humphrey put in, with lofty scorn. 'They're impenetrable by ideas. That means they're animals.'

'We're all animals, stupid,' Noel crossly returned. 'Human animals. It's people like you, Humphrey, talking that kind of muck, who invent and spread this silly myth about women.'

'But the silliest part of it,' added Audrey, 'is when some man says, "Granted that women are mental and moral imbeciles, haven't they a magnificently adequate defence and justification? They are the life-creators, the mothers of the race. Isn't that enough?" Some men just now are trying to spread the legend that parentage is a one-sex business; they try to keep it dark that men are exactly equally life-creators and the fathers of the race. And it's no excuse in either sex for being cretins – quite the opposite, anyone would think. The mistake is thinking that, because most women are stupider than most men, which everyone admits, all women are completely stupid. People like you, Humphrey, need a course of logic and accurate thinking. You think you despise cheap sentimental cant, but really you tumble into it all the time about women.'

'Oh, I'm prepared to admit,' said Humphrey, who saw small hope for the race, 'that the only real disease is being a human being.'

CHAPTER XI

Day and Night

The next day was less wet. Evelyn, Peter, Audrey and Arnold played a foursome all the morning, and Denham rowed up the coast, sounding and charting. She had her lunch with her, and not until she desired tea did she land and climb the cliff and go to the cottage.

It had become a gentle and tranquil afternoon; the green cliff top glistened wet under a yellow sky wherein the sun slid down. There, serenely alone, stood the small white and slate cottage, sufficient to itself, yet welcoming its owner back. Denham's fingers closed round the key in her pocket; she whistled softly as she lounged along. It was her cottage, and in it she would stay. No one should drag her from it again.

She let herself in and made tea. She had brought up a new loaf, and devoured fat slices of bread and butter and raspberry jam, sitting at the open door and looking at the sea and sky. This was the life. Outside she was salt and sticky from her bathe, inside an agreeably full receptacle for hot tea, bread and butter and jam. Undoubtedly this was the life.

Arnold was coming up after tea, to sleep. That would be nice, if Arnold was going to enjoy it, as, with the improved weather, he doubtless would.

After tea she returned to the sea by the underground passage, had another bathe, being of those who like to bathe immediately after a large meal, and came back by the passage again.

2

There were voices above the floor. Arnold's soft, agreeable tenor, Evelyn's clear, staccato treble. Denham, emerging in the cellar, remained there, waiting until Evelyn should have gone, as it was less trouble not to have to talk to her.

As often, Evelyn was talking about the French. Philippe Soupault, Jean Giraudoux, Louis Aragon; a group in Paris. Denham suspected them of being writers, as usual. Or else painters. 'Groups' in London always seemed either to write or to paint. Lawyers, doctors, civil servants, stockbrokers, merchants, or mere idlers, didn't seem to go about in groups, or if they did no one mentioned it. Denham had a faint but definite dislike of groups.

There was a clattering of crockery, a running of water.

'Washing up my tea,' thought Denham, with a grin. 'No accounting for tastes.'

'Denham's incorrigible about washing up,' said Arnold's voice.

'Bless the child,' said Evelyn's. 'She's too terribly lazy to live. This doll's house of a place – she really ought to be able to keep it clean ... See here, Arnold. You don't mind if we talk a little more about Denham, do you?'

More? More than what?

'I've been thinking over what we were saying this morning about her, you see. And believe me, I do see it's difficult. You've both got to the place where the strain begins. It was bound to come, you know, between you and her – you're too different. Besides, Denham's not normal. Not a normal human girl, really. You're very normal; you're an ordinary product of the civilised classes of the twentieth century; she's a primitive. That's part of her attraction, of course. But it makes it difficult.'

'The trouble is,' said Arnold's voice, 'that she hates London so, and the life we lead there. I see it's not fair on her. But what's one to do? I can't publish from a Cornish cottage.'

'It's as I say – she's like a child. She can't understand why she must live in a way she doesn't much care for. More, she can't understand how people who care for each other are bound up together and must each give up something ... I wish she'd have a child, Arnold; it would make a woman of her.'

'She doesn't want one.'

'No, she doesn't; not now. But if she had one ... '

What talk! Denham, hot, resentful and shy, dived through the hole in the wall again and crawled down the tunnel to the near cave, where she sat down and smoked several cigarettes.

What talk! Discussing her like that, in her own cottage. Did Aunt Evelyn never stop? And making Arnold do it, too; Arnold, who shouldn't have talked about her to anyone at all. What damned business was it of Aunt Evelyn's how she and Arnold got on together? Talking her over; chattering about people's private affairs for ever, world without end. It amounted to a disease. Aunt Evelyn ought to die of it, she'd got it so badly. Denham viciously shied her cigarette end at a fissure in the roof. No one was safe from Aunt Evelyn. Denham had heard her discuss and dissect all her children in turn, with casual friends. Even Uncle Peter wasn't safe from her. The love affairs of Audrey and the boys, Noel's temperament, Catherine's marriage ... This idiotic interest in other people's business, this passion to be for ever fingering it; yes, certainly it amounted to a disease.

As for Arnold, Aunt Evelyn had obviously got at him, dragged him into this talking business, made him say things about her and himself. Or did he go about doing it all round? Perhaps he did. To Audrey, Guy, Uncle Peter. These people who keep on talking, you never know what they'll say, they aren't safe. Arnold would be talking about the passage next.

All right, let them talk. For her part, she was going to forget them. They shouldn't spoil the cottage for her. They could jolly well all go back to their precious London; she would stay where she was and have some peace without them.

After a few more cigarettes, two pears, three plums, and a stick of barley sugar, Denham left the cave and took the passage down to the sea. She climbed the cliff and approached the cottage by the overhead route, in case, as was likely enough, Evelyn should be still there.

She was. She and Arnold were sitting outside the cottage. Still talking, no doubt. They came to meet her.

'There she comes at last,' Evelyn called out. 'Arnold was beginning to worry in case you were drowned.'

Denham said nothing to her, but walked moodily into the cottage.

Evelyn had gone. They were frying ham and eggs over the stove.

'What's the matter, old thing?' Arnold asked, carelessly gentle, as he cut the loaf. 'I mean, what made you freeze out Evelyn like that? You quite startled her. Anything wrong?'

Denham bent over the frying-pan, intent on the ham and eggs. She took them off and slid them on to plates before she answered him.

'I came out of the passage into the cellar when you and she were talking. You were talking about me.'

'Oh, I say.' Arnold was taken aback. 'Do you mean you were beneath the floor all the time?'

'Not all. I got bored soon, and went down to the cave. But I heard Aunt Evelyn jabbering away about me. You were doing it too. And she said you'd been doing it earlier, as well. What on earth for?'

'I'm awfully sorry, Den. But we didn't say any harm, did we? I mean, I never would. You know that, don't you?'

'You shouldn't say anything,' said Denham judicially. 'Nor let her, either. It was mostly her, of course; it always is. I suppose she got round you by being sympathetic and interested and all that. All the same, I didn't think you would have.'

'I'm fearfully sorry,' Arnold repeated. 'It was really nothing, you know. She began talking about you and me this morning, when we were out, and I'm afraid I let her. For one thing, it's not easy to stop her; for another, she's so kind and so fond of you and so keen that you should be happy – and, you know, she's really a very wise, clever person, for all that rather wild manner she's got . . . I suppose I *did* talk to her a bit. You see, I'd been doing a lot of thinking to myself, and it was a relief in a way to have someone who seemed to know all about it and to understand.'

Denham was munching a slice of ham, and spoke with her mouth full.

'But what I can't see is, what it's all about. I mean, what is there to talk about, or to think about, or to understand? Your and my affairs are quite simple. You like London and I like the country; you like seeing people and I don't; you like reading and being intelligent and all that and I don't; you want things washed up all the time and meals laid in courses, and I like to eat easily and anyhow; and a few more things like that there are. But there's nothing to talk about in all that, that I can see . . . She dragged in that baby business, too. Aunt Evelyn loves talking about whether people are going to have babies or not, or whether they're trying to do without. She's always talking about it to people, I've heard her. What's it to do with her, anyhow? . . . I've quite got over liking Aunt Evelyn since last May. If my mother was like that I'm glad she died. I call it rotten, people not minding their own business.'

This was probably the longest speech Denham had made in the course of her career. It might have been thought that she was really learning to talk at last.

Arnold was looking at her in surprise.

'I didn't know you felt so much about it, Den. I'm sorry. Evelyn means no harm, you know; it's only that she's a talker, and tremendously interested in people.'

'She shouldn't be,' Denham grunted.

'Well, never mind her. Anyhow, old thing, I'm fearfully sorry for my part in it. But don't let's bother about it any more. Forget it.'

'All right. Pass the treacle.'

They ate.

After supper they played French cricket on the cliff with a stump and an old ball, then sat and smoked outside their house before going to bed. They decided to make a clock golf course close to the cottage, and also to plant some flowers and vegetables and fence them off and make a little garden.

'The more self-supporting we are up here the better,' Denham said. 'It saves going to the village. I must find some gulls' eggs and catch a lot of fish. And one can make bread without much trouble – just flour and water and salt. All that about bread having to rise is stuff. Bread needn't rise at all. People make too much fuss about their food. I believe they *like* work. Anyhow they like other people doing work. Less work is my object. Less work, and more time for other things ... I wonder if a hen or a goat would be worth while or not?'

'Hardly. We've such a short time left now. You see, we have to get back to London next week, worse luck.'

'What for?'

'Well, I'm due at the office.'

'I'm not. I shall stay on here at present.'

'Alone? They'll be leaving the Peewits, you know.'

'Yes. I'm glad.'

'Of course stay on a bit if you want to. That is, if it's decent weather. But I wish you'd have someone from the village in to sleep. Suppose you were ill?'

'I shan't be. I never am. If I was, I suppose I should call to someone passing on the cliff, and ask them to fetch a doctor, if I wanted one. But it's not likely.'

'I was wondering,' said Arnold, 'if Audrey or Noel would stay on with you for a bit.'

'No. I wouldn't have them. I'm not going to have visitors here, they're troublesome, they make work. I like being alone.'

'I gather you do.'

'Except for you,' Denham added.

'I don't appear to be much of an exception just now.'

'It's you who won't stay here,' she pointed out. 'I want you to.'

'And it's you who won't come to London with me. I want you to.'

'It seems,' Denham, always fair, admitted, 'about six of one and half a dozen of the other.'

She considered the situation for a minute.

'Of course,' she said, 'it would be more fun if we both wanted to do the same thing. Still, as we don't, it would be silly to stand in each other's way. The great thing is each to go on in the way we like.'

'Very rational,' said Arnold. 'Though aren't you rather over-looking one trifling fact?'

'What's that?'

'Merely that we married one another, presumably with the object of being together. Don't you want that more than you want to live in this beastly cottage?'

More? How compare? She wanted both.

'Let's both stay here. Arnold, let's.'

Old, fruitless discussions threatened to repeat themselves. It would be better to go to bed. They went.

'You won't stay on here long and leave me alone? You won't –
you can't – you know you can't.'

'No, not long. Only a week or two. Not long.'

'Promise. Promise.'

'I promise. I'll come to London in three weeks, or less.'

'And you'll try to like it, for my sake?'

'Yes, darling. I'll try.'

So easily, so fluently, are promises made by night. And so
strongly and so exquisitely does love by night surge up, tran-
scending its daylight bounds, convincing lovers how greatly
and how faithfully they love.

CHAPTER XII

Living Alone

I

They had all gone away to London. Denham was alone with her cottage, her secret passage, her caves, her boat, her dog. She saw three weeks ahead of undisturbed and tranquil joy. She furnished the cave, little by little, with objects suitable to a cave sitting-room. On fine days she was out from morning until evening, boating, bathing, walking, or motor-cycling. She found sea-gulls' eggs, some good, some bad, caught fish, made what she called and ate as bread, and strolled down to the village to shop. There was no dull moment in her life. She would, had she known them, have echoed the words of Miss Hannah More: 'It is not possible for anything on earth to be more to my taste than my present manner of living. I am so much at my ease, have a great many hours at my own disposal ...'

Arnold wrote of the things he was doing, the people he was seeing. He did not write every day, and she only once a week, not being addicted to the pen, and having, in fact, no writing materials at hand until she purchased a packet of notepaper and envelopes and a pencil (HH) at the post office. Her letters were brief, but full of detail.

> Darling Arnold, – Thank you for your letter. I found three gulls' eggs yesterday, one was addled, the others all right. The fishing has been fair. Isaac caught a rabbit on Tuesday at the point. I caught the boat on a reef and made a hole and it had to be caulked. I have put some linoleum in the cave that I got in the village, as the floor was damp, it's very comfortable now, I sit there quite a lot. Some people came over from Polrew to call, but I saw them through the window and went down through the floor so they didn't get in. It is very nice here, it's a pity you aren't here. I hope you are quite well. I am, so is Isaac.
>   Your loving Denham

2

Arnold was adaptable. He got used to Denham's not being there. Every evening he would do something sociable, have someone in, go and see someone, talk and laugh and discuss, as of old. It was like being a bachelor again. He was even glad, for his wife's sake, that she was prolonging her holiday and having such a good time. In three weeks she would come back, and would begin, as she had promised, to try to like London. She would surely succeed, after this long rest from it . . .

Evelyn talked of Denham and him, but he stopped her.

'I'd rather not discuss Denham, if you don't mind. She wouldn't like it. That time, do you remember, in the cottage – the evening you walked there with me and she was out – she heard it.'

'Heard it? Why, how? Where was she?'

'Under the floor.'

'Under the floor? What in the world was she doing there?'

'She'd just come up from the secret passage.'

'Why, I didn't know there was a secret passage. Where does it lead to?'

'The sea ... Oh, lord, I swore not to mention it. It's a dead secret. Don't ever pass it on, Evelyn. I swore solemnly. Denham attaches great importance to its secrecy. I *am* a fool.'

'All right, the passage is quite safe with me.'

'You're sure? Really, I should hate it to get about, or for her to know I've told you. It was too bad of me.'

'I'm terribly safe with secrets, my dear Arnold ... And of course we won't talk of Denham; in fact, I wasn't going to. It was only that something came into my head, and I just wondered ... But never mind it now ... Which day does the child come back?'

'She hasn't said. In about a fortnight or ten days, I think.'

'Well, till she comes, come over and dine with us whenever you're alone. You'll usually find someone or other in. Arrange it with Audrey at the office.'

3

Arnold thought, lying awake in the night, of the people you can talk to and the person you love. The fact that these are not always the same is an outrage; one of those sardonic flicks at beauty and unity which life loves to give. Men and women have always accepted it, with the cynical, unquestioning patience of their kind. Men go out to talk with other men, come home to woman and child. Girls gossip with girls, take silent walks locked in dumb affection with the beloved youth. What is talk, that curling of the tongue round air to trap ideas, between two people who would kiss? For that matter, what are kisses, what is embracing, what is dumb desire, between two people who cannot know each other's mind? How shall I my true love know? But all the time, thought Arnold, there is love, which comprises, which surely should comprise, both these means of communion, each so foolish and so empty when divorced from the other. How, then, to get through to love, the all-comprehending love of soul and body, without which all else is a snare?

> Two strangers from opposing poles
> Meet in the torrid zone of love,
> And their desires are strong above
> The opposition of their souls.
>
> This is the trap, this is the snare,
> This is the false deluding night,
> And, till it vanish into light,
> How shall each know the other there?

Yes, thought Arnold, this is the trap. We are both caught in it. It won't do. We must get on, into something better. Get on, or get out ...

CHAPTER XIII

The Last Round

I

Denham came home without warning. It had not occurred to her to write beforehand. She clattered up on her motor-bicycle one evening, grimy, dusty and oil-smeared, with Isaac strapped into the side-car, exactly three weeks from the day Arnold had left Cornwall. Winifred opened the door to her.

'Oh, ma'am – we didn't know it was today you were coming.'

'Didn't you? It doesn't matter. Is Mr Chapel in?'

'Yes, ma'am. Miss Arthur, Mr Hunt and Mr Jacobs are here to dinner. They are having it now.'

The artists from downstairs. Bother. Arnold needn't have asked people in just the night she was coming back.

'Don't say I've come till after dinner, then. I shall have something upstairs.'

But Isaac, running round the hall with ejaculations suitable to home-coming, a ritual Denham had omitted, caused Arnold to appear at the dining-room door.

'Den – oh, I say, why didn't you tell me, darling?'

'I did. I said I'd come back in three weeks. Today is three weeks. I'm not coming in to dinner. You've got people.'

'I know; I'm sorry. But we'll pack them off the moment we're through with the meal. They're only Sally Arthur and Jacobs and Hunt. We were all dining in, so we joined forces. But now you've come . . .'

'Can we send them away at once?'

'Well, we've only had soup so far. We can scarcely pack them off till we've fed them. But directly afterwards . . . Anyhow, do come in and eat now.'

Bored, but resigned, Denham followed Arnold into the dining-room in her grimy overalls.

The three guests raised a hub-bub of welcome, of greeting, of inquiry. She was hungry, and ate while they chattered.

One of them said presently, 'Oh, by the way, I forgot – we brought something up to show you,' and produced and read aloud a cutting from a weekly paper.

'We heard the other day a romantic story about young Mrs Arnold Chapel, the wife of the talented author of *Lone Jane*, who is also a member of Greshams' publishing firm. Mrs Chapel is staying in a cottage she has purchased on the Cornish coast, and it is rumoured that she has made the interesting discovery of a long-disused secret passage that runs from the cottage to the sea. Mrs Chapel, who has romantic tastes, can, it is said, scarcely tear herself away from her discovery to join her husband in their artistic flat in Tavistock Square.'

'Good lord,' Arnold snatched the cutting. 'What *is* the rag? Oh, that . . . But how on earth . . . *I* never told them.'

His eyes met Denham's. Pale and sullen, travel-grimed and alien, she looked at him across the dinner table.

'Who did you tell?' Her voice was hard. 'You must have told someone. *I* didn't.'

'Nor did I . . . Well, that is, I did, I'm afraid, mention it once by mistake to Evelyn – but she swore she wouldn't say a word.'

The guests laughed.

'Evelyn Gresham! *She* swore she wouldn't say a word! I expect you wanted to let your cottage, and took the cheapest and quickest way of broadcasting its interesting features. But is it a good passage really?'

Denham said nonchalantly, 'I never noticed it particularly.'

'Quite good. Very good,' said Arnold. He hurried on, talking, covering Denham's resentment with words. She ate her dinner, silent and brooding. He glanced at her from time to time. At least she didn't make scenes. But she was very cross, and no wonder. He had promised. It was a maddening thing to have happened. Curse Evelyn. Who on earth had she babbled to, and who had sent in that ridiculous paragraph? He was stung by anger and remorse.

2

They were alone.

'Den, old thing, I'm frightfully sick about that paragraph. I slipped it out to Evelyn without thinking, then made her promise not to breathe a word. I simply can't imagine . . .'

'*What* can't you imagine?'

Denham was sitting in her arm-chair, smoking Gold Flakes and modelling a lump of Plasticine she had in her pocket.

'Well, why in the world she should go and babble about it, or how that paper got hold of it.'

'I suppose she babbled about it for the same reasons you did.

I don't know what they were. I suppose people who tell things have some reason, haven't they?'

'I just forgot for a second, you see. It slipped out.'

'I don't know what you *wanted* to tell for.'

'I didn't, not really. We were just talking about you, and . . .'

'Oh, about me.'

'I mean she began to, and I said I'd rather not, and . . .'

'All right, never mind; I don't want to hear . . . I expect you can't help it – talking, I mean.'

'Den.'

He was sitting on the floor beside her, and reached up to draw her face down to his.

'Den, old thing, don't let's quarrel, your first night.'

'I'm not quarrelling . . .'

Passively she submitted to his caress. Never had their embracing achieved so little contact.

'I'm only thinking,' she added.

'Don't think, then.'

'I promised to try to like London,' Denham went on. 'And I was going to try. You promised not to tell about the passage. You broke yours. It seems to me that breaks mine too. I don't see why I should keep mine if you haven't kept yours.'

'I've said I'm sorry about that.' He spoke wearily. He had had a tiring, annoying day. He would have liked someone to talk to, to tell things to.

'All the same,' Denham said, 'you keep on doing it – telling things, I mean. It shows we see things all differently.'

'That didn't need any fresh showing, did it?' Anger surged in Arnold and broke out at last. He got up and stood by her, his hands thrust into his pockets, his face flushed.

'We see everything differently, that's obvious. I don't know why you ever thought you could be happy with me at all. You think of nothing in the world but caves and the seaside and doing the things that amuse you. You hate my friends and my life, you don't care a damn how any of my affairs go, you'll scarcely talk to me ... then you round on me because I let out by accident about your tuppeny-halfpenny passage. Oh, what's the good ...'

She blinked at him through the haze of smoke. She was pale and heavy-faced and sullen, smudged with travel, one cheek bulged out with a peardrop; she was not even attractive. Worse, she understood nothing. Blind and crying, their love groped for a door of entry, and turned away defeated.

'I don't want to live in London,' she reiterated, stubborn and dull, like a tiresome child. 'I don't like it.'

'And I've told you a hundred times I *have* to live in London, so that's that.'

'Well, we needn't live all the time in the same place as each other.'

'You mean you don't want to.'

'I want to if it's in the country.'

'Oh, well, what's the use of having all this again and again? I should think we're both sick of it.'

'All right.' She got up. 'I'm sleepy. I shall go to bed.'

Was she hurt? Was she angry? Was she sorry for him or for herself or for both? Who could read that grimy, moody face, cheek bulged out with a sweet, black brows drawn down in a faint scowl?

'Good night,' she said at the door.

'Oh ... Good night.'

198

Arnold sat on by the fire. He was exasperated and jarred, pierced by resentment and remorse.

'It's impossible. We're making it impossible ... We must both be sensible ... *I* must be sensible; she's a child ... But she's no business to be a child ... She doesn't care enough even to ask what I've been doing, or how I am ... Oh, damn.'

In such musings he occupied half an hour, then, feeling a great need of companionship, went downstairs to talk to his three dinner guests.

How dull a London morning was, in a faint yellow October fog. Denham sought about her house for something amusing to do. But all indoor ploys seemed tame after the cottage by the sea. She felt homesick for the passage, the cave, the boat, the plashing of green waves against rocks, the lordly privacy of the cottage, the exquisite meals eaten in the boat or sitting outside her home on the gorsey turf. Winifred and Laura hurried, busy and refined, about the house, doing all those things – what were they? – that servants did, and that went so well undone. Arnold was at the office. Isaac, bored by London too, yawned by the fire. The telephone kept ringing, and Winifred answered it, bringing her mistress each time some redundant and unnecessary message for her or for Arnold or for both. Telephones. The sort of thing people *would* invent, so that even being in different houses shouldn't stop them talking to each other.

Winifred came in.

'Mrs Gresham on the telephone, ma'am. She says will you speak to her.'

'I can't, just now. Ask her to leave a message.'

The message was that Denham was to come to lunch.

'Say I can't. I'm going out to lunch.'

After that, Denham, reflecting that her aunt might call in person, visited the Zoo, and returned late in the late afternoon.

'Let no visitors in, Winifred,' she said. 'And a lot of buttered scones for tea, please.'

She threw off her hat and made herself comfortable in a chair by the fire.

A boring day. Like other London days ... Meanwhile the cottage was eating its head off down by the sea. A quiet, misty October sea, there would be, green in the shadow of the cliff; the boat moored at the Polrew cob, in the charge of Jim Treloar, waiting for her to come; the locked, untenanted cottage on the cliff, its dresser stacked with thick white mugs and plates, its damp corners with fishing-rods, the smell of fried mackerel and tobacco smoke and wet bathing suits still heavy in its little rooms, and beneath its floor the bricked-up passage twisting darkly, secretly down to the deep green cave sitting-room, and beyond this to the shouting, whispering, singing sea ... Fish waiting to be caught, crabs scuttling round in the rock pools, gulls and plovers swooping and crying between cliff and sea ... No Winifred, no Laura, no telephone ... No Arnold either ... but what was the good of having Arnold there if he was bored and wanting London?

She'd promised she would try, when she came home, to like London. Well, she had tried today, and failed. She did *not* like

London. It was a rotten place, and a rotten life. And people made a fool of one. *'Mrs Chapel, who has romantic tastes ...'* Lord! She could hear Aunt Evelyn saying that to some idiot of a young man who was on some idiotic paper. Humphrey, perhaps ... But no, Humphrey wouldn't. It wasn't Humphrey's kind of paper. Humphrey, Denham admitted, would no more write that kind of tosh than she would herself. One must be fair, and make distinctions, even about writers and journalists.

Tea came in, with lots of buttered scones and a new cake. After all, that was something, tea and hot scones coming in for themselves like that, not having to be produced with labour by oneself. There was something in servants; only the nuisance of having them about, making so much unnecessary fuss in the house, easily weighed down their advantages. And, after all, one could have an even larger tea if one got it for oneself. Her lunch had consisted of a doughnut and two mixed fruit sundaes at a Lyons soda fountain, and she was hungry. So was Isaac, whatever he might have had for lunch. He always was. Isaac too was homesick for Cornwall. But homesickness, fortunately, did not impair the appetite, in either of them.

5

The front door bell rang. It didn't matter; she had told Winifred not to let them in. Aunt Evelyn's voice ... heavens, what ailed Aunt Evelyn? She couldn't let her alone; first ringing up, then calling ... You'd think a person wouldn't like to go near another person for some time after they'd let them down the way Aunt Evelyn had about that beastly paragraph in the paper. Aunt Evelyn's cheek was colossal. She probably laboured under the common delusion that you made things better by talking about them. It seemed to Denham that, once a thing had happened, there it was, and you'd better let it alone; talking about it was no use, anyhow.

The next moment Aunt Evelyn was in the room. Damn Winifred ...

'My dear, I made Winifred let me in. I guessed you didn't mean *I* wasn't to.'

She'd guessed wrong, as usual. Denham said nothing while she was kissed and examined. Why did women want to kiss one and look at one? That idiotic habit some women have of exploring the personal appearance, with or without comment, instead of attending to what they and their companion are saying ... There is something the matter with women; they ought to be seen to. They are more interested in people than in things; that must be it.

'You *must* get your hair properly cut, my dear. Why, you've been chopping at it yourself! It looks too fearful. You're burnt a lovely brown, though. I wish the girls went that colour instead of freckling. But really you can't go about London in that old sweater and skirt – *really*, Denham, you know you can't?'

'As a matter of fact,' said Denham, 'I find I can. I've done it all today.'

She had a feeling of having run up a flag of revolt at last. A year ago she would meekly have agreed that she had done a thing one could not do, ashamed of her blunder in the difficult ways of the higher life. A new freedom possessed her; she had shamelessly turned her back on that life, and did not care.

'My dear, you'll be a laughing-stock! Seriously, it can't be done ... But I didn't come to talk about clothes. I was terribly distressed this morning when Arnold rang me up from the office about that silly paragraph in the *Weekly Chat*. It must have been that tiresome Denis Wright – I just happened to drop something about your passage, quite by accident, at dinner, and he went and used it like that. These people are absolutely shameless. Of course I oughtn't to have referred to it. I knew Arnold had told me in confidence, but it tumbled out while we were talking about you ... '

Talking about her. What on earth were they all doing, talking about her? They must be hard up for subjects in London.

'And I'm dreadfully bothered about it, because I feel you must blame both Arnold and me for it. But you mustn't blame Arnold, indeed you mustn't. He *never* meant it to get about.'

'Do you want tea?' Denham asked.

'No, I'm going on to Magda Merrion's at home. But I *had* to slip in on my way and just put things straight with you about this. I can see you're vexed with me over it; of course you are. But you mustn't be vexed with Arnold. I can't go before you promise me that. We must have a good talk about it.'

Apparently they were doing so.

'Why?' Denham asked. 'I can't think of anything to say.'

'My dear child ... ' For a moment Evelyn was disconcerted. Denham had come back odder than ever. Poor Arnold!

'Of course you shan't talk if you feel you can't. So long as you don't let it rankle, and poison your mind, as things will if you aren't firm with them, you know ... One just has to pull one's vexations out by the roots and throw them away. We all have to do it all the time, about one thing or another – some little stupid thing that someone has said or done that has bothered us, and that, if we let it, goes bad in our minds and turns to poison. One has to be terribly firm with oneself about not dwelling on it.'

What about being firm with other people about not dwelling on it, though? That seemed at the moment to be the point. Denham wondered how long Evelyn would go on talking, how soon talkers ran down if one gave them no encouragement.

'You see, child, you're both young, you and Arnold, and I do feel you've come somehow to a rather difficult point on the road, which you've got to get past carefully, d'you see. There are always difficulties in the first year or two of marriage, and in your case there are rather special ones, because you and Arnold are so different, and have been brought up so differently. You've both got to be terribly wise and patient ... Do you know what I can't help hoping?'

Denham felt it safer not to guess.

'That you'll have a child before very long, my dear. It would bring you together so tremendously ... You know Catherine's having one in the spring? She and Tim haven't found it altogether smooth running all the time – who does? – but now ...'

Denham could see nothing for it here but to ring the bell for the tea to be removed. It was really a bit thick for Catherine, having her affairs recounted like this. Anyhow, she didn't want to hear about them. These mushy confidences by the fireside – they made her feel stifled. She turned on the lights, and was pleased to see them glare into her aunt's wide green eyes so that she blinked. They also reminded her of the time, and she rose to go.

'I'm late, my dear, I must fly ... Well, is it all quite straightened out now?'

'Is what straightened out?'

'That silly business about the paragraph, of course. Is it all forgotten and put out of sight?'

'Well, it's not had much of a chance of that this afternoon, has it? You can't well forget a thing if someone's talking about it all the time.'

'Was I wrong to talk, my dear? I felt I had to make you understand, you see ... I wonder if I have, at all?'

'Have what? Oh, understand, you mean. Well, I can't see anything to understand or not understand. I can't see anything difficult about it, I mean.'

'Tout comprendre c'est tout pardonner,' said Evelyn in her favourite language. 'I'll come and see you again, child, and we'll have it all out. I can't stay now; good-bye.'

She was gone.

6

'Winifred,' Denham said sternly, as her handmaid passed through the hall with the tea things, 'I told you not to let them in.'

'I'm sorry, ma'am, but Mrs Gresham said you didn't mean her.'

'Well,' her mistress shortly informed her, 'I did.'

She returned to the drawing-room. It was full of Evelyn's faint, delicate scent and the smoke of her Russian cigarettes. It was redolent of fireside intimacies – horrid. It needed a salt wind sweeping through it, and a smell of fish or tar. Denham crammed on her red tam-o'-shanter and her frieze coat and went out into the misty twilight afternoon. She felt she needed a sea bathe, or a blow on the cliffs, or a conversation with a fisherman about weather.

Aunt Evelyn would be at it again soon. 'We'll have it all out,' she had said. Have *what* all out, in the name of goodness? What was the woman babbling about? Making fools of herself and Denham like that, making fools of Catherine, of Tim, of Arnold . . .

She'd go on about that baby again, of course.

'I'm bothered if I'll have one,' thought Denham, 'while *she's* anywhere about. That would be the last straw, to have her gloating.'

'I *won't* stay and be talked to,' she said presently aloud. 'I won't. I shall go back to the cottage.'

'Well, why not?'

The voice of her cousin Humphrey behind her startled her. She had been walking round the quiet square, and he had emerged from a side street.

'How do you do,' he said, and walked at her side. 'I heard you were back. But I gather from your last words that you aren't going to stay very long?'

She looked at him, half suspicious.

'Don't know how long.'

'Well, I'm off to Italy myself tomorrow. I can't stand London at the moment. It's a sound plan not to stay anywhere longer than you want to.'

A person of some sense, after all, Humphrey was.

'Well,' Denham said, 'I'd rather be in Cornwall than here.'

'Then I should certainly go to Cornwall. I gather, too, that someone has been talking to you too much?'

'Yes,' Denham gloomily agreed. 'Aunt Evelyn has, today. She says she's going on.'

'You'll have to go, in that case. That's the only way I've ever discovered of stopping mother. Even that ...'

'I expect,' said Denham, being polite about his mother, 'she can't help it. My aunt at Torquay has palpitations and hiccups. There's usually something, as people get older.'

'Yes. Or even before they get so much older,' Probably Humphrey was gloomily considering various younger ladies of his acquaintance.

'You go,' he advised, as they swung round the corner of the square.

'I expect I shall. The only difficulty is Arnold.'

'Is Arnold a difficulty? Don't make him so. All this insistence on personal relationships – it's nothing but a disease. Love's a disease. But curable. It passes. Unfortunately also it recurs. One must try hard not to take it too seriously. Plenty of things matter a great deal more. Most things, in fact. Did you ever look through a microscope at a drop of pond water? You see plenty of love there. All the amoebae getting married. I presume they think it very exciting and important. We don't. But we still think our own loves are. We can't bring ourselves to regard them as mere biological impulses, with very little more intellectual or spiritual meaning than the loves of the pond water. We've let love get out of its proper place. We've given in to it. It's a mistake ... Here's your house. Good-bye. I'm going home to pack.'

The fog swallowed him up.

Denham went into her house. Arnold had come back, and was sitting in the drawing-room listening-in.

'Hallo!' said Denham.

'Hallo, m'dear.' What odd clothes she went out in London in, he thought.

'I think I shall go back to the cottage tomorrow for a bit.'

'Tomorrow? At once? Why, you've scarcely got here . . . Oh, all right, if you want to. Don't let me hinder you.'

He was being ironically polite. He was hurt, but only mildly. Love's a disease. But curable. It passes.

CHAPTER XIV

Driven Out

'Black with people,' remarked Denham, as she and Isaac approached their cottage, bicycling along the cliff path from Polrew.

There were, in fact, several persons grouped around the cottage, gazing at it with loquacious interest. Some were children, some adults. They transferred their gaze to Denham as she came towards them. Some of them giggled. Staring and giggling. Denham, familiar with human habits, was not disturbed by them. But it was a bore, the populace rallying round her home like this.

One of them spoke to her as she came up – the wife of the Polrew policeman, with two little girls at her side.

'Good afternoon, ma'am. You've not been long away, then.'

'No,' Denham agreed, unstrapping Isaac from the sidecar and wondering how the lady knew she had been away at all.

'My husband read a piece in a book about your cottage, ma'am. About a passage to the sea . . .'

'In a book? What book?'

'The *Weekly Chat*, it was, I think.'

'Oh, a magazine. Yes, I saw it.'

'And is it true, ma'am? Is there a passage? My husband, he says it must be an old smuggler's way to the sea.'

'No,' said Denham after consideration. 'It's not true. They invented it.'

'There! What'll they say next?'

But Denham was not believed. They all knew there must be a passage, for there had been a piece in a book about it. Pieces don't get into books for nothing. What was the word of this eccentric young lady against a book? Polrew looked at the young lady with suspicion; she was trying to hide something. What, *or whom*, had she got concealed in that passage? '*Mrs Chapel, who has romantic tastes, can, it is said, scarcely tear herself away from her discovery to join her husband . . .*' Thus the book. And, look, here she was back again, only two days after she was gone. That showed. Queer goings on, to be sure. But here were several dozen Cornish folk would know the reason why, however they had to ferret it out.

'I don't know,' said Denham, in reply to the last inquiry, as to what would be the next utterance of the Press. She unlocked the cottage door and entered, with bicycle and dog, closing the door firmly behind her. From inside she glanced out at the besiegers with a grin. Let them wait there all night if they chose; they couldn't get in.

'There's no such thing as speaking politely to people, I suppose.' A tart female voice penetrated through the closed window. 'No such thing as asking people in, of course.'

How oddly people reasoned. How did they come to suppose that, because one person had not been polite and asked them in, this was never done? Denham pondered, not for the first time, on the apparently complete lack of logical sequence in many feminine minds below a certain level of education. Though brought up in continual contact with such minds, for in Andorra, as in Great Britain, they abound, the processes of thought in them had always been a dark riddle to her. She felt towards them as children feel who ask their nurses, 'Why?' and are never told, for the simple reason that these unfortunate women do not understand this small word Consequently they hate it. 'Miss Why was drowned in a ditch,' they will say, or 'Master Why had his tongue pulled out for asking questions.' Thus, easily and glibly, they wreak their dream revenge, and Miss and Master Why are left unanswered.

It was going to be a nuisance if Polrew meant to go on rallying round the cottage waiting for a chance to look for the passage. Damn that paper, and Aunt Evelyn, and Arnold ... Was the whole world engaged in running round with its tongue out chattering? Gloomily Denham got tea for herself and Isaac, while Polrew slowly and reluctantly dispersed.

It was a bad business. The cottage was blighted. Before long, if Denham knew her Polrew, the passage would be located. And then there would be the end of privacy; people would be swarming along it night and day, camping and picnicking in the cave, breaking into the cellar ...

No, the game was up. Arnold and Aunt Evelyn between them had got her fairly in the soup. But they needn't think she was coming back to London because of it. She might have to leave the cottage, but there were other places. One might do worse than travel round on one's motor-bicycle from place to place, putting up where one liked. That would be the life ... One wouldn't get to know anyone that way, either, and they couldn't come crowding round the place, for there wouldn't be a place to crowd round. It needn't cost much, if one put up in cheap rooms, and didn't do immense distances each day. When one got to a good place, one could settle down in it for several days and explore the neighbourhood. Of course that was the life. What a good idea. Why hadn't she thought of it before? Perpetual rest in motion; new places all the time, and no people. And no housekeeping. The only way, outside hotels, workhouses, and prisons, of escape from that.

Why wouldn't Arnold do it too? If he wanted to earn money, they could sell something as they went about – books or pictures or bootlaces or what not. He might peddle his firm's books. People would buy anything. It would be fun if Arnold would come too. But of course he wouldn't, he was too much stuck on London.

Anyhow, the thing was to leave the cottage at once, until the excitement about the passage had blown over. And, if possible, to leave it unostentatiously, so that they should not know. Though, of course, they would soon find out. They have a marvellous gift for knowing all about the doings of others. They do not need to enquire; they merely know, with a kind of heaven-sent intuition. And directly they knew, they would no doubt come about the place, perhaps break in, to look for the passage. Well, it couldn't be helped; one couldn't clutter oneself travelling by taking a lot of things with one, even if it was risky to leave them. They were valuable things, too, thought Denham, regretfully surveying her hardware and chairs. But she would only take the outfit needed for the preparing of food by the way, a few clothes, a brush and comb, soap, towel, and toothbrush. Everything would go on the carrier, and leave room for Isaac in the sidecar.

Whistling softly, she began to overhaul the motor-bicycle.

PART THREE

PAUL AND BARBARA

CHAPTER I

The Creator

Evelyn drummed delicate fingers on the windowsill as she stood looking out on the misty autumn square. Ideas were taking on their shadowy shapes in her quick, restless, creative mind. Phantom figures defined themselves and moved about her lit stage, vivacious with colour, sharp of line, more alive than life. A story was shaping itself in her brain. Her fingers itched for her pen, the fine-nibbed pen that flew so lightly over the paper for her, and scratched when others used it. Her phantom creatures needed, before they were really alive, the chain of small, delicate, upright characters with which she confined them. She felt that if her handwriting had chanced to be soft, flowing and broad, her literary style and her method of creation would have been quite different.

It was now as if the story in her mind, after long germinating, had suddenly burgeoned into flower, so that she must gather it forthwith.

She sat down at her Queen Anne bureau and found her pen and writing-pad.

This is the story that Evelyn began to write, calling it:

CHAPTER I

Was it a week ago or a month that they had parted, wounding one another with that kind of desperate, hopeless impatience that follows spent passion? Barbara, alone by the sea, scarcely knew. Echoes of phrases beat with the waves against the stark rocks, with the salt and bitter tang of tears.

'I've no use for your kind of life – no *use* for it, don't you see. I can't go on, Paul. We're too different.'

'I'm beginning to think you're right. We *are* too different. You hate all my ways and life – why, you won't even bear my child.'

'No, I don't want to bear your child. I want myself, not your child . . . Good-bye, Paul, I'm going away.'

Going away, going away, going away. The waves plashily said it over. Queer, how dead she felt, with no feeling at all. Not sorry that she had gone away, nor glad; it was as if she were waiting to know.

Idly she watched the people in the little cove below her. There was a young couple, a fisherman and his girl, sitting on the edge of a boat. The youth was handsome, bronzed and brawny; he was like a lusty young sea-god. The girl was a jocund Chloe. They teased and romped; then bending her face backwards, he crushed her in his arms, and kissed her on the lips.

Seeing them, Barbara suddenly woke to life. A queer, hot pang stabbed through her. No longer was she dead and neither sorry nor glad; she was now both sorry and glad. Sorry with a new and keen pain, with a sudden blind storming of the senses that shook her as a wind shakes a leaf. She had had love and had torn it from her; and now she knew that she could not go on without it. Glad with a bounding of the pulses, with a rising up of all her being. Love she desired, but no longer Paul. No longer that attenuated, civilised love that cultured persons knew, but the robust, sensuous full-blooded passion of a primitive nature. She had thought that she wanted to be alone. That was nonsense. She did not want to be alone; love of aloneness belongs only to the tired, to the sensitive, to the creators. Barbara in her strong young savagery had no use for it; she wanted her man, whom she had not yet found. Not a player with words, a taster of culture, but someone like herself, who would companion her, play with her, crush her with strong salt kisses, wasting no words. She did not know that, if such a man should come to her, she was even now ready. Inarticulate child, she knew of herself less than nothing. Jacob, the little dog barking at her side, was more awake to his own nature than was she, as, stretched at the cliff's edge, she shot pebbles into the sea below. Softly she was whistling a little tune, and it was the tune that the young fisherman in the boat had been whistling before his young woman had joined him, but whether Barbara had caught it from him or he from her she did not know, in the bitter-sweet, restless unhappiness that drowned her soul.

2

Paul was talking to Dorothea, pacing restlessly about the room. She was listening gravely, her fair young girl's forehead knitted a little.

'What's to be the end of it? What can we either of us do? And, in Heaven's name, what's wrong between us? We did love each other – I swear we did. Oh, yes, we do still, in one way. I think we do still. But now from so many miles apart that it only stabs and hurts. No words can be between us, no understanding, no companionship, *What's to be the end?*'

'It will settle itself gradually.' Dorothea spoke with hesitation, as if she were not sure of herself and her wisdom. 'It will be all right in the end. She'll come back.'

Paul made a sharp gesture.

'And if she does? Are we any further? Won't it be the same again? What have we to build on? That's what I want to know. What have we to build on, Dorothea?'

She hazarded 'Love,' and shrank back, helpless and hurt, from her own word.

'Love.' He repeated it, looking at her vaguely, as if from far off. 'What is love?'

'Oh' – she shrugged. 'Ask me another. That's a worse one than Pilate's ... Anyhow, how should I know? *You* should know, Paul, better than I.'

'I don't know,' he said. 'I don't know. Desire – friendship – kindness – delirium – anguish – joy – all those. Can one build a house on love? I tell you, love shifts and shivers under one's feet like quaking sand. While you look at it it drifts away and is gone. Is ours gone – mine and hers? Sometimes I think that it is—'

Sometimes? The word sang in Dorothea's ears, doubting and bitter-sweet. Sometimes? And the other times? Why didn't he know himself, poor Paul?

'The only thing,' said the girl dryly, 'is to make her come back and see how things go then.'

'She won't come. Not yet. You know she won't … I might go to her …'

'Why not?' The clear dry voice did not falter.

'But I can't stay by the seaside for ever even if she wanted me, and the struggle would only come all over again. Besides, she doesn't want me now. No: we must each be alone for a time, and find out that way how we stand. I believe it's the only way.'

'It's one way.'

She rose. She could not bear this interview any more.

'I must go, Paul. Good-bye … I'm terribly sorry, old thing, about all this mess.'

He caught her hand and held it.

'You're the dearest person, Dorothea—'

She pulled her hand away and left him.

He returned to the room, oddly stirred. She was the dearest person … Her slim, cool hand in his … She had grown so terribly pretty, Dorothea. And so kind … Nothing she didn't understand …

3

Evelyn laid down her pen and looked at her watch. Heavens, it was three o'clock, and she was due at a private view …

For a moment she still sat, with the dazed look of one between two worlds. She passed her thin hand across her eyes.

'Writing makes things come alive. Terribly alive … Oh, why am I made so that I have to see everything always? I'm frightened …'

Then after a moment. 'I must make my darling Audrey go away for a change. She's thinner; she's losing her colour; she works too hard ... Oh, hypocrite, I'm lying. The last sin, the sin against the Holy Ghost – to lie to oneself. Lying to other people – that's a small thing in comparison. One mustn't lie to oneself, ever. I'll say it straight out; my Audrey loves Arnold ... Oh, she must go away. No good can come, only pain. Pain, pain, to everyone ... Oh, what a damnable mix-up it all is.'

4

Denham wrote to Arnold.

Dear Arnold, – I've left the cottage, people came round the place, because they'd read in the papers about the passage, and they wanted to get into it. So I locked it up, but I expect they'll get in just the same, and came away on the bicycle with Isaac. It is a better plan. I go from one place to another, it's great fun. I sleep in inns or lodgings in different places. It doesn't cost much. But you might send about ten pounds, or perhaps twelve, to the Post Office, St Ives. I am there now and shall stay a few days fishing. I have a room close to the harbour, it is very nice. There are some people painting, but I don't know any of them. I've been talking to some of the fishermen, they are nice and know a lot. It is a pity you aren't here, you might be coming round with me, you could sell something if you liked, books or something. I expect I shall go on doing this for some time, it is a very good plan, you get a change all the time and see new things, and lots of air. Isaac likes it and is very well.

Love, yours,
Denham

P.S. – Aunt Evelyn came to St Ives on Monday. I hope
she won't come again to where I am, she talked a lot and
I got bored, I didn't listen much so don't know what it was
mostly about. Stop her coming again.

5

Evelyn, sitting up late one night, wrote chapter 6 of *Paul and Barbara*.

There was something new about Barbara; a new poise, and a kind of glow. She walked towards him across the room, and he thought of a sailor home for a while from strange and joyous adventurings.

'Hallo, Paul.'

'Well, Barbara?'

He would have kissed her, but she held back.

'No. That's all done with. That's what I've come to tell you, Paul.'

'What do you mean?' His voice sounded to himself queer and unnatural.

She sat down and threw off her hat. With her usual direct-ness, she came straight to the point.

'I can't kiss you because I've been kissing someone else. I love him, and he loves me. We're going to be together. We must end our marriage.'

Oddly amaze, anger, pain and a queer, thin, singing gladness mingled in the shock that caught Paul's breath in his throat as he stood staring at her.

223

'End our marriage? Are you asking me for a divorce?'

She nodded. 'Yes; a divorce. Then I shall marry this man – and you can marry again too, if you like.'

'You seem to forget,' he said, bitterness rising in him at her careless calm, 'that we are both Catholics. We can't marry anyone else while the other lives.'

With a gesture she swept aside the Catholic Church.

'I'm through with all that. It never meant anything to me, and now I'm not going to pretend any more. You'd better give it up too. It means nothing.'

'As it happens,' said Paul, 'it does, to me. But never mind that now. I think I have a right to ask who this man is?'

'His name's Jim Tralee. He's a fisherman.'

Paul's short laugh was his only comment.

'And you expect to be happy with him?'

'I am happy with him,' she calmly replied. 'You see, he's my kind of person.'

'And I am not, I am to infer.'

'No,' she said. 'You're not. And I'm not yours. You know it the same as I do. There's no sense in pretending. You ought to be married to someone like Dorothea, who likes the same things you do. I'm all wrong for you. I only disgrace you, and bore myself. Besides . . . '

'Besides?'

'I love Jim now,' she said simply, and in the brief statement throbbed all the stormy music of passion and fulfilment. Before it their own past love seemed to shrink and fade away, a frail thing, dead of exhaustion.

'Have you and he already . . . ' he muttered.

'I'm going to have his child,' she replied.

'His child? You wouldn't have mine . . . '

'No. But I want to have his. It's different. Anyhow, I'm having it, and it can't be helped. So you see, you must divorce me.

'Yes; yes. I'll see to it.' He stood turned from her, looking out of the window, red and ashamed. She had been unfaithful to him. He had kept faith, he would have gone on keeping it to the end, but she had broken it. And now, almost casually, she asked him for a divorce. An immense anger surged in him, at her impregnable childish calm. Did nothing matter to her, was nothing to her right or wrong?

'I'll see to it,' he said, and turned to face her. 'Since you ask me to, I've no choice. Though you seem to be managing all right without it so far.'

'Oh,' she returned, 'I don't mind. But Jim does. He wants us to be married. And I want you to be free, too.'

'I've told you already I can't be free.'

She remembered the Church.

'Paul, does that really matter?'

Violently he flung at her, 'Yes, it does.' Violently, in contradiction not only of her, but of the clamorous voice in his own soul that cried, 'It doesn't, it can't.'

So, across the dark, bright worlds of forgotten passion and remembered pain, of conflict, of love dead and love newly born, these two trapped children faced one another as from a great distance.

'It matters more to be free,' Barbara protested, and it was as if she flung the challenge to the universe of impeding things. 'Free to do what one wants. That's *all* that matters, I think.'

Pagan and Christian, they spoke from opposing camps.

Paul shrugged his shoulders.

'As to that – who is? But at least I'll do what I can to set you free, my dear. I suppose I should apologise for not having been able to make you happy.'

'I don't see why we should either of us apologise. It was just that we didn't suit.'

'True, and spoken with your usual common sense. No apologies then, on either side ... This is the end, then. You're going straight back to Cornwall, I assume.'

'Yes, straight back.'

6

Peter Gresham came into his wife's room at one o'clock; he had been out to dinner.

'My dear! Writing so late? What is it just now?'

Evelyn laid aside her glasses and her pen. Her big green eyes were full of dreams.

'A story, Peter. A story out of real life. But so entirely out of real life that I shall never, never be able to publish it, I'm afraid. It's too near the quick, d'you see; too near the quick.'

'Whose story, my sweet?' Peter spoke a touch uneasily.

'The story of those two unlucky children, Denham and Arnold. It suddenly swept over me, all the inwardness and the truth of that tangle, and what's happening and going to happen, and I had to write it. But – you *see* ... '

'Oh, quite. Quite impossible to publish it, of course,' he ardently agreed.

'Still, Peter – I'd like you to read it, when it's finished. Or even before. When I've done a little more, you might. Just to see what you think about the possibility of disguising it enough ...'

'No, my dear. You can't publish stories about the matrimonial troubles of your niece and my junior partner, you really can't ... Not, for that matter, that *she'd* read it – but he would.'

'Yes. Oh, it wouldn't do; of course it wouldn't do. There's Audrey, too.'

'Audrey? What's Audrey got to do in it?'

'Oh, my poor precious Peter Simple, what d'you think?'

'I don't think anything; certainly not. Really, Eve ... Don't get telling me that Audrey and Arnold ...'

'Oh, there's nothing yet – nothing definite or admitted. But it's all there, waiting. Don't you see it, Peter?'

'No, Eve, I don't. But I suppose if you say so, you omniscient woman ... Well, look here, I'm going to bed. I've been talking all the evening, and I'm not going to talk all night ... For Heaven's sake don't go leaving that story about, or Audrey'll see it. She wouldn't like it, you know, if you've gone and put her in.'

'I wonder how much Audrey would mind? In a way, she might be glad. Relieved, you know. It might show her things she hadn't admitted to herself, and that's always a relief. It lifts inhibitions, enables one to face the truth.'

'She'd not be pleased,' said Audrey's father, briefly, and went to his dressing-room.

He hoped Evelyn would be careful. She never would realise that people resent being talked about and written about; she always seemed half to think that they liked it. And of course they didn't like it; no one did. Fact was, it was impudent, yes, rather impudent, writing stories about the private affairs of the people one knew. If you wanted to do that, you should frankly write reminiscences, and call them *About My Friends* or something, which was quite the fashion now. Then the victims could write and contradict what you said of them if they didn't like it. But not fiction; that was hitting below the belt, thought Peter, for even publishers have their own code of honour.

'How are you making it work out?' he called through the open door.

'Well, I've not got it all clear in my mind yet. But Barbara – that's Denham, you know, of course that's Denham – gives herself to a young fisherman in Cornwall, and ...'

'Gives herself to a fisherman? *Gives* herself ...' What an expression!

'I say, my dear, you mustn't say that so loud, you really mustn't. And, you know, I don't think that'll do. Not a fisherman ...'

'Why not? It's just what she *would* do. It's *right*, don't you see.'

'No, I don't see. Seems to me quite wrong, when she's married to Arnold.'

'Artistically right, of course I mean. It's what she'd do. It's what I believe she is doing now, Peter.'

'Doing now? Giving herself to ... Why, who said so?'

'No one said so. But I feel it's true. I feel it, d'you see? I'm never wrong about things like that. What's more, I saw the man. He was there when I went down to St Ives. I knew it from her manner and his. She was tremendously happy and at peace. He was terribly good-looking. They were out fishing together when I got down there. Well, I ask you. It was all completely obvious.'

'Too many things are completely obvious to you, my love.'

'I, tell you I *felt* it, Peter. *Felt* it, do you see. I'm never wrong about things like that.'

'Well, for Heaven's sake don't go saying it about. I mean, it gives a girl a bad name, that sort of thing being said of her. Let's hope for the best till we know, shall we?'

'What is the best?' Evelyn enquired. 'And how can we judge? It may be the best for Denham to find her mate and her happiness that way. Best for everyone, you know. For her, for Arnold, and . . .'

'And for the fisherman,' Peter put in hastily, to prevent her saying, 'for Audrey,' which he didn't care about.

'Well,' he concluded, as he got into bed, 'don't leave the things about, anyhow. And, of course, that puts the lid on as regards publication – the fisherman does, I mean.'

'No harm in fishermen,' Evelyn murmured drowsily. 'I say the child's right to do it. To cut the knot that way.'

She was asleep, and to Peter's, 'But you don't know that she *is* doing it,' she only returned slow and gentle breathings and the clear knowledge of the truth that dreams give.

CHAPTER II

Evelyn and Arnold

I

Peter caught up the piles of typescript he had been reading, crammed them into his dispatch case, and hurried away to his office through the white Advent fog. He was one of those industrious publishers who take home manuscripts to read during weekends.

He bustled into his room at the office, flung out the manuscripts on to a desk, summoned his secretary, and began his usual energetic day's work, for it was twelve o'clock, and he had to get it all done by lunch time. 'Mr Gresham's here.' The news ran through the office, and everyone, from the advertisement manager to the office boy, braced up and began to work at double rate, so infectious was Mr Gresham's energy.

Peter hurried about the office, seeing to everything, hurried back to his room, dictated six letters, had eleven interviews over the telephone and three with authors in person, looked into Arnold's room to say, 'You might look through that manuscript of Condover's that I've marked for cutting and see what you think,' sent a messenger for a taxi, fired a quick round of last orders at his secretary, and dashed off to lunch at the Fishmongers' Hall.

His secretary, a little exhausted by the crowded hour and relieved that it was over for the day, went out to lunch herself, after carrying the pile of typescripts on Mr Gresham's desk to Mr Chapel's room upstairs.

2

Arnold came in, after lunching with Audrey at a Spanish restaurant in Soho. He was full of rice and fried banana and things of that kind, that Peter would not have admitted to be lunch at all, for Arnold liked being reminded of abroad, and talking to Spanish and Italian waiters in places that more nearly resembled their native haunts than the ordinary Westend restaurants wherein they serve.

A pile of typescript lay on his desk, and he remembered that Peter had asked him to look through Condover's book that he had been cutting. He sat down to it. It was not apparently only Condover's book that had been brought him to look at; there was also something much shorter called *Paul and Barbara*. Obviously one of those long stories or short novels, that never went well. He turned over the pages; some kind of a love story, apparently. His eye caught passages.

'*Are you going to let the rules of your Church spoil both our lives then, Paul?*' cried Dorothea.

He looked at her as she stood there, young and fair and fresh, her dear face powdered with childish golden freckles; looked at her as in a dream. Then suddenly he awoke.

'My God, no.' *He caught her hands in his and drew her to him, and at the touch of her lips the Catholic Church shivered into fragments.*

'Audrey, Audrey, my dear, my dear——'

'Arnold . . .'

Arnold paused, surprised. Arnold? Audrey? He had thought that these persons were Paul and Dorothea. He looked on, and sure enough, they *were* Paul and Dorothea, except in that one passage, when they seemed to have forgotten themselves. Why, he wondered? And the Catholic Church . . . that was odd too.

He turned to the beginning of the story, and began to read.

4

Evelyn Gresham was sitting alone in her little, softly lighted, Morris papered book room, writing letters and waiting for Arnold, who had telephoned from the office to ask if he might come and see her.

Evelyn was agreeably interested. Arnold's voice had sounded as if he had something on his mind. Perhaps he had had a disturbing letter from Denham; perhaps the situation was developing, working to a crisis, in his own mind. Anyhow she would listen to him, and help so far as she could. Life was full of these crises, and a great number of them came her way, perhaps because she saw things without needing to be told, which made it easier for people to talk to her. Anyhow, disturbed young wives and husbands needing counsel were all in the day's work to her, and by no means the part of the day's work which she found least stimulating. And of Arnold, poor worried boy, she was very fond. They had for years been great friends.

'Mr Chapel,' said the maid, showing him into the small, lit room, that shone gently, like a dim golden flower, in the fog, and smelt of Russian cigarettes and of burning logs and heather, like a bonfire on a heath, for all Evelyn's rooms, like herself, had a lovely vivid grace.

Arnold came in, pale and chilled and dirty with fog, his dispatch case in his hand. He shook hands and sat down by the log fire, and opened the dispatch case and took out a pile of typescript which he held out to her.

'There's no name on it, but it must be yours, I think?'

She made a quick movement towards it, taken aback.

'You've read it, Arnold?'

'Yes, I've read it. It was brought me by Peter's secretary, probably by mistake, with another manuscript. I read it through. I inferred it was yours. But I didn't quite get the idea – or why it was lying about the office.'

'My dear – Peter must have taken it by mistake this morning. It was never meant to leave the house, of course. Forgive me, Arnold. I wouldn't have had you come on it by chance like that for the world.'

'Who typed it?'

'My usual typist, the girl who does all my stuff. Oh, *that's* all right – she lives out at Turnham Green and knows nothing about any of us.'

'I suppose the occasional variations in the names of the characters she copied from your manuscript, then. Arnold and Audrey for Paul and Dorothea, I mean.'

'Oh, Arnold – I've not done that, have I? How terrible of

me. Yes, of course, the typist would copy it – they don't think, you know, they can't, they just type everything they see, or think they see ... I can't think how I came to slip into that, though, and not see it when I read it through. I suppose it was because they were so vivid to me. But you'd have known who they were meant for without that, wouldn't you?'

'I might have guessed. Only I shouldn't perhaps have read it but that I came on that. Why did you have it typed at all, I wonder?'

'I get all my stuff typed, Arnold. I wanted Peter to read it, and he won't read manuscript, you know. That was all; I just wanted Peter to read it, to see ...'

'To see?'

'Well, to see, you know, if there was any way of wrapping it up that would make it possible to publish it ever – perhaps in America.'

'Oh.'

He was looking at her owlishly, the light from the shaded lamp glowing on his glasses. He seemed to be trying to understand.

'Publish it ... But you can't publish it, can you? I mean, it's about us – that is, you meant it to be about us ...'

'I know, my dear. And *of course* I can't and shan't, not without your permission, and not without such changes as really would disguise it. You can trust me, can't you? It was just that I had to write it, to get it out of my head. It's done now, and I'll put it on the fire if you like.'

'If you don't mind,' said Arnold, gently and distantly.

She hesitated. 'You don't want even Peter to see it, do you mean?'

'Naturally, I would rather no one saw it.'

'The only thing is, Peter was in the middle of it, and he'll want to finish it. Shall I just let him do that? Oh, I won't if you say no. If you tell me to, I'll burn it here and now – both copies. She did two copies, of course.' Evelyn was not the woman to keep that back; according to her lights she was a gentlewoman, truthful though inquisitive.

Arnold considered for a moment before saying: 'No, I don't mind Peter finishing it, if he cares to. Of course, no one else must see it; it mustn't be left about, I mean.'

'Indeed, no. The other copy is in a locked drawer. It was terribly careless of Peter to leave this about the office; *anyone* might have got hold of it.'

'They might,' Arnold grimly agreed.

There was a moment of silence. What was he feeling about it? Evelyn put out the feelers of her mind towards him, groping, trying to discover. How much, of what she had told him in that story was new to him? How much had he already, in his heart, known?

'You didn't *mind* my writing that story, my dear?' she said, leaning forward to see his face, her long amber cigarette holder between two white fingers. 'I mean – it didn't hurt you?

'You must write what you like, of course.' He was courteous and cold. 'Hurt me? . . . No, it didn't hurt me, exactly. I thought it a mistake, and that one shouldn't perhaps write fiction about the people one knows best . . . The part about Audrey, for instance – she wouldn't like it, would she? I mean, however absurdly remote you've made it from the truth about her, still, it *is* meant for her, and she'd know it. Denham, too . . . No, I don't care for it, I must say.'

'I'm sorry. But you know, Arnold, all writers work that way – taking real people and letting them develop and grow. Real life has such a deadly fascination – drama ready made to one's hand.'

'I suppose so. Though in this case there wasn't much drama about till you wrote it up, was there ... I wonder, by the way, though it's of no consequence – why you made Denham behave in such a fantastically improbable manner? I suppose a wife merely taking a tour on her motor-bicycle would scarcely have made a dramatic enough situation. But anyone less likely to turn a situation into a triangle than Denham one can't imagine, can one? You got right out of her line of country there.'

Evelyn watched him curiously through wreathing smoke. Compassionate interest was in her eyes. How the boy hid from his own knowledge! Oh, she'd better say it right out, not leave suspicion to rankle in his soul. Be cruel to be kind; so often it was the only way.

'My dear, *no*.' She spoke with a greater gentleness than usual in her clear tones. 'Not out of her line of country, I'm afraid. I didn't invent that, Arnold; I wrote it from what I saw when I went down to St Ives.'

'From what you saw ... ' He was staring at her, a tide of red slowly surging over his neck and face.

'Yes. What I saw. I saw the man, Arnold; I saw the man.'

'*What* man, in heaven's name?'

'The young fisherman. I saw him myself. It was obvious what they both felt ... Oh, I don't know how far it had gone, but I do know she cared.'

'You're speaking of *Denham*,' he shot at her.

'Denham's human, Arnold. A woman who's once been in love isn't content without love again. You and she had come to an end – yes, really to an end, however you might manage to jog along together – and she found her man down there. I don't blame her; I blame no one. The thing's inevitable. I came home and wrote it all straight down; it developed and took on detail in my mind as I wrote, and I seemed to see it all. But it was all there before I wrote a word ... Didn't you guess, my dear, that Denham wouldn't stay away from you all this time unless there was that?'

'She's bicycling,' he stammered. 'She likes the country, and that kind of life. You – you don't understand Denham.'

'Are you sure *you* do, Arnold,' she gently answered. 'Or rather, my dear, are you sure you *don't*, in your heart? Hasn't Denham, beneath all that rather crude simplicity and childish love of open-air amusements, got a very human, passionate side? Even we, from outside, can see that, you know ...'

He was silent, staring on the floor, his forehead on his hand. Yes, Denham was human all right ... How sure Evelyn was, and how wise she seemed, and how utterly wrong she must be.

She had seen the man. How, in God's name, did she know it was the man? What was this occult power of divination to which women such as she laid claim, and which led them along such wild paths of fantasy? Feminine intuition, people called it ... Damn the lot of them. Meddling busybodies ... Yet he had always liked and admired Evelyn, and he still did so. She was kind.

He got up.

'You're quite wrong, you know,' he said. 'Is it too much to ask that you should destroy that thing without letting anyone but Peter see it, and not talk to anyone about it, or about Denham and me, or about . . .'

About Audrey, he meant, but, trying to say her name, he flushed and stuck. Evelyn had embarrassed him about Audrey for ever, creating that absurd situation between them. If Audrey were to read the thing, she too would be embarrassed for ever. Their relations would be spoilt. Audrey, of all people mustn't see it.

Evelyn, as always, understood.

'I won't talk of it to anyone,' she said quickly. 'And I'll destroy it – or lock it away in my desk – at once, and only Peter shall see it. Will that do?'

'Thank you. I shall be glad if you will do that.'

She took his hand in hers, holding it with her light, caressing touch.

'Good-bye, my dear. Forgive me when you can, for all this. I wouldn't, for the world, have had you stumble on that tale like that. Though I might have told it you sometime; I expect I should if I could have found courage at the right moment. Because, however hard things are, one ought to face them – put them in the light, and try to understand, not hide from them. Then they work out somehow to some end – make a pattern, you know, even though one can't see it at first. But it's terribly hard going for a time; I know that.'

'Thank you,' said Arnold. 'Good-bye.'

'And Arnold,' she added, 'another thing. Be gentle with that child. Go down to Cornwall and see her yourself, and talk it all out face to face. It's the only way.'

Arnold murmured something and went.

Evelyn sat on in the small fragrant room.

'Poor children,' she thought, 'poor dears; what a mess it all is. How will it work out? How little help one can really be, for all one's experience, and for all one's goodwill. But one has to try, and to trust for the best.'

4

The square was now full of cold grey fog. Someone was approaching the Greshams' house as Arnold left it; they met outside.

'Hallo, Arnold?'

'Oh – Audrey. Hallo.'

They stood for a moment face to face, wrapped by the dense evening as by blankets. Through it he saw, dimly, her pale, fair face under the soft hat she wore pulled down to her eyes.

'Have you been to see us?'

'Yes. Only your mother was in.'

'I know. Daddy's gadding round all day today. I'm sorry I missed you.'

'Yes, I'm sorry. I've got to get home now . . . Good night.'

He left her abruptly.

What's the matter with Arnold, she wondered, as she went in.

That damned story of Evelyn's, he said to himself. He couldn't forget it. It spoiled his ease with Audrey, the best of companions. The best of companions, of friends . . . the dearest person. So kind, so clever . . . nothing she didn't understand. She had grown so pretty, too . . . No, that was Dorothea in the book. All the same, Audrey *was* pretty, and clever, and kind, and dear. One could talk to her about anything; she was like an intelligent youth, with a girl's grace added.

Oh, why had Evelyn written that, invented all that, made something come alive between them? It had been such a good friendship, and now it was spoilt. These creators of situations – they created more than they knew. If it should be created for Audrey too, what then? It must not be ... Yet, if Evelyn were right, it was already recognised by Audrey. *If* Evelyn were right. But of course Evelyn wasn't right; no more right about Audrey and him than about Denham.

Denham. His thought jerked back to her. What did Evelyn mean by that vile nonsense about the fisherman? Of course she'd see a fisherman if she visited Denham by the sea; Denham always talked to fishermen. What sickening rot ... It was time Denham came home to give the lie to it. He would go down and fetch her back.

But where was she? She hadn't written lately. Her last picture postcard had been from St Ives again; she must have gone back there for a time. But she had given no address, and had probably left it before this. She was very bad at giving addresses. She didn't care, apparently, whether she heard from him or not. And she didn't mean him, obviously, to come and see her ... I can't, he thought, go about Cornwall vaguely looking for her. I must wait till she writes.

Or he might have an S.O.S. broadcasted. Will Mrs Chapel, last heard of at St Ives, Cornwall, come to Tavistock Square, London, where her husband is waiting, seriously anxious ...

Well, he thought, it's no good getting into a stew. The only thing is to put all this nonsense out of mind and go on as usual. Denham will come back when she thinks she will, and if she won't let me know where to find her I can't find her, so that's that. I'm not going to let Evelyn put us all about with her rubbish.

5

He let himself into the flat. A picture postcard lay on the passage table. On one side of it was a coloured view of a bright blue sea laving a bright yellow beach, and a pier black with a pleasure-seeking populace jutting out from the latter into the former. Under this was inscribed 'Newquay; the Pier.' On the reverse side was his address, an illegible postmark that looked like Padstow, and 'It has been very wet lately. We have stayed several days in Padstow, going on today. Fishing fair. Shall go through St Ives sometime soon, you might write to the P.O. there. Hope you are well, I am, D.C.'

It was the first communication which Denham had emitted for some days. Arnold sat down to write to the St Ives Post Office. He would ask her to come back at once; she *must* come back at once. He would say to Evelyn, 'Denham is coming back this week, by the way. I've just had a letter.'

Then they would settle down as before, and try again to make a job of it, try to be happy together, as they had been at first. They could be in the country more; if Denham liked they would go and live at Gerrards Cross or Missenden, or one of the other Londoners' dormitories, and he could come up every day, though he hated trains. Would that please her, he wondered? He added to his letter, 'Shall we give up the flat and live in Bucks or Surrey, some place from where I could get up to town easily? We will if you like.'

He was bribing her to come back, to come back and destroy Evelyn's situation, this monstrous thing which Evelyn had called to life with her novelistic imaginings.

A good letter, and he went out and posted it at once. But he never had any answer to it.

CHAPTER III

Noel and Audrey

I

It was mid-December. Noel was back from Oxford. The comparative warmth of London, where houses stand huddled together, street on street, each glowing with its heart of fire, and chimneys belch heat and dirt, and human creatures jostle and press one another, thawing the air with warm breath, the greater warmth of this genial city over university towns that stand congealed in cold fogs on their chill rivers, enveloped Noel with its gay comfort, even as its restless, vivid, many-coloured life dazzled and stimulated her mind with a wit, culture, learning and experience more adult and more comprehensive than the wit, culture, learning and experience of even the cleverest young gentlemen and ladies round about twenty years of age.

Certainly London was amusing and instructive, and certainly the Greshams' circle was not less so than the rest of London. They were so bright, so funny, so graceful, so informed, so *alive*, thought Noel, watching her family as they made happy the guests who had dined with them and the few more guests who had been requested to look in after dinner. Suppose the few more guests should actually only look in, thought Noel, look through the door or peer through chinks between the rose damask window curtains, smile at those within, and flit away. Suppose, she speculated, that people always did literally and precisely what they were bidden to do, took what was said to them at the foot of the letter, what a different world it would be, and how oddly it would behave. A world of people all behaving rather like Denham, who was at present perhaps the only literal adult person in it.

'Oh, she's left him. Hadn't you heard that?'

How often the delightful people said that! Noel always counted it one of their lapses into dullness, if not into bad taste. Someone had left someone, had joined some one else . . . Well, it seemed quite their own concern. And what could be less interesting as a topic? It wasn't even interesting that two persons should be together, still less so that they should have ceased to be together. What is interesting in personal relationships is the action and effect of persons on one another when they are together, the interaction of character, not the fact that they are together or that they are apart.

'Yes, she's gone off with a Cornish fisherman. That's the tale, anyhow. Evelyn Gresham saw the fisherman. It all sounds most suitable. Now she can catch pollock all day, or whatever it is one tries to catch in Cornwall. She always seemed so inappropriate as the wife of a London publisher . . . '

Noel crossed the room, to be out of earshot, a little frown on her childish forehead.

Guy passed her, carrying meat and drink to someone. She put out a hand to stop him.

'Guy.'

'Noel.'

'I want to speak to you.'

'Is it urgent? I'm being busy and polite, as you see.'

'Yes, it is rather urgent. Just for a moment, only.'

'Well, let me deliver this food and liquor first.'

He was back in a minute, standing by her, graceful and dark and lithe, looking like a gentleman of the eighteen-thirties and taking snuff from a silver box.

'Well, my child? What am I to do for you? Is there someone feeling solitary whom I ought to charm and solace?'

'Guy, come over here; it's private. They're talking about Denham – Mrs Waters and Mr Ansell over there. She was saying that Denham's left Arnold and gone away with someone in Cornwall. Can we stop them?'

Guy lightly shrugged his shoulders.

'I should think it improbable. Everyone's saying that just now. It's the talk of the moment. Didn't mother or Audrey tell you in their letters? I wonder at their restraint.'

'Audrey said she was still in Cornwall, bicycling about, and wouldn't come home or give an address, that's all. Now there's a fisherman come into it. They said mother'd seen him.'

'She did. She went down there on purpose to.'

Noel was silent for a moment.

'I suppose the story started from mother, then?' she said.

'It's not the first, is it? You must allow mamma her triangles. She'd be as lost without them as Euclid would.'

'Then,' Noel concluded, 'there's probably nothing in it at

all. I mean, mother just thinks of things. In any case, it's no business of any of ours, and we oughtn't to let people talk about it here. It's not fair on Denham or Arnold. Besides, it's cheek, talking about them like that. Will you tell them, Guy, that there's nothing in it and they mustn't say it?'

'It's not my part to interfere with the conversation of our guests, my dear. It would be inhospitable. It's our job to entertain them, not to check their innocent amusements.'

'Then I shall get daddy or Audrey to tell them.'

'You can, if you like. But it won't do the slightest good. It wouldn't be believed. Besides, we all believe the tale ourselves, you know. It sounds so probable. Mamma's quite positive about it. She's keeping it secret, but tells her friends in confidence, so it's done a little travelling about ... If you take my advice, Noel, you won't worry; after all, everyone's talking all the time about something and someone, and no bones are broken. It's a parlour game; there's no sense in barging into the middle of it and upsetting it all. No one takes it seriously, and no one cares whether or not Denham has eloped with a fisherman. For Arnold's sake and her own, I rather hope she has.'

'Whether she has or not,' Noel asserted, obstinately, 'is no one's business but hers and Arnold's—'

'And the fisherman's,' Guy put in.

'And I think it's rotten to talk about it when we don't know that it's happened. If you won't, I shall go and tell those people it's all a mistake.'

'Do what you feel you must, of course.'

Guy watched her, a smile in his eyes, as she crossed the room. He would have rather liked to have heard the interview, but he decided discreetly not to be involved in the affair, and returned to his son-of-the-house duties.

Noel, a faint pink rising in her face, approached the two talkers, who were now on the Diaghelev ballet, and said,' I'm awfully sorry to interrupt, but I heard you speaking just now about my cousin, Denham Chapel.'

They looked at her, polite, startled, uncertain of her meaning.

'Why, yes – I'm afraid we did ... I'm sorry – perhaps we oughtn't to have ...'

'There seems,' said Noel, in her clear-cut voice, 'to be a mistake about her. She's only on a motor-bicyling tour in Cornwall, you know, for a time.'

'Oh, my dear – of course. One repeats the nonsensical gossip one hears, you know – it's unpardonable, but one does.'

The man said, 'Hear, hear. It *is* unpardonable, and I've often said so. Do it myself all the same. So much for your romantic Cornish fisherman tale, Mrs Waters. He boils down to a bicy-cling tour in Cornwall. Half these stories burst if you prick them; I've often said so. Thanks very much, Miss Gresham. If I hear that story again I'll set it right.'

'Of course,' his companion agreed. 'I must say it didn't seem a *likely* story. But you know how one picks things up, likely and unlikely. I promise I won't pass that one on again, anyhow.'

They were nice people. But they didn't believe Noel. Next time, Mrs Waters repeated the story it would be with Noel's amendment, dubiously and amusedly proffered. When a dull story and an interesting story conflict, the dull one has no chance. To Noel's taste the duller tale was the one about going off with a fisherman, but to most people this seemed more interesting than bicycling in Cornwall. There is no accounting for tastes.

'Thank you,' said Noel, and turned away.

2

From the window recess Noel looked across the room at her mother, who sat on the sofa talking, all bright animation, to a little group. How graceful she was, leaning forward, one slim leg crossed over the other, her cigarette in its immoderately long holder in her hand, her small white face uptilted from her long white neck, her dark, closely cut head, her thin, lithe body, of the shape commonly and oddly described as 'boyish' – (oddly, since it is the way in which about half the British female sex are constructed, which gives them a bad name on the Continent, and it has, in its flat slightness, little of a boy's solid robustness) – well, anyhow, how charming and how exquisite Evelyn was. It was scarcely credible that she was the elderly mother of four adults. Her wide green eyes looked from under their black lashes, shining in the soft shaded light. How large they were ... People with large, wondering eyes will believe anything. They are often religious; sometimes even spiritualists; oftener still, they believe anything they find interesting. Really believe it, thought Noel; the people with smaller eyes and less belief should not judge them as liars, for they are only believers. Sceptics, who do not believe easily, should be fair. Noel had smallish grey-green eyes, so had her father; Guy's dark eyes were not large, and Audrey's clear grey-blue were medium size. Denham's were small, and set far back and deep; Denham believed very little indeed.

Of course mother may be right, thought Noel. Denham may

have left Arnold and taken up with a fisherman. There's nothing to show, either way. It's not more likely because mother thinks it, and, added Noel fairly, not actually more unlikely. The people with large eyes are sometimes right. Often they have a queer talent, an uncanny knack of pitching on the truth. Often they are abnormally silly. In either case, they speculate and talk about other people's concerns, and that's revolting. They ought never to be allowed alone with another person, for that makes them worse. They should always be in lots of several at once, like Japanese.

Evelyn's clear laugh rang out.

Well, of course, she was charming, and amusing, and clever, and a darling ...

'What are you thinking about, little 'un?' Peter was at her side, smiling at her grave, intent face.

Noel took a cigarette, and lit it at his.

'I was looking at mother, daddy.'

'Worth looking at, eh?' His fond and proud glance followed hers.

'Yes. Mother's lovely ... I was just thinking, suppose her eyes had been half the size they are ...'

'Then she'd be less lovely, wouldn't she. Like big green lamps in her face, aren't they. The finest in the room, eh? Oh, no, it would never do to have them half the size; what a blasphemous notion.'

His own eyes dwelt on his graceful wife with proud love. His girls were pretty dears, and Noel rather lovely, but they were nothing to their mother. When *they* were five-and-forty, they couldn't hope to have her style ...

'Anyhow,' Noel said practically, 'that's the size they are.'

The people who had dined and the people who had looked in had all looked out and gone.

Noel was in Audrey's room, smoking a last cigarette in her pyjamas and dressing-gown, and eating marrons glacés taken from the party, while Audrey crouched before the gas fire, drying her short waves of light brown hair. They were talking, as girls talk in the evening.

'But it's quite likely true, Noel,' Audrey mumbled, her head muffled within folds of towel. 'Mother's certain of it, from what she saw when she was there.'

'I didn't say it wasn't true,' Noel mumbled back, her mouth full of marron. 'I don't know and I don't care. Why should I? It may be true and it may not. Denham may have gone off with twenty fishermen, a whole flight of fishermen—'

'You say a shoal,' Audrey corrected, 'when it's sea creatures.'

'Shoal, then. She may, and she may not. All I mean is, I don't believe it in the least more because mother's sure it's true. Don't you remember when mother said Dick Grantham had left Margery and gone to Biarritz with a woman, and it turned out it was his aunt? And when she got worried and told everyone she thought Molly Harding was taking to drugs and drink and going dotty? And when she got it into her head that I had something wrong with my lungs, and that Babs Prittie had gone abroad to have a baby, and all the times she imagined people were in love when they weren't?' Audrey began to say something behind the towel, and stopped. 'The fact is,' Noel went on, 'mother *magnifies*. She can't help it. I think things should be *minimised*. I like them small, and it does less harm ... Anyhow, we've no business to say that Denham's left Arnold when all we know is that she's away in Cornwall for a bit. Mother hands round stories because she believes them and is interested and can't help sharing confidences, and Guy because gossip amuses him, and you don't stop them, you often help. Why do you? I can't understand about you, Audrey. I can't make out whether you like that sort of thing or don't. But it seems to me you do,' Noel concluded, with dispassionate younger sisterly severity.

Audrey, rubbing her tousled head, considered herself.

'I don't actually understand myself,' she said, with interest. 'I'm mixed, I think. Partly I get interested in the stories, like mother, and partly I'm amused, like Guy, because they're so silly, and partly I think I get hypnotised by mother, like daddy, and only a bit of me sits apart, scornful and gentlewomanly and disapproving. I see it's low and underbred to gossip, but I do gossip; I've even passed on secrets sometimes, just to amuse or interest people. That's terribly caddish. When I'm mother's age, I dare say I shall go on talking about people all the time. Still, I expect I'll always know it's low ... It's this infernal interest in *people* that women have. The only safe way, if one's a woman, is to be like Denham, and not want to talk about anything but the weather, and food, and things like that. Only it would be awfully dull, Or to be like you, really pure. (*Don't!* you disgusting sticky little pig; I take it back, then, you're not pure a bit.) My lower nature gets back on me all the time, and one moment I talk about books or politics or places or ideas quite respectably, and the next about someone's liaison. I expect it can't be helped.'

251

Audrey finished analysing herself, and began to rub Pond's cold cream into her face and neck.

'Don't you find it refreshing and delicious?' Noel absently enquired, 'and that its pure oils sink deep into the pores, thoroughly cleansing them and bringing to the surface all impurities, leaving the skin clear, supple and rejuvenated and removing that tired, lined look? ... Look here, Audrey, we've got, somehow, to stop this romance about Denham. We must make her come home.'

'And desert the fisherman? She won't even send Arnold her address, my dear. He hasn't an idea where she is. She hasn't written for ages, I believe. Really, you know, it does begin to look rather suspicious.'

Noel got up and stretched.

'I shall go and find her,' she announced.

'Where? Somewhere in Cornwall? You might look for a month.'

'I shall go at once,' said Noel, 'and bring her back. She's a perfectly prize ass, but I shall make her come.'

'Shall you bring the fisherman, too? It would be nice to make his acquaintance, now we've heard so much of him.'

'No. The fisherman can stay and go on fishing. I shall tear them apart.'

'There'll be a parental fuss when you suggest starting off alone in mid-winter to explore the Duchy for Denham.'

'I don't propose to suggest it, ass. I suppose I can go away by myself for a few days on my own concerns without anyone objecting. You're not to tell anyone, Audrey.'

'All right, old thing, I wish you luck, but don't expect it. How shall you get about Cornwall, by the way?'

'Train and legs.'

'The weather will be rotten. Where shall you start looking?'

'I've not thought yet. I shall collect what data I can from Arnold.'

'Arnold? You'll tell him, then?'

'I shall tell him I'm going to see Denham, if I can find her. He won't mind. I don't know why he hasn't gone himself, long ago.'

'He doesn't know where she is. And he's feeling rather hurt, I suppose, and proud, and doesn't want to bother her if she doesn't want him. Mother says he knows about the fisherman. I expect she told him, but she seems to think he had some independent knowledge of it.'

'Bunkum. Of course she told him. Mother's always telling people things and then saying they knew already. Usually it grows into *their* having told *her*. The fact is, when mother and anyone with at all the same gifts get together, things don't need to be told; stories simply build themselves up, like genies out of smoke wreaths, and there they are, and no one knows who started them. It's a funny trade ... Has Arnold spoken about it to you at all?'

'No. Arnold doesn't talk to me much these days. He's queer – somehow shy. He only talks about books and things.'

Noel nodded approval.

'Very sensible of him. If we all kept to that ... Well, good night. I shall probably go to Cornwall the day after tomorrow.'

4

Audrey, getting into bed, thought of another example which she could have added, only had not, to Noel's list of their mother's imaginings. It had been a fortnight ago.

'Darling child, you don't suppose I don't know ...'

'Know what, mother?'

'All there is to know, sweetheart. You; Arnold; the whole tangle of it ... I'm inclined to think you should go away, dearest, for a bit. Why not go with the Barringtons to the Riviera?'

'Mother, why should I? There's nothing to know about me and Arnold – you've imagined it all. Oh, for goodness' sake – you've not talked to Arnold about it?'

'Oh, no, child, no. But I know, I can feel, that Arnold knows I know.'

'Oh, mother, please drop it. I tell you there's nothing to know. I suppose you mean Arnold and I are in love – or that one of us is. Well, we're not. We're great friends, as we've always been. He's in love with Denham, I suppose, and I'm in love with no one. Mother, you *mustn't* talk like that, it's too bad.'

'My dear, you don't suppose you can't trust me. But I won't mention it again, even to you. In fact, I wasn't going to. These aren't things to be talked about.'

'But you must get it out of your head, mother. It's simply not true.'

'Oh, Audrey, you can trust me.'

'Darling, I don't trust you farther than I can see you. You're hopeless. But for God's sake, don't set people talking about me and Arnold. It would be such a dreadful bore, and we'd both hate it so. It's not fair on Denham, either.'

'Oh, Denham. Denham's got her own affair to run; Denham's counted herself out ... But of course, sweetheart, you can trust me not to set people talking, or to talk myself. Only I wanted you to know that I knew and cared ...'

'I'd much rather you *didn't* know and care. But I suppose

you must have it your own way, you'll never believe me. Only if I find you've been talking to Arnold about it, I shall go and live alone in rooms in Shepherd Market. Or else marry Mr Brigham, the dentist, if he'll have me. He's much handsomer than Arnold.'

'Silly child. Give me a kiss and go and get ready for dinner.'

No; Audrey hadn't told Noel that. It cut too near the bone. It had gone far to spoil her friendship with Arnold, for she divined his new shy aloofness to be the outcome of an embarrassment like her own, caused by perceiving her mother's thoughts about them. Consciously or unconsciously, Evelyn had created a new relation between them, destroyed the old frank affection and camaraderie, destroyed it by the simple process of calling it something else. It hadn't turned into anything else; it had merely wilted away, leaving a void. In time it might revive again . . . Or something else might . . . At present, each, having been assured that the other loved, held back doubting, startled and shy, yet oddly moved. They builded better than they knew, these fictionists.

CHAPTER IV

Noel and Denham

I

Noel walked along the cliff path from Polrew in the dark of the December afternoon. A soft fog folded sea and land. Through it pierced the shrill cries of gulls and the deep cries of ships at sea.

The gorse and turf round the path dripped with mist. Only a few yards in front and to the sides were to be seen; the path ran twistily into a blind country. The mist beaded Noel's coat, her rucksack, her bare head, her brows and lashes. She was a wet phantom alone in a wet phantom world. As she walked she hummed whisperingly a cold little stave from Bach, that was like the cold whispering of the winter sea.

From out the hidden distance came the yap yap that small dogs utter when excited. Something came scuttling and tumbling through the gorse scrub, and a damp little rough creature flung himself at Noel's legs.

'Isaac! Good boy, good old man. There, calm yourself. Yes, all right, I'm coming.'

Isaac dashed ahead, looking over his shoulder to call her. A square mass loomed out of the mist; the cottage defined itself. There it stood, its slate roof shiny and dripping, and at its open door stood its owner, looking out, a mug of tea in one hand, a slice of bread and jam in the other.

'Hallo,' said Noel.

'Hallo,' said Denham. 'Have some tea?'

'Thanks very much.'

They went inside. Noel took off her wet coat and sat by the fire, drying the fog off her, while Denham filled another mug with hot tea.

'Bread and jam?' Denham cut a slice, spread it, and handed it to her guest. Then she sat down and went on with her own tea.

'Are you alone?' she enquired.

'Yes. I came down to see you.'

'What made you think I was here? I hadn't told anyone.'

'I know. But I guessed you might be. Anyhow, I came here first to look. I hope you don't mind much.'

Denham considered this, as she spread some more bread and jam.

'No. Not as you're alone I don't . . . I didn't tell Arnold I was here again because I was afraid he might mention it to people who might come.'

'Mm,' Noel agreed, and neither alluded more nearly than that to Evelyn.

'How long have you been back here?' Noel asked presently.

'Ten days . . . They've been in while I was away. They picked the lock of the door and came in.'

'Did they take things?'

'Yes, a few.'

Denham's glance strayed to the boarded floor.

'They'd no business in here.' Old, unspent resentment was in her voice. 'Prying about. They'd read about it in that paper, and came to look.'

Noel nodded. 'I heard about the paper.' No personal sympathy, but impersonal distaste for papers, for those who tell things, for the inquisitive, for those who repeat and those who pry, was discernible in the faint, amused twist of her brows. She set down her empty mug, and seemed to be going to say no more about the paper, its readers, what they had read, or what, if anything, they had found when they came to look.

As the two young girls sat together in silence, something in each, something virginal, childish and remote, found response in the other, and, without words, the young barbarian and the product of a fastidious civilisation became friends, as children become friends, suddenly, with tacit recognition.

Denham stood up.

'Shall I show you the passage to the sea?'

'Yes, please.'

Denham pulled up the boards of the floor and descended into the cellar, torch in hand. Noel followed her hostess. A few minutes later they were in the cave sitting-room.

'Frightfully useful,' said Noel, sitting on one of the camp stools and looking about her with approval.

She was the only person except Denham who had used that particular adjective about the cave. It was the right adjective, but most people wouldn't apply it; they would say 'thrilling,' or jolly,' or 'romantic' or something.

'It's been useful all right,' said Denham. 'But they've found it now. They came exploring into it while I was away.'

'Bad luck. But they may forget about it later on.'

'No,' said Denham gloomily. 'It will never be safe again. Now come on to the sea.'

They crawled down the slimy tunnel to the cliff cave. Looking out through the hole, they saw and heard the mist-bound sea. Its cold, hidden whispering shivered in their ears. They dropped down into the cave, and the rising tide slapped the rocks at their feet.

'Shall we go back through the passage,' Denham asked, 'or over the cliff? There's an easy way up along there.'

'I'll go through the passage,' said Noel, 'and you the other way. I'd like to see which is quicker.'

'The cliff is. But we'll try. I won't run.'

She scrambled along the sea's edge to the way up the cliff, and Noel climbed again into the tunnel.

2

Denham had been in the cottage for five minutes when Noel emerged through the floor.

'Walking is quicker than crawling, you see,' Denham explained, replacing the boards. 'Are you going to stay the night? You can. There's a bed and food.'

'May I? Thank you, I'd like to.'

'You can stay two nights if you like,' said the hostess, after a moment's consideration.

'No, thanks. I shall go home tomorrow.'

'All right.' Denham felt the relief that follows unaccepted hospitality.

'But,' she added, 'you can stay if you like, you know. I don't

mind your staying.' There was a faint emphasis on the posses-
sive pronoun.

'Thanks awfully. But I'm going home. I only came to see
you. When are you coming, by the way?'

'Well, I don't quite know.'

'Arnold asked me, if I saw you, to say he wished you'd come
soon. He says he wrote to St Ives, but you didn't answer.'

'I expect I didn't get his last letters. I didn't call for them.
I came here instead. And I didn't write from here because I
didn't want people to know I was here. I was going to write,
though, soon.'

'Arnold said he'd written to you that he wanted to go and
live in the country, near enough for him to catch a train to
London each morning. Bucks, he seems to be thinking about.'

'Oh!' Denham, too, thought about Bucks.

'I wonder which part.'

'I don't know. He probably wants you to help him in finding
a place. There are some good places in Bucks.'

'Yes.' Denham had walked and bicycled in this county.

'Not a bad idea,' she said.

'Well, you'd better come up and see about it, or he'll be finding a place for himself.'

'Yes,' said Denham. 'I shall come ... As a matter of fact, I
was thinking of coming before long, anyhow for a bit. I got
rather tired of being on the move, and the weather's rotten
now. And now they've found out about the passage, it's not
quite so private here as it was. And it's time I saw Arnold
again ... If you like I'll take you up in the side-car tomorrow.
Isaac can sit on your knee, if you'll hold on to him.'

'Yes, let's.'

Noel said presently, 'Shall I wash up the tea-things?'

'If you'd rather they were washed before supper. I don't usually wash up myself till the day's meals are over. But you can, if you like.'

Noel did so. She was a very clean, neat girl, and washed and dried with beautiful care and precision. Denham sat by the fire smoking, with Isaac dreaming at her feet. Both were torpid, and undisturbed by the activities at the sink.

Noel, placing the clean crockery on the dresser, glanced at Denham in passing, and thought she had a heavy, pale kind of look.

'You don't look up to much,' she commented.

Denham raised her eyes from the fire.

'Don't I?' She paused, and added absently, 'I've not had enough exercise lately.'

She had a queer, vague, strayed look about her, thought Noel; somehow she wore a new air, less defined, as if she had lost her way and was tired, too tired to find it again for the moment. An odd new look for Denham ... Perhaps it was a trick of candle and firelight, throwing their blurred shadows on the pale face and deep eye sockets. A *helpless* look; yes, almost that was the word.

'Nothing to do with me,' thought Noel, and lit a cigarette and sat down.

'What way shall we go tomorrow?' she enquired, seeing the map on the floor.

Denham picked it up and spread it out. Whatever ways she might have lost, no way traceable on a map was among them.

CHAPTER V

The Fisherman's Child

Every year, in the deep mid-winter, there descends upon this world a terrible fortnight. A fortnight, or ten days, or a week, when citizens cannot get about the streets of their cities for the surging pressure of persons who walk therein; when every shop is a choked mass of humanity, and purchases, at the very time when purchases are most numerously ordained to be made, are only possible at the cost of bitter hours of travail; a time when nerves are jangled and frayed, purses emptied to no purpose, all amusements and all occupations suspended in favour of frightful businesses with brown paper, string, letters, cards, stamps, and crammed post offices. This period is doubtless a foretaste of whatever purgatory lies in store for human creatures.

But it is only the naturally idle who find Christmas terrible. The active and industrious enjoy scrambling about streets and shops and doing up parcels and waiting in post offices and giving pleasure by their gifts. They are exhilarated by the bustle and the scrum, and by the thought of the Little Children's Joy. They find Christmas a season of cheer and goodwill, and welcome it each year with a brave and generous smile.

Among these admirable beings was Evelyn Gresham. The seasonable crowds in the streets did indeed get on her nerves and tire her physically and mentally, so that she came home after each day's shopping a disintegrated wreck, but she remained a happy wreck. Her sense of Christmas exhilaration never failed to revive her again in a few hours. She might kill herself in the battle, but, dying, her spirit would still greet the spirit of Christmas with a gay smile of fellowship. She loved to spend and to give. She would think out delicate and lavish gifts for each friend, each relation, plunge into the maelstrom, and emerge with some object, not that she had thought of, but more brilliantly fantastic and charming. She was a shopper of charm and distinction; she made of the tedious business a gay and lovely game.

So now, at five o'clock on the feast of poor dubious St Thomas, she came home to Mulberry Square in the dark, frosty afternoon, laden and hung about with packages, her voice broken and hoarse from exhaustion, feeling and looking like an all but extinguished lamp that yet indomitably glows.

In the drawing-room, Peter, having fled early from the storm of Christmas books under which his office lay drifted deep, sat, as men will at Christmas time, above the battle, drinking tea with his daughters. Evelyn sank on to a sofa and closed her eyes.

'My dears! I love you, you know I love you all, but I can't talk. I'm like a frog. The fog and the fatigue ... The shops are terrible. I never saw them worse. And I've been hearing the most dreadful news. Tea, Audrey, please. Noel, darling, disentangle these parcels from my arm.'

'What news?' they asked.

'About Joan Ashley's husband. It seems he's the worst man ever. Cocaine, morphine, drink, women, disease ... everything there is, don't you know. And there's that poor child tied up to him only last week. It haunts me. Yet what can one do about it?'

'Obviously nothing,' said Peter. 'So don't let's worry. It's probably all exaggerated, too. Very few men are as bad as all that.'

'Anyhow,' Noel put in serenely, 'he's not our husband, so we don't have to think about his crimes. I suppose Joan likes him, or she wouldn't have taken him.'

'Oh, that's simply unkind, Noel. You none of you care a bit about people's troubles. I think it's too awful, and someone ought to tell the Ashleys.'

'They probably know,' Audrey suggested, 'if he's really as bad as all that. I mean, they saw quite a lot of him before the marriage. You can't go in for all those amusements and keep them dark.'

'No. No, they don't know. He took them in. He kept decent during the engagement, and now he's relapsing again. It's too terrible, poor child.'

'I wouldn't let it spoil my tea, mother darling. It's Joan's funeral, after all, not yours. And she can always divorce him if she wants to.'

'She won't want to; she's head over ears in love with the fellow. That's the worst part of it ... I do think life's dreadful, but none of you care a bit. And I called at Tavistock Square and saw Denham.' Her hoarse voice had almost died away, but with the last sentence it revived, taking on body and import.

'The door was open, so I went in. She hasn't been at home

264

any of the other times I've been, but this time I found her. I don't think she much wanted to meet me. And when I saw her, I knew why. You didn't tell me that, Noel.'

'Didn't tell you what, mother?'

'That Denham is going to have a child.'

'I didn't know she was. She didn't tell me.'

'She wouldn't, of course. But it's quite apparent. Of course I knew it the moment I saw her. But she wouldn't talk about it.'

'Well, why should she? After all, there's nothing to say. Either you are going to have a child or you aren't, and in either case there's nothing to say about it except that.'

Evelyn gave her younger daughter a pitying glance as she left the room with her book.

'There may be a great deal to say. But Denham, naturally, wouldn't choose to say it, in this case.'

'How do you mean, in this case?' Audrey asked.

But Peter knew what she meant, for he remembered Chapter Six of *Paul and Barbara*.

'*I'm going to have his child.*'

'*His child? You wouldn't have mine.*'

'*No. But I want to have his. It's different . . .*'

That confounded fisherman again.

'Really, Eve,' began Peter, and stopped.

'Oh, yes, Peter, it's all right. I'm not going to say a word to anyone about it; you needn't be afraid . . . Anyhow, there it is, and talk won't mend it, whatever's happened.'

'You mean you think the child won't be Arnold's,' said Audrey, with the indifferent candour of her generation, which always worried Peter. He broke out uneasily. 'Don't talk in that improper way, either of you. It's revolting.'

'It is, quite,' Audrey calmly agreed. 'You'd better go back to the office, daddy; the drawing-room is no place for you.'

'It's all right, Peter. No one's going to talk of it. In point of fact, there's nothing to say. And we can't know, of course; we can only guess ... I do wonder how much she's told Arnold – if she's told him anything at all, which I doubt. I've not seen Arnold since she got back. How does he seem?'

'Quite well, I think,' Peter answered. 'Just as usual. I've not noticed him particularly. I've had too much to do, and so has he.'

'We've all been rather irritable at the office,' Audrey added. 'We always are at Christmas, aren't we, daddy?'

'Oh, and that house at Great Missenden,' cried Evelyn. 'The Cliffords *are* giving it up this Christmas. I must tell Arnold. It will suit them exactly. In metro-land, and such nice people all about. A darling little house and garden. They *must* have a car, though; relying entirely on the Met. is too awkward, with so many strikes and so few late trains. They must go down and see it before the Cliffs turn out. The Cliffs will give them introductions, so they'll start off knowing the people worth knowing; that makes a move so much more cheerful at first. I'm afraid Arnold may feel it a bit lonely for a time, even coming up every day. After all, it's not London; metro-land can't be London. But it will suit Denham better, particularly with this baby coming on ... The question is, will she let it come, or will she be as reckless as last time? That's it; will she let it come? There are quite two sides to the question this time ...'

The baby was still the fisherman's, her husband and daughter perceived.

'Of course,' Evelyn pursued her line of reflection, '*if* it's not

Arnold's, she *ought* to tell him. Absolutely, you know, she *ought*. What I mean is, he ought to know.'

'Well,' said Peter, 'that's between her and him. Anyhow, no one else can butt in with unfounded allegations. Even if the thing was a certainty, not a fancy, no one else could butt in. That's quite obvious, isn't it?'

'Of course it's obvious. There's no question of anyone else butting in. All I say is, she ought to tell him. If she hasn't, you know. But I wouldn't be surprised if she had. Denham's terribly truthful really. Reserved, you know, but honest. I don't believe she *could* conceal a thing like that from him, even if she wanted to. I believe she'd blurt it straight out, and I shouldn't wonder if she has.'

'Well, you'd better stop talking and thinking about it, hadn't you, or *you* might blurt it out sometime when someone else was there. That would never do, you know. Never do at all.'

'Of course not, Peter. You know I'm safe as the grave. But you're right; it *is* best not to speak of it, even among ourselves. There it is, and talking won't mend it if it is so. And, after all, life moves on. Yes, life moves on all the time. One has to trust life, or where are we? Good could come, even out of that.'

Even out of Denham and Arnold bringing up a fisherman's child in metro-land, she meant.

CHAPTER VI

Go and Live in Metro-land

I

It was a dear little house, standing in a dear little garden, well back from the road, at the station end of Great Missenden village, and it was called Well Cottage. Arnold and Denham moved into it at the end of January. Evelyn came down from town to help them to settle in, together with Arnold's mother, just back from Luxor, who was to spend a few days with them, helping to get things straight. They had a cheerful, bustling day, hanging pictures and curtains and dragging furniture about the rooms and disputing about its position. Denham was inert and silent through these activities. She felt listless, and did not care whether the bureau stood against the window wall or the opposite one, or whether the Cézanne looked its best over the fireplace or elsewhere, or what the spare bedroom was like (except for an impulse, not uncommon among hostesses, to make this as repulsive as possible, in order to spite visitors from coming to stay). Denham thought she could have managed the move more expeditiously by herself; there would, somehow, have been less of it. In her cottage, things had been soon settled. 'They,' when moving, hustle and bustle and make a to-do. Things settle themselves all right if you leave them alone; this is a maxim which 'they' too often overlook, in house moving as in other departments of life.

2

Denham left them to it after lunch, and went out with Isaac. The important thing about a home is not what it is like inside, but what country surrounds it. Denham knew the Missenden country already; it lacked excitement and was over-built, but it had a quiet Buckinghamshire charm, and there were some small woods near, and what pass in metro-land for hills.

She ascended the lane that led over the railway, and entered a dripping grove of trees. Here, in the chill, secret January hush, she stood concealed, looking down at the villa-dotted valley and the long line of Great Missenden village. It all looked very civilised, very cultivated, very residential. The country abode of hundreds of professional Londoners – lawyers, doctors, publishers, journalists, business men, all catching an electric train to Baker Street five mornings a week, an electric train back from Baker Street five evenings. Except when they, with or without their females, stopped the night in London, for some of those nocturnal activities which Londoners practise. Metro-landers have *pieds-à-terre* in London. Arnold had retained for himself and his wife a room in the Tavistock Square house which they could occupy when they chose. It was all very convenient. Arnold could be in London as much as he liked, and Denham as little as she liked.

'But I expect we'll both pretty often want to be up, for theatres, and to see people, and all that,' he had said to her.

'Yes, I expect so,' she had agreed.

For Denham was getting back, numbly acquiescent, to acceptance of the Higher Life. What was the good of revolt? Life was too strong; it forced one. One was trapped by love, by that blind storming of the senses, by that infinite tenderness, that unreasoning, unreasoned friendship, which was love. This was the trap, this was the snare ... It had been the undoing of Mr Dobie, and it was now his daughter's. Love broke one in the end, ground one down, locked the fetters on one's free limbs. If you had never loved, you could be happy, loafing, idle and alone, exploring new places, sufficient to yourself. Once committed to love, you couldn't; it came baldly, to that. You had to go back. Love was the great taming emotion; perhaps the only taming emotion. It defeated all other desires in the end. You might struggle and rebel but in the end love got you.

Further, to make quite sure of you, love set its seal on you by giving you a child. When Denham had first perceived that this occurrence had again overtaken her, she had known that the struggle to live in her own way was over. She must have this child; she could not again fight against it. Arnold must have his way. Because she loved Arnold, she would go and live again as he lived, surrounded by people, civilisation and fuss, she would bear his child, tend and rear it, become a wife and a mother instead of a free person, be tangled in a thousand industries and cares, a thousand relationships, instead of soaking in idleness alone.

Then the plan of a house in the country had brightened this prospect. Living in Bucks, one would be freer, less civilised and polite, more alone. Perhaps, except for the servants, one need see no one much. One could dress as one liked. The Greshams would be miles away. One need no longer accept invitations, no longer have people dropping in by day and night. The room in town was dangerous, but of course, Arnold must be able to stay up when he wanted to. Oh, yes, one could surely be freer in Bucks than in London, even if the residences of Londoners were dotted all over the landscape like currants in a crowded cake. The thing was not to get to know any of them, if possible. Once you know your neighbours, you are no longer free, you are all tangled up, you have to stop and speak when you are out and you never feel safe when you are in.

Then had come Evelyn's, 'The Cliffs have told everyone about you; all their friends will call early. I believe there's a terribly nice set down there,' and Arnold's pleased, 'Oh, good.'

A cold fear had grown in Denham. What if Bucks should be as sociable, almost as sociable, as London? Almost as sociable, and with fewer ways of escape, for at least in London you don't meet your friends much in the streets, but on the bare and rolling roads of Bucks what shelter have you from encounters with the terribly nice set, who will engage you in conversation and cast perceptive glances at the holes in your stockings? What if Great Missenden should be but another compartment of the trap? Oh, life itself was the trap, and love the piece of toasted cheese that baited it, and, the bait once taken, there was no escape.

The bait ... Even that had lost some of its savour. Arnold had welcomed back his wife, but rather with gentleness than ardour. Moments of ardour had come since, but between these moments was a kind of puzzled questioning of her, of himself, of their love, that would have been more apparent to a more conscious and perceptive mind than Denham's. Vaguely she had supposed that he was vexed with her for staying away so long, and left it at that. As the days went by, his gentleness and kindness deepened, the shade of doubtful hesitation disappeared. He seemed to take her and their coming child into his affectionate, solicitous, and almost remorseful care, and to be striving to recapture the love that had so shaken them only a year ago. They were dead, those old ardours and raptures, and an unexuberant ghost did duty in their stead.

What did it matter? The bait had done its work; these two were safe and snug in the trap, and had no more need of toasted cheese.

Denham and Isaac left the damp copse and went down to Well Cottage, shivering a little in the dank air.

3

Denham rang the bell of her front door, for she had taken no key out with her. Winifred admitted her, and from the hall she heard voices conversing in the drawing-room – Mrs Chapel's loud and brisk, Evelyn's, loud and clear, and two strange new voices, loud and polite.

'They' had got in, then.

'Two ladies have called, ma'am,' said Winifred, and, sure enough, their cards lay on the hall table – a Mrs Someone, a Miss Someone else. The vanguard of the terribly nice set.

As Denham stood in the hall, the drawing-room door opened, and they all came out together, talking away, loud and brisk, loud and clear, loud and polite.

'Why, here she is,' cried Denham's mother-in-law and aunt, and introduced her to Mrs Someone, to Miss Someone else.

'We're such near neighbours, we're hoping to see quite a lot of you,' they said. 'You know, the path leading to your house from the road behind runs *almost* through our garden. The Cliffords spoke of you to us; dear things, we knew them so well, we and they were always in and out of one another's houses. You'll find Great Missenden a very sociable place, Mrs Chapel, so I hope you haven't come to the country for a retired life!'

'If you're going, go,' said Denham to them silently, behind her passive, acquiescent face. 'If you're going, go; don't stand about the hall like that. If you're always in and out of this house it's the time now for being out of it, you've had your go at being in.'

'Good-bye,' she said, taking the friendly offered hands.

'And I hope we shall be seeing you often, too,' they said to Evelyn, whom they had met before.

'Oh, I expect I shall be running down quite often, if these children will let me,' Evelyn brightly replied.

They went at last, after the usual dairyings with politenesses, coats and umbrellas.

The three ladies went into the drawing-room.

'Nice of them to call quite at once like that,' said Mrs Chapel, standing before the Cézanne, her head at a critical angle. 'They thought we'd got it all wonderfully straight in the time, Denham, and that it all looked charming. They're hoping to see quite a lot of you, with Arnold so much in town . . . I *think* this is right here, don't you, dear?'

'Quite all right,' Denham replied. She was not looking at

the Cézanne, but at the door and windows, with a kind of dull, half-dazed expression.

She'd come back stupider than ever, both ladies thought, not unkindly. Too stupid, almost, even for metro-land . . .

Evelyn said she must go. She kissed Denham, and said she would be down again soon.

'It's no distance, really; in the car it's no way at all. You'll be always running up and we running down.'

Mrs Chapel went with her to the garden gate.

Denham stood in the little hall, her arms hanging loosely at her sides, and Isaac nuzzling against her legs.

Mrs Chapel came in, brisk, stout and competent, rubbing her chilled hands together.

'Well, that's been nice, having your aunt down. She has such a good eye for a room. Now, Denham dear, you mustn't stand about like that, you're doing quite too much. I'm going to put you on the drawing-room sofa with a rug, and you're going to have some tea and a good rest, while I hang the little etchings. I shall send Winifred up for a rug and a hot bottle. And for your slippers – my dear child, those shoes are soaking, that will never do. You really must be very, very careful this time, you know you must, don't you . . . That's it, let me tuck you well in. Quite comfy? That's good. Now we've time for quite a nice long talk before Arnold gets home.

'First, a little about house management, if it won't bother you. Because you know, child, you've got a good deal still to learn about that. It's not an easy business, running a house and servants; you've got to put brains into it, if it's to be done well. It used to worry me dreadfully, I remember, when I first began it. I wasn't naturally good at it, and it seemed to take such a big slice out of one's time and energies. In a way, of course, you've more time to give to it than I've ever had, because I've always been at work on some book, or digging with my husband, or something. But anyhow, much time or little, a married woman's got to do it. One's got to see to it that things aren't all hugger-mugger in the house, and that one's man has a comfortable home to come back to from his day's work. Servants won't do it by themselves; the mistress of the house *has* to see to things ... Of course it's worse when the babies begin coming; one has one's hands full then, I can tell you. I had to give up my other work altogether for a time, while the children were little. You'll be a better mother and house manager than I was, I hope, because you've no other job dragging at you. But you won't mind my giving you a few hints now, will you? It seems the moment for it, now you've just got into this dear little house and settled into it. And after all, what *is* the good of one's painfully amassed experience if one can't pass it down to the younger people?

'Well, first, then, you should really make out a time-table for the maids' week's work. It's the only way of getting everything done in order. Monday morning clean the silver, Tuesday the knives, Wednesday, the paint, Thursday, the taps – and so on through the week. No day without something cleaned. And one room thoroughly turned out each day, too – that's most important.'

'Turned out ...' Denham repeated it vaguely.

'Yes, turned out. The things all taken out of the room and put back again, you know.'

What for, Denham silently wondered. The same result would surely be achieved, with less effort, by leaving the things where they were. But the maids would not then have done a morning's work; that was of course important.

'Oh, I know you're going to make a capital housewife, my dear,' said Mrs Chapel, enthusiastically reaching up to hook brass hangers over the picture rail.

'You see, it should be easier, in one way, for you than for many girls, because you're not the booky type, so you've fewer counter interests to distract you. Though, as to that, the more intelligent a woman is, the more brains she ought to bring to bear on her home. The Cambridge and Oxford Colleges are excellent training schools for housewives. No, I know you weren't at them – they wouldn't be in your line – but a woman can be quite intelligent without a university education ... Can you tell me if that's straight? A little too much to the left, isn't it? I thought so ... And, you know, they should really take out the hall rugs and thoroughly shake them on the lawn at *least* once a week ... I'll tell you what we'll do while I'm here, Denham dear – we'll make out a time-table together. We might have a good go at it tomorrow morning, while you lie down. I shall enjoy that, ,and I think you'd find it quite interesting too, wouldn't you?'

'Yes,' said Denham.

'And,' continued her mother-in-law kindly, 'it needn't only be the maids who have a time-table, either. I'm quite sure it's a great help to one's own life to have some kind of scheme mapped out for the day, to which one tries to keep. It's wonderful what a help it is to see it written down. One should begin it right after breakfast – 9.30–9.45: see the servants; 9.45–10: do the flowers; 10–11: read the papers and write one's letters; 11–1: serious reading; 1–1.30: lunch (an early lunch is nice in winter,

I think, it leaves a longer afternoon); 1.30–2.30: lie down; 2.30–4: exercise or gardening, either alone or with friends; 4–5: tea and see friends ... And so on, do you see? It regularises the day so, and prevents one drifting and idling the time away, as one's often inclined to do ... By the way, I was thinking it would be rather nice if you were to learn a little Greek in the mornings for your serious reading. Wouldn't that surprise Arnold?'

It would surprise me a good deal, too, Denham thought.

'You see,' said Mrs Chapel, stepping lightly, though stoutly, from a chair on to the floor. 'There needn't really be *any* empty moments in one's day, if it's properly schemed out. Think of that! Not one empty, idle, useless minute.'

Denham thought of it ...

virago

To buy any of our books and to find out more
about Virago Press and Virago Modern Classics,
our authors and titles, as well as events and
book club forum, visit our websites

www.virago.co.uk
www.littlebrown.co.uk

and follow us on Twitter

@ViragoBooks

To order any Virago titles p & p free in the UK,
please contact our mail order supplier on:

+ 44 (0)1832 737525

Customers not based in the UK should contact
the same number for appropriate postage
and packing costs.